Praise for
Indestructible Object

A *BookPage* Best Young Adult Books of 2021 selection
An ALA 2022 Best Fiction for Young Adults selection
A 2022 Rainbow List selection

★ "Lee's journey toward even the hardest truths plays out with
stunning emotional depth. This is a layered and vulnerable
examination of everything that makes a heart beat—or break."
—*BookPage*, starred review

"A thoughtful exploration of love and identity."
—*Kirkus Reviews*

"Printz Honor Book author McCoy offers a nuanced coming-of-age
story about a complex heroine with her heart on her sleeve."
—*Booklist*

"Beautifully messy and real. A raw look at what it means to actually
live as the person you truly are."
—Amy Spalding, bestselling author of *We Used to Be Friends*

"With wisdom and fearlessness, Mary McCoy's *Indestructible Object*
is not just a novel, but a manual for a life well-lived—it will leave
readers wanting to make Art, to fall in and out of love, and to
bravely reveal the parts of themselves kept hidden."
—Iva-Marie Palmer, author of *Gimme Everything You Got*

"A moving and masterfully drawn love letter to art, found family,
and all of the messy but always wonderful shades of love, filled
with as much soul as the city of its setting."
—Jeff Zentner, Morris Award–winning author of *The Serpent King*

ALSO BY MARY McCOY

Dead to Me

Camp So-and-So

I, Claudia

INDESTRUCTIBLE OBJECT

Mary McCoy

PRINTZ HONOR AUTHOR

SIMON & SCHUSTER BFYR

NEW YORK   LONDON   TORONTO   SYDNEY   NEW DELHI

SIMON & SCHUSTER BFYR

An imprint of Simon & Schuster Children's Publishing Division
1230 Avenue of the Americas, New York, New York 10020

SIMON & SCHUSTER BOOKS FOR YOUNG READERS
and related marks are trademarks of Simon & Schuster, Inc.
For information about special discounts for bulk purchases, please contact
Simon & Schuster Special Sales at 1-866-506-1949 or business@simonandschuster.com.
The Simon & Schuster Speakers Bureau can bring authors to your live event.
For more information or to book an event, contact the Simon & Schuster Speakers Bureau at
1-866-248-3049 or visit our website at www.simonspeakers.com.
Also available in a SIMON & SCHUSTER BFYR hardcover edition
Interior design by Hilary Zarycky
The text for this book was set in Bell.
Manufactured in the United States of America
First SIMON & SCHUSTER BFYR paperback edition July 2022
2 4 6 8 10 9 7 5 3 1

The Library of Congress has cataloged the hardcover edition as follows:
Names: McCoy, Mary, 1976– author.
Title: Indestructible object / Mary McCoy.
Description: New York : Simon & Schuster Books for Young Readers, 2021. | Audience: Ages 12
up. | Summary: In the city of Memphis, eighteen-year-old Lee and her boyfriend, Vincent, make
a popular podcast on artists in love, but Lee learns that stories of happily-ever-after love do not
always mirror real life.
Identifiers: LCCN 2020030125 | ISBN 9781534485051 (hardcover) |
ISBN 9781534485068 (pbk) | ISBN 9781534485075 (ebook)
Subjects: CYAC: Love—Ficton. | Dating (Social customs)—Fiction. | Bisexuality—Fiction. |
Podcasts—Fiction. | Memphis (Tenn.)—Fiction.
Classification: LCC PZ7.1.M43 In 2021 | DDC [Fic]—dc23
LC record available at https://lccn.loc.gov/2020030125

To the people I love

CHAPTER 1

Artists in Love

ARTISTS IN LOVE, EPISODE #86:
"I Hope I Gave You a Good Love Story"
Hosted by Vincent Karega and Lee Swan

VINCENT KAREGA:
The first time we met, you told me I had the kind of voice you'd follow down a dark alley.

LEE SWAN:
Oh yikes, did I? I can't believe you had any romantic interest in me after that.

VINCENT:
I liked it. It was the first time anyone had ever suggested that I might be trouble. I liked that someone like you would think that about someone like me.

LEE: (laughs)
I think what I meant was, you have a trustworthy voice. I wouldn't have followed a dangerous voice down an alley. What did you think the first time you met me?

VINCENT:

You were wearing a T-shirt that said, THERE IS NO MUSIC UNDER LATE CAPITALISM. I thought it was really pretentious.

LEE:

Because I am really pretentious, Vincent.

VINCENT:

Only about things you really care about. That was what I liked about you right away, Lee. That's what I still like about you.

Every week for the past two years, Vincent and I have met in my attic to record our podcast, *Artists in Love.* This episode, we are the artists in love. And we are about to break up.

VINCENT:

Have you heard about the performance artists Marina Abramović and Ulay? They were lovers, and they made art together for over a decade. For their last piece, they walked from opposite ends of the Great Wall of China, and met in the middle, and then they broke up. That's what this feels like to me.

LEE:

So is this performance art, or is it life?

VINCENT:

Can't it be both?

Twenty-four hours before Vincent and I went up to the attic to record Episode #86, "I Hope I Gave You a Good Love Story," I knew what my life was going to look like for at least the next four years.

We'd been accepted to the same college, right here in Memphis, and the plan was that I would major in recording technology, with a minor in music business, and he would major in creative writing, with a minor in graphic design. We would funnel everything we learned back into the podcast. He would write our stories, and I would make them sound beautiful. We would get an apartment together. And after that, who knows? We talked about starting a new project together, or traveling the world, or moving to New York.

We talked about how we'd avoid turning into our parents—his, so traditional and conservative and terrified of anything outside the airtight corridor between their home and their church; mine, a pair of feuding conjoined twins, too miserable to stay together, too codependent to mercy-kill their marriage.

Case in point: my parents had announced their separation the day after I graduated from high school, and now two weeks later, neither of them had so much as packed a suitcase.

I will not lie, there were times during my relationship with Vincent when I might have flaunted our love a little bit, as if to say to my parents, *For fuck's sake, I'm eighteen and I'm better at having a healthy relationship than you are.*

Shows what I know.

LEE:

I have an artist breakup story for you, too, Vincent. It's very self-serving. It's about Lee Miller and Man Ray.

VINCENT:

Ah, your namesake, to whom you would dedicate every episode of this podcast if I would have let you.

LEE:

Well, ha. Last episode, and you can't do shit to stop me now.

VINCENT:

I wouldn't dream of it.

In the South, people name everything Lee—streets, schools, parks, entire neighborhoods. People plaster Robert E. Lee's name on so many things here, it's like they forget he was the bad guy in this historical narrative.

Thankfully, I am not named after a Confederate general. My parents named me after the photographer Lee Miller, who started off as a model in *Vogue*, before she decided she wanted to be on the other side of the camera. She moved to Paris, joined the Surrealist artists, and had a series of passionate and scandalous love affairs, then became a photojournalist on the front lines of World War II. Nobody here knows about her, however, and people tend to assume I was named after Robert E. Lee like everything else around here is, so I guess my parents' cheeky little joke backfired.

I do like being named after her, though. She went where she

wanted to go, lived how she wanted to live. She was the kind of person who would photograph her lover in a gas mask or organize a topless picnic in the woods for all her friends. I guarantee you that Robert E. Lee never once organized a topless picnic.

LEE:

In 1923, the artist Man Ray attached a photograph of an eye to a metronome. He set it in motion and painted to the rhythm. The eye on the metronome tracked his every move in the studio, letting him know if the work was any good or not. He called it *Object to Be Destroyed.*

When Lee Miller broke up with him a decade later, he remade the object using a photograph of her eye, and included the instructions for its use, which read: *"Cut out the eye from a photograph of one who has been loved but is seen no more. Attach the eye to the pendulum of a metronome and regulate the weight to set the tempo desired. Keep going to the limit of endurance. With a hammer well-aimed, try to destroy the whole at a single blow."*

This time, he called the piece *Object of Destruction.*

Because that's what Lee Miller became. Once, she'd been the object of his affection, and then she destroyed his heart. It was like she took aim with a hammer, and laid waste to it.

VINCENT:
That's intense.

LEE:

He was devastated.

VINCENT:

Is that how you're feeling right now?

LEE:

It's just a story.

VINCENT:

I don't know if I could handle it, knowing that my leaving would cause you to suffer like that.

LEE:

That's the thing about breakups, Vincent; the whole point of them is that you don't get to know. Because you're not there.

When we finish recording the last episode of *Artists in Love* at one in the morning, we stop and hold each other, and for a moment, I wonder if he's going to change his mind. But then he lets go of me, he wipes the tears from his eyes, and we go back to work.

VINCENT:

I should probably explain to our listeners. This week, I was accepted to Howard University off the waitlist. For our listeners who may not be familiar, Howard is a historically

Black college, or HBCU, in Washington, DC, and it's where some of the greatest Black scholars, scientists, politicians, and artists got their education. Toni Morrison went there, and Zora Neale Hurston, and Kamala Harris.

And now, I guess, me.

That was amazing enough on its own, but then something else happened. National Public Radio has a paid summer internship program. I was sure I wouldn't get it. I was so sure, I didn't even tell anyone I'd applied—and then I got it. So I'm moving to Washington, DC, next week.

LEE:
I'm happy for you, Vincent. I know it sounds cliché, but I really am. It's a great opportunity.

VINCENT:
It's a lot to process. Since I got the news, I've been having five feelings at once, at all times. I'm excited about the challenges; nervous I won't be up to them; dazzled by the possibilities; terrified at the prospect of uprooting my entire life with a week's notice.

And of course, my heart is breaking to leave you, Lee.

LEE:
But I don't want you wondering, *What if?* I want you free in the world. I want you to go after the things you want. I'd be

7

pissed if you never found them because of me.

That's some pretty evolved shit right there, isn't it? Even in the moment, it surprises me. My voice becomes this center of eerie calm, even though the rest of me feels like a flooded wasteland.

What I don't say to Vincent is that I wish he'd told me about the things he wanted sooner. It might have occurred to me to want other things too.

I don't know what I was thinking, why I'd bothered getting idealistic about any of this when I had a lifetime of hard evidence that love doesn't last forever and that tying your future to another human being is the surest way to end up regretting all of it.

VINCENT:
Lee, can you promise me you're going to be okay?

LEE:
Can you promise me you're making the right choice?

VINCENT:
Can you promise me you'll keep doing this without me?

LEE:
Can you promise me you're going to be happy?

VINCENT:
I can't.

LEE:
Me neither.

VINCENT:
I guess you can't ask other people to make promises like that.

LEE:
But Vincent, if this is the last time we're here in my attic, telling each other love stories, I'm glad we're ending with ours.

VINCENT:
I hope I gave you a good love story, Lee.

And then Vincent and I sign off, the way we've always signed off at the end of each episode: *"Until we meet again, make art, make beautiful love stories."*

Around four in the morning, I almost forget we've broken up. We're in our flow, me editing and mixing, him listening, rewriting, making us do it again when it's not good enough. We're both completely focused on the work at hand, and it's nearly finished when I say the thing that's been tugging at my sleeve for the past hour.

"What do you think about cutting the last line, the part where you tell me you hope you gave me a good love story?"

"Why?" he asks. "So we can end with the part *you* say?"

"It's not about who says it, Vincent. It's about how, maybe some things should stay personal. Some things we should keep only for us."

He goes quiet for a minute, and it seems like he's about to agree with me until he shakes his head and says, "But it's a good line."

I don't want our last episode, our last night together, to have a disagreement in it, and besides, we're breaking up. We don't need to keep anything for us because there is no us anymore.

"It is a good line," I admit.

"Actually, it would make a good title for the episode," he says.

"Let's leave it in, then," I say. "Screw it."

"Yeah, screw it!"

Vincent doesn't swear. He has no vices that I'm aware of, so when he says "Screw it," I know he is not fucking around.

We upload the final episode of *Artists in Love* at six in the morning. We sneak down the attic steps together for the last time. I drive him home, and we hug goodbye, and he walks up the sidewalk.

I keep up my eye-of-the-hurricane calm until he turns out the porch light, and then I fall apart because for two years of my life, this was everything, and now it's over.

CHAPTER 2

Love Is Dead

Eventually I drive home. After I park in the driveway, I sit in the car for a minute, running my hands up and down my arms like my parents used to do when I was little, whispering "I am calm, I am calm," until it almost feels true.

When I open the front door, the alarm on my mom's phone is going off, and my dad is yelling at her to do something about it, because he's sleeping in the office and isn't there to reach over and turn it off like he always did before they decided to split up.

If someone told me they were going to continue on like this for another year, without either of them moving out, I wouldn't find it shocking. Twenty years of misery is a hard habit to break.

My dad lumbers out of the office in his plaid pajama pants and Goner Records T-shirt, his hair matted to one side of his head. He has no idea I've been up all night, no idea that Vincent and I broke up, and I decide it's much too early to tell him that story.

"What's a combined breakfast food that hasn't been invented yet, but should be?" he asks.

This is how my dad talks to people. Most of the time he comes across as quiet, or even shy, but then out of nowhere, he looks you in the eye and asks you a question like that, and he really wants to know what you, specifically, think. People are generally flustered by these questions. They can rarely answer them, but are nonetheless flattered to have their opinion sought on such matters.

"I don't know, Dad. It's too early to know. I'm going back to bed."

"I was thinking bacon-wrapped Apple Jacks."

He seems disappointed, so I decide not to leave him hanging entirely. "Seems like a lot of work. Would you do all of them, or just the green ones? Or just the pink ones?"

"It's too early to know," he says, and continues on his way to the kitchen to make coffee, like we've just exchanged normal morning pleasantries.

Soon my mom will get out of bed, and the two of them will start getting ready for work, ignoring and avoiding each other, but unable to resist making passive-aggressive, shitty comments. I decide to avoid the scene entirely and go up to the attic to hide out until they leave and I have the house to myself.

I pull the attic steps up behind me, turn on the window air conditioner, and sit down at the computer to check the traffic on the new episode of *Artists in Love*. Over the past year, we'd attracted an audience of people we didn't know, but our most vocal fans remained a group of underclassmen from our school, who were in love with the idea of Vincent and me. We were a power couple in a limited, niche way, aspirational to the theater, band, and poetry crowds, relationship goals for freshman girls who loved art and hated going outdoors. Or maybe they listened so they could swoon over Vincent's sexy voice and lush descriptions of Frida Kahlo paintings.

There are already comments from our fans in other time zones:

Last episode? What happened?

Ohhhhh noooooooo. Lee & Vincent broke up!

Love is dead, and there's no hope for any of us.

I scroll farther down and see that at least one of our haters has weighed in as well. Or specifically, one of my haters. Nobody hates Vincent. They generally seem to agree with the commenter:

He deserves better than her vocal fry ass.

I delete the comment, like I always do. When people post things like this, I always wonder, who do they think moderates this thing? Interns?

Maybe there are more, but that's as much as I can handle reading. I lie down on the attic floor and realize that our breakup is real now. It's out in the world, and there's no taking it back. I listen to my parents moving around below and try to imagine whether I could endure this kind of cold war if it continues for the entirety of my college career. Before last night, it wouldn't have mattered how much they hated each other because I was going to be moving out and getting an apartment with Vincent. But now I'll probably be here, sleeping in my bedroom down the hall from them like a kid.

At last, my dad's friend Harold pulls up outside and honks the horn for their morning carpool to the Poplar–White

Station Library, and then a half hour later, I hear my mom backing the car out of the driveway, and then I'm alone in the house. All I want to do is crawl into bed and stay there until it's time for college to start, until the raw, pulpy exposed nerves of my heart have calloused over. I'll sleep through the pain all summer, and when I wake up, maybe I'll have missed it.

I climb down from the attic and am on my way to my room, to carry out this brilliant plan, when I pass my parents' office. It's always been my parents' office in name, though my mom hardly ever uses it, and even less now that my dad sleeps in there. I haven't gone in much myself, and when I look inside, I gasp.

My dad is not personally tidy—he tends toward wild hair and scruffy fashion—but he is fastidious in his habits and surroundings. When he's bored, he cleans grout or wipes down the blades of the ceiling fans, but the office looks like it's been boarded by pirates and ransacked. The couch is still made up like a bed, the sheets wrinkled, and there's a stale sweaty-sock smell in the air. The floor is covered in dirty clothes and wadded-up notebook pages, and crumb-covered plates and half-empty jam jars full of various beverages litter the desk. If his usual, real self could see this, he'd be appalled.

Since he has spent the past eighteen years cleaning up after my mom and me, I decide to return the favor this once. I fold up the sheets and toss the dirty clothes in the hamper. I'm not sure what to do with the paper on the floor, though. I uncrumple one of the pieces and recognize lines of dialogue between two characters I've known longer than I've known most people, from a play my dad has been trying to finish since I was twelve. I don't read it, but I don't throw it away either. We don't do things like that in my family, not when it comes to one another's art.

Instead I gather up the plates and jam jars, and I'm about to take them out to the kitchen when I notice a passport in the middle of my dad's desk. This is curious because my dad hardly ever leaves Memphis and has never, to my knowledge, set foot outside the United States. Is he going to start now? Now that he and my mom are splitting up, is he going to run off to another country, change his name, and live in a garret with a cot and a hot plate and a stray cat? I open the passport. This isn't private like a diary or a notebook—this is a government-issued document, and if my dad is skipping town, I have a right to know about it.

He's not going anywhere with this passport, though. It's long expired, and my dad is young in the picture, still scruffy, but no gray in his hair or beard. He's wearing a moth-eaten wool sweater, and he's grinning with a sweetness that I sometimes see when I play him a song that I like or show him a story I've written. I wonder, when is the last time I've seen that grin? And then I notice the date that the passport was issued: six months before the day I was born.

I sit down at the desk, push the plates to the side, and begin to flip through the pages of the passport. Not a single stamp.

If you weren't going to use it, why get it at all? I wonder.

But of course, the obvious answer is that he *had* meant to use it. Until I came along.

I open the desk drawers and begin to dig through them, through the stacks of old notebooks, filled with drafts of his plays; the pens he likes; the old checkbooks. Then I go through my mother's desk on the other side of the room. Does she have an unused passport, too? Were she and my dad about to run away together before I came along and ruined everything?

She almost never uses the office, so her desk is more symbolic than anything. Some kind of Virginia Woolf thing about having a room of one's own in which to make art. The drawers are empty, except for the bottom one that only opens halfway. I reach inside and my fingers wrap around the spine of a small, thin book with a rough paper cover. The cover sticks in the drawer and tears a little as I pull it out.

It's a collection of poetry. My mother's poetry, titled *Map Room Love Songs*. Unlike the rest of her books, I've never seen it lying around the house before. Unlike the rest of her books, it's not professionally published. The cover is a screen-printed image of a man lifting a coffee cup to his mouth, cropped just beneath his eyes. There's a notation on the bottom corner, *1/25*, which I realize is probably how many copies were ever made. I feel bad about ripping the cover of a limited edition. There is a date inside, the year I was born, and a dedication that reads, *For Greg, for everything.*

Here is the story, as I've always been told it: my parents met in college, at an artists' salon that they and their friends started, and after they graduated, they found out that my mom was pregnant, so they decided to get married and have me.

"It seemed like a subversive thing to do at the time," my dad said.

"It was very romantic and exciting," my mom said.

"And we were very much in love," my dad continued.

I put the passport and the poetry book back in the desk, in the drawer that only opens halfway.

Fuck being subversive, I think.

Like anyone was watching the poses you struck. Like anyone cared.

Fuck romance.

Romance was a lie you built with another person. It rotted your judgment.

And while I'm at it, while I'm heartbroken, while I'm sitting in the sad remains of my stupid life, *fuck love*, which took away all your choices and tied you to another person and made you forget who you were without them.

Fuck love, because it always ends up the same way, because it always ends.

CHAPTER 3

Hot Mess Island

I go back to bed, I don't know for how long, before I become hazily aware of my mom standing in the doorway to my bedroom, saying, "Lee. Lee. Are you up? Hey, Lee, are you up?" over and over, until I stir and rub my eyes and sit up.

"What is it, Mom?" I ask, equal parts groggy and annoyed.

"Lee, I listened to the podcast. I came home as soon as I heard."

This wakes me the rest of the way up. She comes in, sits down on the edge of the bed, and strokes my hair.

"You poor girl. That was . . . hard to listen to. It was a lot of your heart to spill out on the pavement." She says it with a pity that pisses me off, but which I also sort of appreciate.

"Yeah."

"What I'm saying is, how's your heart, Lee?"

"Fine, I guess."

Poets won't let you get away with saying you're fine. I mean, why do that when you could drag a rake over the coals of *fine* and stir up a nest of cinders? My mother takes my hands, folds them into hers, and waits for me to excavate my feelings for her.

"The two of you had made a lot of plans together. Are you angry with him?"

"I don't want to be," I say, and that part is true. When I said I wanted him to be free in the world, I meant it.

"But you are."

"Mom," I say, and that's all I get out before my voice cracks and I start sobbing, my tears landing on her hands. She wraps her arms around me and holds me until I stop crying.

"You're allowed to be angry, sweetie. Even if you still love him. Better to be honest about it."

There is at least one wonderful thing about having a poet in your family, which is that when you suffer some ordinary human setback like heartbreak, they can generally rise to the occasion and whip up some good tempestuous feelings on your behalf. Besides, my mom is definitely a person who can say something like "You can be angry and still love him" and sound like she's speaking from experience.

"But I wasn't honest," I say. She frowns, not quite understanding, but I don't feel like elaborating and she doesn't press.

"When does he leave?" she asks instead.

"A week."

"Ugh. Well, get up. I'm taking you out for treats."

"Can we have treats here? I don't really feel like leaving the house."

"Understandable," she says. "*Hot Mess Island*, then?"

Hot Mess Island is the name we made up for *The Bachelorette*, a show where a woman with perfect hair and very white teeth seeks her ideal life partner from a field of shirtless hunks, all of whom are down to wed. Our love for this show is intense and secret. For two seasons, we didn't even let on to each other that we were obsessed with it. I watched it on my phone in my room, and she watched it on the iPad in the living room, until gradually, we began to drop cryptic, exploratory comments at the breakfast table: *Tyler wore the salmon jacket again. A dream date on a horse is objectively less romantic than a dream date on a boat.*

My dad would look at us like we were spies. But my parents announced their separation right before the new season started, and now my mom no longer cares about concealing her trashy television-watching habits from anyone. We watch it openly together, on the TV in the living room.

I don't think there's ever been an artist in love on *The Bachelorette,* but the intensity with which the contestants talk about their romantic feelings makes Lee Miller and Man Ray look almost boring by comparison. As my mom and I watch the most recent episode, both of our romantic lives are in shambles, and yet, we are totally stone-faced, while the contestants on *The Bachelorette* are sobbing over people they barely know.

At the beginning, they go in joking and self-aware. *I'm looking to make a connection,* they say, but they have no idea what they're in for, what that even means in the context of *The Bachelorette.* Three weeks later, after all the rose ceremonies and choreographed dates, they're completely bewildered by the power of their feelings.

This is real, they insist every time.

"If I got paid to live in a mansion, drink wine, and snorkel, I'm pretty sure I could fall in love with a management consultant from Boca Raton too," my mom says.

We're almost to the end of the episode when my dad walks in the door holding his afternoon cup of coffee from Java Cabana, the shop down the street. He pauses in front of the television for a moment, then asks, "So, what's happening on *Hot Mess Island*?"

We ignore him until he leaves the room. Only we are allowed to call it *Hot Mess Island*.

When the episode ends, my mom says, "I'm taking you out of this house for treats now. Real ones."

"But I don't want to."

"It's four in the afternoon, and you haven't left the house all day. Besides, I need to talk to you."

And you don't want to be here with Dad, I think.

Grudgingly, I go to my room, pull my hair back, and put on a sundress, for reasons of survival rather than aesthetics. The moment we set foot outside, I'll be engulfed in the thick, raw hamburger–smelling humidity that is Memphis in the summertime. Maybe Vincent wanted to escape that, though is the weather any better in Washington, DC? And god, you don't even get Congressional representation if you live there. It's like throwing your vote away—what a stupid place to move.

For our first treat, my mom takes me to the nail salon, where we both get pedicures, a bright blue polish for me and black for her.

"Are you goth now?" I ask, teasing.

"Actually, I was thinking of joining the Church of Satan," she replies, much too loudly for a Midtown Memphis nail salon.

The woman who's doing her nails sucks in a breath and closes her eyes, and I see her lips moving, as if in prayer. Growing up with my artsy, heathen parents makes me, if anything, more aware of how much we don't belong in Memphis. People go to church here. They say *sir* and *ma'am*. They have monogrammed towels, and while they think that Midtown is a nice place to go out to eat or see a show, you wouldn't actually raise a child there. As a city, Memphis is just big enough to accommodate my mother's strangeness, but even so, at least half the people who meet her suspect she's not entirely on the level.

After our nails are finished, she takes me to our favorite dim sum place for steamed buns and tea, even though there is a leftover casserole in the refrigerator that we are supposed to finish. My dad hates wasting food, hates when we deviate from planned menus, but my mother insists. It will keep another night, she says, and besides, it would be cruel to feed tuna casserole to someone with a broken heart.

"Lee," she says, pouring each of us a cup full of jasmine tea, "I wanted to talk to you about the separation. The timing's horrible, and I'm so sorry, baby."

"You don't need to apologize," I say. Like, were they supposed to stick it out another six months to spare my feelings? Then again, if they'd already stuck it out this long, what difference would another six months make?

"What I mean is, I'm leaving town tomorrow," my mom says. "Just for a week or so. I'm going to teach a workshop in New Orleans, do a couple of readings, give your dad some space. But we've agreed that when I get back, he's going to move out of the house."

I wrap my hands around the cup of tea, let the heat sear my palms as her words sink in.

"What about you?" I ask. "Are you moving too?"

"I don't know, but for now, he's going to get a new place, and I'm going to stay in the house. You can stay too, as long as you like."

"What if I'd rather live with Dad?"

It's a petulant and bratty thing to say, and as soon as the pained expression crosses her face, I know the only reason I'd said it was to hurt her.

"I thought you'd want to be closer to school. But of course, you can live wherever you want," she says quietly. "I'm taking the train to New Orleans with Maggie. She and Sage and Max are already on their way from Chicago. They'll be getting in late tonight."

Maggie and Sage are my parents' friends from college, and Max is their son, whom they adopted when he was eight. He's my age now and going to college in the fall like I am, though his plans were never as crisp and ironed as mine. Over the past three months, Maggie and Sage have told us that Max is planning to major in theater, psychology, global labor studies, and video game design.

"Why are Sage and Max coming?"

"Sage is going to stay with your dad, help him look for a place."

"If I'm supposed to be Max's driver and tour guide, I feel like someone should have talked to me about that."

I'm doing it again, being difficult because I can, because I am an objectively wounded party, whose bad behavior could briefly be excused. I don't even mind the idea of having Max around. We only see each other once or twice a year, and so every time we're a different iteration of ourselves, but all of those versions more or less get along. At the heart of it, we knew what it meant to grow up with parents like ours, how art museums were cool, but sometimes you wanted to be taken to *Disney On Ice* without your family having an aesthetic crisis over it.

However, the last time Max came here, he spent the weekend playing video games in my room while Vincent and I camped out in the attic, working on the podcast. And the last time Maggie and Sage came to visit, he'd just turned eighteen, and they let him stay home on his own. Which makes me wonder why he's coming along this time.

"Max will take care of himself. We didn't think these plans would affect you when we made them. Honestly, I thought you'd probably be off with Vincent most of the time," she says with an apologetic wince, like she's not sure she should have uttered Vincent's name around me. "In any case, it would be kind of you to entertain Max a little bit, if you're feeling up to it, but I'm sure he's not expecting it."

Maggie and Sage were a couple in college, too, though unlike my parents, they spent a decade traveling around the world, living in Berlin and New York before Maggie's sister—Max's biological mom—died, and they moved back to Chicago to raise Max.

Maggie's family emigrated from the Philippines before she was born. Maggie grew up in a quiet Chicago suburb until someone slipped a Flannery O'Connor novel into her aspiring-writer hands and she ended up in Memphis out of macabre fascination. She's intense, like my mom, and writes doorstopper-thick novels about nineteenth-century women in desperate circumstances. Sage is white and grew up in Tupelo, Mississippi, and still has the thick, drawling accent to prove it. They're a tattoo artist now, their arms covered from shoulder to wrist in dragons and whorls and waves that look like stained glass, ending in a dagger on the back of each of their hands. Sage has identified as nonbinary for as long as I've known them, and though Maggie used to identify as a lesbian, she pretty much uses the term "queer" now.

When Maggie and Sage visited, or any of the other friends from that college literary salon circle, my parents always turned into completely different people. They acted happy and youthful and fun. They stayed up too late, drinking wine and smoking weed in the backyard, having deep, intense conversations on the front porch until two in the morning.

"Well, I'm glad you're at least getting a party out of it," I say.

My mom looks stung. "That's not what this is, Lee. This is getting the people we love most together to hold us upright, because this is really hard."

"I'm sure Maggie will be holding you upright on Bourbon Street."

"I'm sorry I've left you with the impression that I expect to enjoy any of this."

"Then why are you going?"

"Because I'm afraid that if I don't, neither of us ever will," she says.

After we finish our tea, I say, "We should get home. I have work in a little bit."

"Lee, I didn't mean to talk so much about your dad and me. I don't want to drag you into our stuff. Really, I wanted to talk about *you* this afternoon. How are you doing? Are you going to be okay?"

I let out a short bark of laughter. "What choice do I have?"

"There's something I want you to do for me while I'm gone," she says, smiling sadly when I tense up, already unwilling to comply with whatever her request is. She continues anyway.

"You were planning to make things when you thought Vincent would be making them with you. I think you should make things whether he's here or not. Make something for yourself."

We drive back to the house in silence. At a couple of red lights, she starts to turn toward me like she wants to say something, but she always changes her mind. My dad isn't home when we get there, which means that Harold must have taken him out for a drink. More college-friend stuff. They have been doing this since I was little, and to my knowledge, Harold is the only person who can nudge my dad out of his grout-cleaning, four p.m. coffee-ordering routines.

I go up to the attic to pack for work. I run sound at Java Cabana, for their weekly open mic nights, poetry slams, songwriters' showcases, and other gigs, and while the soundboard and monitors stayed in the coffee shop storage room, I treasure my microphones and cables too much to let them out of my sight. I know how people treat gear that isn't theirs.

The attic feels haunted, and my eyes flood with tears as I look at the side-by-side chairs where Vincent and I had worked just hours before. We were never going to be like that again. *I* was never going to be like that again. Which is upsetting because that's the only person I know how to be.

The podcast and my job at Java Cabana were my only extracurricular activities. I can't remember the last day that had passed without me thinking about *Artists in Love*, without writing for it, recording it, mixing it. What was I supposed to do with that part of my brain, now that the thing it was used to doing, the thing it was good at doing, was gone?

I log into the social media accounts for *Artists in Love*. Vincent designed all the graphics for them, but I did all the posting because his parents hovered over his shoulder anytime he used the internet, like they were waiting to slay any demon that slipped through the screen to corrupt his soul.

I haven't even used my own social media accounts in a year. Anytime there was something clever or interesting I wanted to post for myself, I posted it to one of the *Artists in Love* accounts instead. Eventually, it was easier to let all my personal accounts atrophy and throw my energy into getting more followers for the podcast until my personal brand was indistinguishable from *Artists in Love*. I was it, and it was me, a thought that didn't seem gross or problematic at the time, but does now.

Sometimes I got the feeling that Vincent thought most of the work I did was just clicking buttons and tuning virtual dials, that he was the artist and I was the engineer, though of course, not a real engineer. I wonder if Vincent will have to do this kind of work during his internship, whether he'll think there's any art to it when he's the one doing it. Then again, I won't be there. I won't get to know.

As I monitor the accounts, I tell myself I'm just doing my job, even though it's wallowing, self-inflicted torture to read every message, every mention of our breakup. I sign out without responding to any of them.

When I come down from the attic, my dad is home, and he and my mom are sitting on the couch together, closer than I've seen them sit in weeks.

"Your mom told me that you know," Dad says. "And she told me about you and Vincent."

"Hello to you, too." I smile to give the remark plausible deniability of being a joke with no real malice in it.

"I'm sorry, Lee. Is there anything you need?" he asks. "Anything I can do to help?"

"I'm fine," I say. I know this is probably the full extent of my dad's check-in with me over the Vincent situation. He isn't going to ask me how my heart is.

"So, I'll stay in the bedroom, Sage will be in the office with Max. Harold can crash on the air mattress or wherever if he stays over, and Greg will sleep on the couch," my dad says. He brings it up like these are casual logistics, but when he gets to the last part, he runs all the words together as quickly as possible.

"You invited Greg?" my mom asks. Her head whips around, though she keeps her face in a pose of forced calm. This is the kind of thing that, until recently, she would have been consulted about ahead of time. But when you're supposedly separated, I guess you lose the right to have an opinion about who your ex invites over when you're out of town.

And what was my dad thinking, inviting him here? Surely, he knew about *Map Room Love Songs*, about "For Greg, for everything." Why would you want *that* guy around while your wife was leaving you?

Even though he is the least reliable of my parents' artist friends, Greg is also the most successful. He worked on a Tim Burton movie. He made big, loud art that involved disrupting city council hearings and building roadblocks out of Perrier bottles. All the other artists I know have other jobs to bring in most of their money, and make art on the side. My mom and Maggie teach, my dad and Harold work at a library, and Sage does neck tattoos in Old English script for drunk guys on Saturday nights, but all Greg does is make art. He's an artist full-time.

"Maya, he's my friend, and I want him here."

"He's not actually coming, though, Arthur. He never comes."

This was not exactly true. He'd come once, when I was eight, right after Maggie and Sage adopted Max. He spent the whole weekend drawing robots with us, and from then on, he sent me a box of fancy Blackwing pencils every year on my birthday, along with a hand-drawn card. *Save those cards*, my dad always said. *They'll probably end up funding your college education.*

"He says he's coming."

"Greg always says he's coming, and then he never does," my mom says, then turns to ask me, "Is all of this okay with *you*, honey?"

Maybe she legitimately cares, or maybe she's just trying to influence things through me.

My dad, who clearly suspects the latter, asks, "Why wouldn't it be okay?"

"I only mean, the house will be very crowded with all those people."

This is not what she meant at all, and we all know it.

"Sure, I don't care," I say.

"Sounds like a regular slumber party," my mom says, barely concealing her disgust. I mean, I guess if their friends had chosen sides, my mom got Maggie, while my dad got Sage and Harold and Greg. Maybe she's mad because they're all on his side.

"Anyhow, Lee, let me know if there's anything you need," my dad says. "I'm here for you."

"We both are," my mom adds.

"But I'll be *here*," my dad points out, and my mom narrows her eyes and draws in a sharp breath.

"I should go," I say. "I'll be late for work."

"I love you, Lee," my mom says.

"I love you, too," I say in a perfunctory let's-end-this-conversation-now kind of way. Still, she looks relieved when I give her a hug, then my dad.

"I'll see you before I go tomorrow," she says, and I nod and go out the front door, and I'm not even in the car yet when I hear them yelling at each other in the living room.

CHAPTER 4

Unhelpful Neural Messages

laire is the barista on duty when I arrive at Java Cabana. She can tell I'm in a bad mood and leaves me alone, cleaning the espresso machine while I haul gear out from the storage closet. Claire is one of those coworkers who's also sort of my friend, although it's more complicated than that. We went to high school together, but we weren't really friends there. It was more like we were just friends here. I wasn't sure how to feel when she didn't acknowledge me in the hallways at school, even though I never said hi to her either. Mostly these days, we just treat each other like coworkers, which I think feels like a relief to both of us.

I finish setting up the monitor and the mic stand, and have just gotten settled behind the soundboard when Claire wordlessly delivers an iced mocha with a shot of peppermint in it, my favorite, and a day-old ginger cookie from the half-price bakery case. Coming from her, it's such undeserved kindness that I nearly burst into tears on the spot.

"Vincent came by a little bit ago," Claire explains. "He told me. I'm sorry, Lee."

"He was *here?*" I ask. I try to make the question sound

casual, but inside I'm panicking. "What did he want? What did you say to him?"

Claire gives me a weary look. "I told him I was sorry. That's all I said, Lee."

"He can't just come by here while I'm at work and disrupt my life."

"Well, technically he didn't. You weren't here."

"But I *might* have been," I say before I realize how irrational I sound. I do not sound like an evolved, cool person who is calmly moving forward from a breakup.

It would have to take something serious for Vincent to come to Java Cabana. Suspicious as his parents were of the internet, even they could admit it had educational and possibly even religious applications. Java Cabana, on the other hand, attracted people who played secular music, read poetry, and said provocative things just to get a rise out of nice people. And even though Vincent didn't necessarily feel the same way, he never set foot in the place. It was almost like he knew they'd be able to smell it on him when he came home, and he didn't feel like explaining to them that it was just the coffee shop where his girlfriend worked, not a den of iniquity.

School, the podcast, every other part of my life had Vincent in it, but Java Cabana was this walled-off place he never visited. There were places in his life I'd never been either. He'd never invited me to his church, or introduced me to any of his friends from there. I'd never been in his bedroom. We never talked about *why* that was—it just was.

Although now that we're broken up, none of those unspoken rules apply anymore.

Just then, there's a tap on my shoulder, and before I can turn around, I hear my least favorite voice on the planet asking me, "Have you started the sign-up sheet yet?"

"Give me five minutes, Brent," I say.

"I don't want to go first. I want a good spot. I want to go fourth."

"If you're the fourth person who signs up, you'll go fourth, Brent."

"You always give me a shit spot."

"She doesn't," Claire says in a voice that shuts Brent up for half a second. Java Cabana doesn't have a bouncer or a door guy on staff, but Claire is so punk and disaffected, it's almost like she could kick your ass with nothing more than her poor opinion of you.

"You're on Java Cabana parole," I say to Brent. "And if you play the donkey-jism-squirt-gun song again, or anything like it, I will ban you."

"You can't ban me. You're, like, twelve."

He says it like he's joking, but underneath I detect the outrage that I am preventing him from doing whatever he wants. Maybe if a sound *guy* told him not to play the donkey-jism-squirt-gun song, he would have been more agreeable, or at least had the decency to feel ashamed of himself.

And I'm still being civil to him! I'm still giving him a chance! A sound *guy* probably would have told him to go away and inflict himself on some other open mic. That's probably how we ended up with him at Java Cabana in the first place.

Eventually, Brent leaves me alone and orders a drink, and

I set up my tabletop mic stand in the back so I can introduce the acts from the soundboard.

As people start approaching me to sign up, it occurs to me that I shouldn't be so hard on the scene at Java Cabana open mic. For example, I don't hate Desmond, who had been in a semi-famous band about ten years earlier and now worked as a teacher's aide at an elementary school. I don't hate Laura, who played folksy feminist anthems that sounded like they'd been written by Dolly Parton, if Dolly Parton was a Memphis hippie who made her own kombucha. Ian hasn't gotten here yet, but I like him because he looks like one of the shirtless *Bachelorette* suitors, and I like looking at him. This could not have been a secret to anyone, because I was all easy chitchat with Desmond and Laura, and I usually told Brent to go to hell, but every time Ian came to sign up for his open mic spot, I'd get tongue-tied and my hands would start to shake. Even when I was dating Vincent, this still happened.

A white girl I've seen before in the audience comes up to me carrying a guitar case and asks if she can play. I remember her because she always sits by herself, sipping a cup of tea, nibbling a scone, and studying every performer intently. Most people at open mic come to listen to themselves play, and only stick around for anyone else's set out of etiquette, so a legitimate audience member stands out.

"It's your first time, right?" I ask.

She nods nervously, tucking a strand of thick black hair behind her ear, so it curves around and grazes her jawline.

Okay, I've also noticed her before because she is very, very pretty. It's not just Ian who does this to me. I don't talk about it because it makes me feel like a weirdo or a perv, how often I notice people and find myself admiring their faces, their voices, the way their hair curls around their earlobes. It's one of the great things about people, how there's something shimmery about nearly all of them, something that gets my attention and draws me closer.

The girl nods and tells me her name is Risa, and I say, "I'm going to have you go first."

Risa's eyes widen in terror, but I say, "Trust me on this. You're going to do great."

At seven thirty, people start to come in. Brent waits until he sees a few other people sign up. I take his name and put him fourth even though I know there's a decent chance he'll clear the room with his "songs." Then I call Risa's name and go up to the front to help as she checks the mic and tunes her guitar, to give her a reassuring nod and let her know it sounds good. Once I can tell she's comfortable, I go back to the soundboard and introduce her.

Someone like Brent would see going first as a shit spot, and it seems like a scary thing to do to a new person, but I know this open mic, and I know it will be the perfect spot for Risa. The crowd isn't intimidatingly big, and she doesn't have time to get in her own head and panic.

Risa has a beautiful voice, even though it trembles during the first verse, like she's not quite used to the sound of it. Maybe this is the first time she's played a song outside her own bedroom, but even so, it's clear she can *play*. The way she holds the guitar is assured, her fingers attacking the strings, hammering out one inventive lick after another. She sings with her eyes closed, and she doesn't look at her hands once.

I look over at Desmond and Laura, and see them nodding their heads along to the music, grinning the way real musicians do when they recognize one of their own, when they hear something fresh that makes them sit up and take notice.

I clap extra hard when she's done, as do Desmond and Laura, who play next.

And then it's Brent's turn. I call him up, but instead of worrying about what he's going to play this time—hopefully not the one about his balls, or the one called "Title of Your Sex Tape"—I find myself wondering why Vincent had come by the coffee shop. Had he wanted to see me? Was there some message he'd come to deliver, only to lose heart at the last minute? Claire said he'd told her what happened. How had he told her? Like, what exact words had he used to describe what had happened between us, and what exact words had Claire said back? I wish she was the kind of friend I could have interrogated a little more thoroughly without being terrified it would backfire.

I obsess over this through Brent's set, through the girl with the pink hair and the red Gibson 335, through the guy who plays bluegrass mandolin. I'm about to announce a fifteen-minute break when Ian comes in, carrying his acoustic twelve-string in its giant case. He glides up to me, smiles, and asks if I can put his name on the list.

"Can you go on after the break?" I ask. I look away while I talk to him, because I know if I look into his smoky gray eyes, I'll start stammering like an idiot.

He must think I'm annoyed with him rather than nervous because he says, "No, it's cool. I can go after."

And then he sits there next to me while the bluegrass-mandolin player finishes up, and I call for everyone to give him a hand, remind the crowd to tip their barista, and say we'll be back shortly. Just when I've managed to get through that without hyperventilating, Ian draws his chair up close to mine and says, "I wanted to ask you something about guitars."

I nod because I'm still too tongue-tied to speak. Ian never talks to me during open mic, not more than to say hello and sign up. He never sits next to me, and he certainly never asks me about guitars.

"I'm thinking about getting a new guitar, and I wondered which ones you thought had the best sound."

This I could do on autopilot—the virtues of Telecasters, Rickenbackers, and Les Pauls come reeling out of my mouth, and I'm grateful to have accumulated so much information over the years. I play a little, but most of what I know comes from watching musicians struggle with floating bridges or guitars that refuse to stay in tune. I've had dozens of conversations about action and hot pickups. I tell Ian that the guitar is only one variable. I tell him the amp matters; the pedals matter; what he plays on it and how he plays matter.

Something I admire about my namesake, Lee Miller, is that before she was a surrealist photographer, she was a theater geek. Light crew, to be precise. She could have acted or written or directed, but what really got her excited was playing with gels and amassing a team of electricians to carry out her brilliant visions.

This is how I feel about doing sound production. It takes away the pressure you might sometimes feel to insist upon your own personality. I find the spotlight somewhat distressing, though I'm willing to aid and abet those who seek it out and make them sound as good as they deserve to sound.

While I'm telling Ian about guitars I love and hate, my throat finally loosens, my heartbeat returns to a normal rate, and I notice that he keeps looking away while I'm talking. At first, I'm a little bit annoyed—like, am I that boring? And then I realize that occasionally he does make eye contact with me, and that every time he does, something like panic registers on his face. His cheeks are flushed and he's talking too fast, and one of his knees is bouncing up and down, periodically jostling the table leg, and I think, *Oh. You're into me.*

Why does this happen? Why does the desire to be attractive to another person make you completely incapable of doing that very thing? I'm sure it's hormones, your body sending out all sorts of unhelpful neural messages. But also, when you want someone cute to like you, there's this thing where you start being YOU *as hard as you can*, like you're trying to push your essential being at this person, but cramming it through a pinhole of human interaction, and it builds and builds, until suddenly, it comes exploding out in a messy, unexpected spray.

It would be completely understandable, maybe even charming, to tell a person, "I'm sorry. I'm very twitchy because you're pretty and I like you."

Reasonable people would do this; evolved people in touch with their own brain chemistry and emotional states would do this. A person like that would acknowledge that a recent heartbreak, followed by her parents' clumsy announcement of their long-overdue yet still-upsetting separation, might have caused her to be a little bit more volatile than usual. She would make corrections for the variables: less caffeine, no unnecessary eye contact, no knee touches and arm brushes, no flirting.

One day post-breakup, two hours post–family tumult, a reasonable, evolved person would not abandon her post at the open mic, then lean over and whisper into the ear of a boy she barely knows, "Enough about guitars. Meet me outside in five minutes."

CHAPTER 5

Just Let the Kissing Be Enough

I don't drink, but there is a kind of hangover I know about. You get it when you wake up the morning after you've made a stupid mistake, and it comes with a headache of regret and a churning stomach full of shame, as you realize that what happened the night before wasn't a dream, but something you now have to fold into your waking day.

It hits me as soon as I open my eyes and makes me want to put my head under the covers and stay like that forever. Only, as soon as I do that, all the events of the previous night play back in my mind, starting from the moment I snuck out the back door of Java Cabana and met Ian in the alley. We didn't speak. I put my arms around his neck and he pressed me up against the brick wall, and we started kissing, which was where things began to go wrong.

Something I had forgotten in two years of kissing one guy exclusively was that many guys are bad kissers. It's so sad, because they never get any better, and there's no language in place to correct them without hurting their feelings, though that's probably the fault of humans, not language.

I should have called it off right there, said, *Hey, shouldn't we go back inside?* Instead I motioned for Ian to come with me to the lot where my car was parked, following some kind of stupid horny logic that insisted a guy who was a sloppy kisser might do a better job given access to other body parts.

Ian in the back seat of my car was no better than Ian in the alley, and it didn't take long before the novelty of hooking up with someone new disappeared entirely. I pulled away, refastened the buttons on my shirt, and told Ian I didn't think this was working. He shrugged, and at first I thought, *Okay, it's cool, no harm, no foul.* But then, Ian suggested—seemed to expect, in fact—that I would "take care of him," to use his words, intimating that what I had done was somehow unfair and that my unfairness to him was going to result in some kind of great physical pain.

"How is that fair to me?" I asked.

"It's not a big deal. It's just relief."

My parents were probably getting divorced, and my boyfriend had dumped me for public radio. I did not have time for this shit.

"If it's not a big deal, then do it yourself," I said. "Don't let the specter of blue balls hang needlessly over my car."

Then I made an *Oooooooo* sound and waved my hands in the air like a ghost, the Specter of Blue Balls in this case, which he did not find as funny as I did, and then I told him to get out of my car and I drove home, even though there were three other people on the open mic sign-up sheet scheduled to play after the break, and all my gear was still inside, and Claire had no idea where I was.

Kicking him out of my car was the only part of the whole encounter that *wasn't* a mistake. And now, in addition to feeling annoyed, disappointed, and filled with dread about the idea of returning to Java Cabana to face Claire, I also feel out of practice at all of this stuff, and decidedly off my game.

I should probably mention, all this time I've been talking about how deep and passionate a love affair Vincent and I had, we never actually had sex. I have had sex with people who were not Vincent. Not a lot of them, but there had been times when the possibility of sex, or at least enthusiasm about it, was part of the equation.

Not only did Vincent and I never have sex, but he never even seemed like he wanted to. Eventually, I stopped asking him to touch me in different places, or asking if he wanted me to touch him, because the answer was always the same. He'd shake his head and look away and we'd stop kissing and never talk about it. Since I didn't want to lose the kissing, too, I stopped bringing it up at all and just let the kissing be enough. Which sometimes it was. That's the other thing—I mean, yes, I was frustrated sometimes, but that wasn't Vincent's problem. And unlike Ian, I didn't think that was Vincent's job to take care of.

And that's the most confusing, irritating part of what happened with Ian and me last night. As poorly as it had gone, I'm surprised how good it felt to want a guy to put his hands on me like that, to feel excited about what might happen next.

Of course, having those exciting, sexy feelings tied to a guy who'd proven himself to be wholly undeserving of them makes me wonder if Vincent's way is right. Maybe desire is something to put in a jar for later, and my life would be happier and simpler without sex in it.

I emerge from my bedroom to find the house empty, two notes addressed to me on the kitchen table. My dad has left for work, taking Sage and Max with him. My mom and Maggie have left for the train station. They're all very sorry to have missed me, and I feel alone in a way I've never experienced before. Ordinarily, I'd call Vincent or work on *Artists in Love* or go to Java Cabana, but now I have no one to see, nothing to do, and nowhere to go.

I know I *should* go to Java Cabana and apologize to Claire for skipping out on the second half of open mic and leaving my gear behind. I don't flatter myself thinking that she wasted any energy worrying about my sorry ass, but she's probably furious that I left her to close by herself.

I feel too ashamed to face her, so as a kind of penance, I lie down on the floor, let my back ache on the hard wood. I don't know what my mom was thinking, suggesting that I make something. There isn't a single idea in my head, and I realize that maybe I was never an artist at all. Artists are supposed to feed on experiences like this. They're supposed to make beauty out of tragedy, art out of heartbreak. These things are supposed to charge you up and give you something to make art about. But me? At the first setback, I give up, let all the life go out of me.

I don't know how long I've been on the floor when I hear a knock at the front door, and when I get up and answer it and find Vincent standing there with a cup of coffee and a bag of pastries from the bakery near his house, I'm so happy, so relieved to see him, that I fling myself into his arms. The coffee slops over the lid on impact, splashing down my leg, and the pastry bag is smashed against my chest, but I don't care because Vincent is hugging me back, hugging me like his life depends on it.

I start crying, and then he's crying, and even though there are so many things I want to say to him, I don't allow myself to say any of them first.

Not *I miss you*, not *I love you*.

I don't say those things because he's the one who is leaving, and because I still don't know what he's doing at my house.

Finally, we let go of each other, and I take the coffee cup from his hand and set it on a coaster, inspect the pastries, which are not unsalvageably crushed, and go to the kitchen for cups and plates and forks. I'm weirdly formal as I lay it all out on the coffee table, put a pastry on each plate, and divide the coffee between two cups and saucers, folded paper towels on the side. I feel his eyes on me, on my every move and gesture, like he's memorizing them.

Because there is nothing else to do, and because I'm still waiting for him to say something, I sit and take a bite of my pastry, a sip of my coffee, and finally, Vincent asks, "How are you?"

I think about the past twenty-four hours, about my parents and Ian and fucking up the open mic night and the crushing emptiness of standing alone in my living room with no ideas. It's been less than two days since we broke up, and he wants to know how I am?

"Not great, Vincent," I say, and then I start to laugh, and he starts to laugh too. At first, he laughs like he's not sure whether he should, but then we both lose it and our laughter becomes almost unhinged.

Eventually, I pull myself together and ask, "And what about you? How have you been?"

I'm being formal again, like he's someone I barely know, someone I've forgotten how to talk to. His face grows serious and he takes a deep breath and says, "Lee, I think I made a mistake."

My heart starts to beat faster, and a surge of adrenaline shoots through my body and sends my muscles quivering, even as my brain whispers, *Settle down, slow down, you don't even know what he means.*

"I was at church last night, and everybody was congratulating me, making a big fuss, but the whole time it was like they were secretly thinking, *Really? You?*"

I've never met the people at Vincent's church, but they've known Vincent his whole life. They watched him grow up.

"Isn't it possible they're genuinely proud of you?" I ask.

"Or it's possible they think a spot at Howard should have gone to someone a little more Black."

"Vincent, that's bullshit," I say, not knowing how much exactly that means coming from me, a white person who didn't even know about Howard University until her boyfriend applied there.

"I used to worry that I was the wrong kind of Black for Memphis, and now I'm worried that I'm not Black enough for Howard. Or talented enough, or smart enough. They put me on the waitlist for a reason, Lee."

"They took you off for a reason, too," I say.

I've never seen Vincent like this before. I think back to the other night when we were recording the last episode of our podcast. He'd admitted to feeling nervous about not being up to the challenges and terrified about uprooting his life. The way he'd said it was so rational, like he was just acknowledging some unpleasant feelings before getting the better of them, but still, it should have tipped me off. Everything Vincent puts out into the world is so polished and positive and assured. Even his feelings.

Especially his feelings.

"I've been so unhappy, Lee. I haven't eaten. I haven't slept. I keep thinking about what my life will be like without you, and it is intolerable to me."

I like that he said "intolerable."

It's such a certain word, it sounds like the Vincent I'm used to. When I imagine what my life will look like without Vincent in it, I can't muster language that certain. What I know is this: before Vincent and I broke up, I could see a future that was very big and full of all the things I wanted most; and now it was an empty room, silent and still. My life without Vincent is unimaginable to me. Which is also intolerable.

"What are you thinking, Lee? Please, say something."

Sitting next to him on the couch, I study his face, his golden-brown eyes, the sweat beaded adorably on his nose.

"I love you," I tell him, "but you're leaving."

"That doesn't change the way I feel. I love you, too."

"What's going to happen?"

"I don't know."

"Vincent, I'm so tired. Will you hold me some more?"

He knows what I mean when I say this. It's an old code between us. We go down the hallway to my bedroom, and I close the door behind us, turn on the air conditioner, and pull the curtains closed. And then, Vincent and I slide under the covers of my bed, our arms and legs intertwined, our faces pressed together. It feels like home, just like it always did. Even though we never take our clothes off, every time we hold each other like this, I think, *I will never feel this close to anyone again.*

"What do we do now?" I ask, my eyes half-closed, drinking in the smell of him. After he leaves, I know his smell will still cling to these sheets, and I can bury my face in the pillow and remember that this happened, that it was real. I thought I'd lost him, and then, there he was.

"Come with me," Vincent says.

"Really?"

"I don't want to do this without you."

Tears begin to leak from my eyes. This isn't supposed to happen. He isn't supposed to come back. I'm not supposed to get him back.

The lump in my throat, the tears in my eyes, the feeling in my heart all tell me to nuzzle into his shoulder and say, *Yes, yes, yes, I love you, and I will come with you.*

But when I open my mouth to say the words, nothing comes out.

The first time Lee Miller met Man Ray, she walked up to him in a Paris café and said, "I'm your new student." He said, "I'm afraid that's impossible, as I'm leaving Paris for the summer," and Lee replied, "Then I'm coming with you."

Nothing about this story seems true, yet neither of them ever deviated in their telling of it for the rest of their lives.

It would feel so good, and so free, to give myself over to Vincent like that, and I don't know why I can't just say I'll go with him. Vincent doesn't seem to mind. He reads the language of my body, all weepily joyful and wrapped up together with him, and takes it for my answer.

"I love you so much," he says, and he kisses me.

Maybe the words will come later, when I'm less overwhelmed, when my head is clear. I'll be able to say them then.

I kiss him back, and it feels like home, and without meaning to, we fall asleep in each other's arms.

CHAPTER 6

Head in the Game

Lee!" I wake up to the sound of my dad's voice, a sharp voice he never uses, and the glare of my bedroom light. I dig myself out from under the sheets and sit up, at which point I notice that Vincent is still in my bed, a few seconds behind me in consciousness, his cheek still resting in a small spot of drool on my pillow. I check the clock on my dresser and realize that it's four thirty, and that Vincent and I have been asleep for hours.

My dad is standing in my doorway with Sage and Max. Sage studies my dad, waiting to take his cues on how to react, though my dad seems not to know.

"Our guests are here."

Behind him, Max stifles a laugh. He looks different from how I remember him. The last time I saw him, he was wearing Banana Republic shorts and deck shoes. Now he's wearing a mesh shirt and eyeliner. I wonder what this newest iteration of Max makes of me.

Modest and discreet people might go back out to the living room and give Vincent and me a moment to collect ourselves, but Max, Sage, and my dad make no move to leave. Vincent shudders awake, then sits bolt upright in bed, a look on his face like he might perish on the spot. If this had happened to us at his house, his parents would be dragging him out of bed by the ear and taking him straight to church. They would have looked at me like I was some kind of biblical temptress, come to cut off their son's hair or sell his birthright.

"Vincent, will you be staying for dinner?" my dad asks in an uncharacteristically frosty tone. As far as he knows, this is still the person who broke up with me less than two days ago.

"I'm so sorry, sir. I had no idea how late it had gotten."

"That doesn't answer my question, Vincent. Will you be joining us or not?"

"Yes, sir. Thank you," Vincent says, because he thinks he's supposed to, and in his effort to be polite, inadvertently does the thing no one wants.

"Very good," my dad says. "I'll order the pizza."

"Hi, Lee. Hi, Vincent. Congratulations on Howard," Max says, waving from behind our parents.

"And NPR," Sage calls from the doorway. "And congratulations on graduation, Lee. Do you have any plans for the summer?"

"Not really," I say.

"It's a wild time," they say. "Limbo land. Your old life isn't entirely over, but your new one hasn't entirely started. That's how I remember it, at least."

Sage and my dad exchange a look, and he snorts, and I realize that the three of them are enjoying the shit out of themselves, making this as awkward and embarrassing as possible.

"How about you, Max?" my dad asks. "Have you figured out your life yet? Have you picked a major?"

Frozen beneath the sheets, Vincent blushes furiously.

Max, who is still grinning, turns to my dad and says, "I'm going to major in Mortification Studies with a minor in Napping Until the Food Gets Here."

"Are you sure you don't want to visit with Lee and Vincent?"

"I think maybe they need a minute."

"Yeah, a minute would be nice," I say.

My dad says, "Then I'll see the two of you in the living room in a minute."

"Actually, sir," Vincent says, probably considering the prolonged awkwardness of joining my family for dinner and dialing back from his gallant etiquette, "I should probably go home."

"Are your parents expecting you?" Sage asks.

"Yes, ma'am."

"Just Sage is fine. I'm not a ma'am."

"Yes," Vincent says, and I can tell he's barely caught himself from saying *ma'am* again. Sage gets clocked as a guy about as frequently as they get clocked as a woman. It's worse in the South with all the excessive *sir*-ing and *ma'am*-ing that goes on. Like people can't figure out how to be polite to you unless they can determine to their satisfaction where you belong.

"If you have to call me something, call me *Captain*," Sage says, and they and my dad finally leave, closing the door behind them. I look at Vincent and laugh while he puts his head under the covers.

"I'm so embarrassed," he says.

I run a brush through my hair, fix my face in the mirror,

smooth the fabric of my sundress. In the mirror, I catch Vincent looking at me.

"You're so beautiful," he says. "And I'm so happy."

"What are you so happy about?" I ask. I already know, but I want to hear him say it.

Vincent swings his legs over the side of the bed and comes up behind me, puts his arms around my waist as we stand together in front of the mirror.

"I'm glad I came over, I'm glad you let me stay. I'm glad about everything that happened this afternoon. I love you so much."

"I love you, too."

We go out into the living room, and Vincent pulls himself together and says his awkward goodbyes. The detritus from our morning, the half-empty coffee cups and plates covered in crumbs are still on the coffee table. It feels weirdly intimate, having it out there for everyone to see, and I clear it away in a rush.

When the pizza arrives, my dad, Sage, Max, and I sit down to dinner like nothing has happened. No one asks me what Vincent was doing in my bed; no one asks me how my heart is.

Instead Sage pulls out their notebook and begins to page through it with my dad, showing him some of their latest tattoo designs.

"Do you see anything you like?" they ask.

"I've been thinking," my dad says slowly, "could you do a bridge for me?"

"Like London Bridge? The Golden Gate Bridge?"

"The M Bridge," my dad says. I know he's talking about

the Hernando de Soto Bridge, which stretches from down-town across the river into Arkansas. Everybody calls it the M Bridge, though. *M* for Memphis. *M* for Mississippi River.

M *for Maya, my mother's name,* I think.

"I can do that for you," Sage says before turning to me to ask, "What about you? Have you ever thought about getting a tattoo?"

"I can't think of anything I'd want on me permanently."

"A tattoo doesn't have to say something about the rest of your life. It only has to say something about your life right now."

"But it's on you for the rest of your life."

"Well, there's that," Sage says, then rolls up their sleeve and points to a tacky four-leaf clover inked on their bicep, right in the middle of the beautiful dragons and stained glass swirls. "Looks like it came out of a cereal box, right?"

"Can you cover it up?"

"It's part of my story," they say.

It makes sense to hear it that way, sort of. If you covered up part of your own story, wasn't that like saying you were ashamed of it?

"I thought you and that guy broke up," Max says, chewing on a mushroom-and-pepper slice.

Sage and my dad let their conversation slow to a trickle so they can hear how I answer.

I nod, to indicate to Max that we are being monitored, then whisper under my breath, "It's complicated."

"Isn't he leaving town in a few days?"

"Geez, Dad, did you air my business to everyone?" I ask,

in full voice, before turning back to Max and whispering, "We sort of got back together. I'll tell you everything later."

Max gets this world-weary look on his face, sympathetic but skeptical.

"Lee, maybe you could take Max to work with you tonight," my dad suggests.

"What's your work?" Max asks.

"I'm a sound guy."

"Cool," he says, to my surprise. This current iteration of Max seems possibly too cool to acknowledge that other things are cool. "I'll go."

I'm glad my dad mentioned it. I haven't even thought about work until this moment, and now I'm wondering whether Ian will show up again and how angry Claire will be when she sees me. I'm glad Max wants to come along. It will be nice to have a buffer.

Harold arrives around the time Max and I are getting ready to leave, and he, my dad, and Sage set up on the front porch with a bottle of bourbon. I'm sure they'll pull out their vape pens later on too. However, this evening doesn't have the party atmosphere of their usual raucous college reunions. They all look miserable. If my mom was worried about Dad having more post-separation fun than her, her fears were misplaced. I wonder what she and Maggie are up to, whether they're holed up in their hotel room, writing, or flirting with musicians, or sobbing in their daiquiris on Bourbon Street.

"How's the podcasting thing going?" Max asks as we get into the car. "You still do that?"

Do I? I wasn't sure. Would Vincent still want to make *Art-*

ists in Love with me when he was working on real shows on NPR? Would he still have time when he started college? And what was I supposed to do while he was off doing those other things?

Running away with Vincent felt very romantic until I started thinking about the details.

"I listened to some of it," Max continues. "It's good, really professional. But I wanted to ask you, why artists in love? What makes them so special?"

The anxious questions in my brain evaporate as I remember the day Vincent and I came up with the idea. It was the first time he'd ever been to my house after school, and I remember how he froze in the middle of the living room. I thought he was nervous because we liked each other but hadn't done anything about it yet, but then I realized he wasn't looking at me. He was looking at the walls, covered with art by my parents' friends. He was looking at the crates full of records, the hundreds of books, overflowing their shelves and stacked on every surface in the room. His face lit up as he spun around slowly, taking everything in, and then he kissed me right there in my living room.

We spent the rest of the afternoon pulling art books off the shelves, poring over them together, talking about the work we liked, trading artist love stories, and when my parents came home from work, they found us sitting on the floor, our fingers laced together over a book about Christo and Jeanne-Claude.

"Because artists have the best love stories," I say to Max.

"Bullshit," he says. "What about Barack and Michelle

Obama? Prince Harry and Meghan Markle? Oscar Wilde and Lord Alfred Douglas?"

It wasn't just Max's clothes that had changed, apparently. The Banana-Republic-shorts-and-deck-shoes Max would have nodded his head agreeably and left it at that.

I step up to his challenge. "Artists have a process that allows them to create. And some of that process gets into their love stories as well—that's what makes those stories more interesting."

"It sounds like you're saying artists are better than other people."

"I never said that. It's just that, the kind of love you're supposed to want, the romantic-comedy, Hallmark-card, royal-wedding mainstream idea, is so fucked up that I've always thought maybe artists have a better idea of how to do it."

"Even now?"

"Especially now," I say, but Max doesn't look convinced.

Claire doesn't make me any special drinks or give me treats from the day-old case when I come in, and she gives Max a suspicious look when I introduce him.

"I'm sorry about last night, Claire," I say. "It won't happen again."

"Whatever, we're good," Claire says in a terse way.

It's not the first time Claire has told me *We're good*, and I know what she really means is we'll be good in another day or so, but we aren't good *yet*.

Max buys an iced latte and sits at a table in the corner

while I set up. He puts earbuds in and starts messing around with his phone; meanwhile, I'm trying to look as professional as possible, like showing Claire how seriously I take my job will make her forgive me faster.

Then our manager, Trudy, shows up with that night's musician, a one-man band who performs under the name Wire Mother, but whose name is actually Steve. Steve looks like an accountant, and I steel myself for a night of boring Beale Street knock-off blues or sad divorced-dad basement music.

But because I'm trying to show Trudy and Claire how much of a pro I am, I take notes while Steve describes his set and realize that, while he may be wearing pleated khakis, Steve is possessed of a deeply unusual mind.

"Can you mic a coffee can full of nails?" he asks.

"No one's ever asked me to before. But I can try."

The coffee can proves to be the least daunting thing Steve throws me, as his set also involves a glockenspiel, a kazoo, and a light-activated oscillating drum machine that sounds like a 1950s sci-fi movie. It's fun having a challenge like this, figuring out how to mic the oddball mix of analog and digital instruments. And a decent distraction as well.

Trudy pulls me aside while Steve chills out in the storage closet, waiting for the set to begin. In addition to managing Java Cabana, Trudy books all the bands that play there. There's so much music in Memphis, so many venues, it's not like bands are exactly lining up to play at a Midtown coffee shop with no stage and no cover that seats fifty people if they're packed in shoulder to shoulder. Trudy wants a club of her own someday, the kind of venue that bands are falling over themselves to book. The nights she isn't working, she goes to shows, meets everyone, tells new local bands to send her demos. In that way, Java Cabana books bigger and better bands than we have any business attracting.

"Claire told me you disappeared last night," she says.

"I'm really sorry, Trudy. It won't happen again."

Trudy gives me a hard look. "Is everything okay, Lee? Claire also mentioned that there was some personal drama."

"It was a one-time lapse in judgment."

"Then who's that?" she asks, nodding her head toward Max.

"He's my dad's friends' kid. I promise, he's the opposite of trouble."

"He looks like a postapocalyptic rogue you picked up at the club."

"He's from Chicago," I say, like that explained things. Max is dressed like someone who's spent a lot of time in Europe, which he has. His eyebrow is pierced and so are his ears, and right now, he's wearing bright yellow pants and patent leather boots that come up to his knees.

"There are two rules, Lee. Don't electrocute anyone, and don't wander off. I mean, there are more than two rules, but those are the ones I really can't let slide."

I'm mortified. I should have saved up some of my breakup goodwill instead of squandering it all with thirty-six hours of questionable behavior that sent me running back to the safety of Vincent's arms.

Although, now that I think about it, I'm not the one who's been running. Vincent was the one who'd ended it, the one who was leaving. Vincent was the one who wanted me back. And I'd gone along with all of it, like I was waiting around for him to decide whether we were going to stay together or not. The thought worries me. How had I ever accomplished anything up to now, without someone else prodding me along, telling me what to do, shoving me in front of opportunities I would have daydreamed past?

"Is your head in the game, Lee?" Trudy asks.

"Yes," I say, determined to prove it to her.

Wire Mother, aka Steve, comes out of the storage room and gives me a set list and a list of cues to listen for.

"I'm worried it's going to be muddy," he says. "Do you have any ideas for that in a room like this?"

"I was going to ask you to scoop out the mids," I say, and Wire Mother looks at me like I have asked him to saw off his thumb.

"I'll lose my tone if I scoop out the mids."

"You'll lose everything else if you don't. In this room, you've got to punch out a hole for the vocals and the sampler and the coffee can to come through."

I speak with enough authority that Wire Mother nods and makes the adjustments on his guitar amp. The café is beginning to fill up, and both Trudy and Claire are behind the counter slinging drinks when Wire Mother slings his guitar strap over his shoulder and steps up to the mic.

He's the wrong musician for this venue, too loud, too complicated. There's no room for the sound to bounce around in a pleasing way, and if I'm not careful, he'll drown everyone in a sea of sludge. But my head is in the game, and

I'm holding it together, sorting out the different threads of sound, disentangling them so each one rings out clear, so the vocals cut through. He sounds as good here, in this makeshift space, as he would in a bigger club with a real stage and a real sound guy.

My head is in the game so much that I don't lose my focus when Ian walks in during the set. I don't panic when Vincent walks in a few minutes later and orders a coffee from Claire. I don't do anything except whisper "thank you" when Vincent brings me the steaming mug between songs, kissing me on the cheek.

I refuse to let myself get distracted by the fact that the guy I'd been in bed with that afternoon and the guy I'd hooked up with last night are sitting within spitting distance of each other. *Nobody knows,* I tell myself, until I remember that Claire knows.

So what, I think. *Claire can keep a secret. Nothing's going to happen.*

Wire Mother's set takes up all my attention, and I don't even look over my shoulder until it's over. That's when I finally take a moment to survey my handiwork—a long line of people waiting to talk to Wire Mother and buy his merch, a busy coffee counter, nobody complaining or holding their ears, a full house of happy people. Trudy catches my eye from behind the register and gives me a thumbs-up.

That's when Ian leans over my shoulder and whispers in my ear, "You didn't say you had a boyfriend."

I doubt that explaining the complexities of the situation will make him any happier, so I ask, "What are you even doing here?"

"Maybe I was coming to apologize for last night," he says, though he doesn't sound sorry for anything.

"Were you?"

"Not anymore," he says, his voice getting louder. "That's a shitty way to treat someone."

"Well, it's shitty to assume a girl owes you a hand job just because you hook up."

And of course, that's when Vincent joins us.

"You okay, Lee?" he asks. "Who's this?"

"No one."

"That's right," Ian scoffs. "I'm no one."

"What's going on here?" Vincent asks.

"Ask your girlfriend."

Vincent gives me a look, and I realize he's waiting for an explanation. If my sweet, trusting boyfriend hasn't taken Ian's side outright, he's at least decided it's worth hearing him out.

And judging by Ian's defiant stance, he's not going to leave until he's succeeded in making some kind of a scene.

"I don't know what he's talking about."

"You were saying something when I walked up," Vincent says, and his voice drops to a whisper when he says, "about hand jobs."

"It wasn't anything," I say, and when he doesn't look reassured, I add, "That's not even what I said."

Ian and Vincent both stare at me with disgust. Behind the register, I see Claire watching all of this unfold. I meet her eyes, looking for any kind of help, but she looks away.

Ian turns to Vincent and says, "Good luck with that," before he walks out of Java Cabana.

I give Vincent a nervous smile, as if to say, *Whew, thank goodness that's over, can you believe that guy?* He doesn't smile back.

"I heard you, Lee," he says. "I heard most of it, I think."

"Oh."

"Did you really hook up with that guy last night?"

"It wasn't like that," I say.

"What was it like?"

"I didn't like it. That's why I didn't let it go any further."

"What if you *had* liked it?"

"The point is, nothing happened."

"Well, not nothing."

"Vincent, we were broken up. I didn't do anything wrong."

"I didn't say you did."

"Are we okay?" I ask.

"I don't know," Vincent says, looking like he's about to cry. "I mean, you just lied about it to my face until I called you out. And I know there were things you wanted, but, Lee, we'd been broken up for a *day*."

"I didn't think you were coming back, Vincent."

"Did you even want me to?"

"Of course I did."

Too late, I see Trudy approaching. She looks at Vincent and me and says, "Maybe finish this later?"

Vincent seems like he's thinking about arguing with her, but I cut him off.

"Can we talk when I get home?" I ask.

He holds up his hands and starts to back away, then shakes his head and says, "You know, Lee, maybe not. Wait a day. See if some other guy comes along."

Then he storms out of Java Cabana, and I sit down like I've been slapped. Trudy looks at the long line of people waiting for drinks, gives me an apologetic look, and joins Claire behind the counter.

Stunned, I start breaking down the gear, winding up cables and folding up the mic stands. I hadn't started it, I hadn't intended for any of it to turn out this way, and still, I'd done exactly what Trudy had warned me not to do.

"You were right about the mids."

I turn around to see Wire Mother, aka Steve, standing behind me. He's transformed from an avant-garde rock star back into an accountant in pleated khakis.

"You sounded good," I say, like a zombie. "It was a good set."

"Thanks to you. Do you have a card?" I shake my head, and he shrugs. "No worries. Maybe we'll get to work together another time, though."

I make some blandly agreeable sounds, then hide in the storage closet until the crowd thins out and it's time to go home. I'd been hoping to slink out the door unnoticed, but Trudy catches me and pulls me aside in the middle of the coffee shop.

"Lee, I want you to take some time off," she says.

My eyes widen as I realize what she's saying, that I'm no longer wanted at the one place left that I have to go.

"Please give me another chance," I beg. "What happened tonight, I swear it won't be a problem again."

"Lee, I'm not mad at you, but you're going through a lot. Call me in a couple of weeks, and we'll see where things are."

"This isn't fair!" I say, my voice growing hysterical. "If I was a guy and my ex showed up and made a scene, you wouldn't be punishing me for it. Trudy, please. I need this."

Trudy's face goes cold, and I can tell that she's reached the end of her patience with this conversation.

"Lee, come back when you understand why I can't let you come to work like this."

I'd hoped that maybe Claire would come to my defense, but she stays behind the counter, washing dishes. The only customer left in the café is Max, at the same table where I'd left him two hours before, still fooling around with his phone.

He looks up when I come over to his table, takes the earbuds out.

"What'd I miss?" he asks.

CHAPTER 7

Your One Wild and Precious Life

Max doesn't try to make small talk on our drive home. When we pull up to the house, my dad, Sage, and Harold are still on the porch, still somber, but talkative as we go inside. They're putting on a performance to demonstrate to us, their children, how sober they are. We know exactly how sober they are. The bourbon bottle is half-empty, and though my dad hugs me and tells me that he loves me when we say good night, he looks like he's about to break down or pass out.

As I follow Max to the kitchen, I take out my phone and see that I have texts from Vincent and my mom. I'm not sure which ones I want to read least.

I open the one from my mom, which says:

I saw this Mary Oliver poem today, and it made me think of you. Love you, baby. Miss you.

Her next text is a photograph of her holding a sheet of paper where she's written a message in Sharpie. She likes to do this with me for some reason. I have a phone full of her selfies, holding messages that say things like *Creativity takes courage* and *Please fold the laundry in the dryer.*

This time, she's written a line from the Mary Oliver poem,

and it glares at me like an accusation: *Tell me, what is it you plan to do with your one wild and precious life?*

Thus far, my plans for my one wild and precious life had amounted to getting fired and crying over boys.

I sit down at the kitchen counter and take a deep breath as I look at Vincent's texts, which I know will be long and well punctuated and upsetting:

Lee, I'm so sorry that I lost my temper, but it doesn't change the fact that I hate that it happened.

I wish I could find some way to explain it to you. Sometimes I feel like my parents and Jesus and the world get all mixed up together, and I can't tell who I'm really listening to. All I know is, it's too much noise in my head.

I thought that if we could just get away from here it would all be different and I could be the person you want me to be.

I guess I was wrong.

I put my phone facedown like that will make Vincent's texts go away. I can practically see the disappointment and frustration on his face as he typed them. Disappointment and frustration with me, with the world, with the whole stupid situation that could have been avoided if I'd had enough self-control to avoid kissing one feckless coffee-shop rando. I wonder what kind of person he thinks I want him to be—someone who would do more than just kiss me? I don't understand why that part would be different if we lived in Washington, DC, instead of Memphis.

Max sets a bag of chips and two cans of soda on the counter in front of us and takes a seat next to me.

"I listened to the last episode of *Artists in Love* during the set," he says, cracking open his can. "Were you and Vincent always like that?"

"Like what?"

"So serious about everything."

"We took it seriously. We took each other seriously."

"I liked the metronome."

"The one that watched Man Ray while he worked, or the one he wanted to smash with a hammer?"

"*Object of Destruction.* So fucking metal."

"Yeah, I guess."

"I'm sorry about what happened with you two."

"Thanks."

We eat and drink in silence for a minute, before Max adds, "I'm sorry about your parents, too."

I feel so grateful to have him here, someone who already knows what happened, understands the people involved.

"It's kind of my fault," I say. "Not that I'm wishing myself out of existence, but if you think about it, there's an alternate universe where I was never born, and therefore, there was no reason for my parents to spend eighteen years making each other miserable."

"That's not on you," Max says pragmatically. "They're adults. They made their choices."

"Can I show you something?" I ask.

Max nods, and I take him into my parents' office, open up the desk drawer that sticks, and pull out my dad's expired passport and my mom's poetry chapbook.

"All of this was happening around the time that my mom got pregnant and my parents got married."

"What was happening?"

"My dad was thinking about leaving the country, and my mom was dedicating books of poetry to Greg, *'for everything.'* Your parents must have known at least something about that."

"Maybe they didn't want to get involved. Or maybe they thought it was a bad idea for your mom to end up with Greg. Or, very likely, they had their own shit going on."

"But the thing is, nobody knows. There's a story in these objects. Not the kind that they tell at parties and everybody knows by heart. There's a story in here that nobody ever talks about."

Max gives me a teasing grin and starts to back slowly out of the room.

"What?" I say.

"You just seem a little worked up is all."

"I am worked up! This is serious!"

"It's also . . ." He takes some time choosing his next words. "You've had a pretty intense day, Lee. Are you thinking about *this* just so you can avoid thinking about that?"

"That's not what this is," I say. I pull out my phone and show him the Mary Oliver poem that my mom had texted me. "Do your parents talk to you like this when you break up with someone?"

Max lets out a bitter laugh. "I wish."

"This is my one wild and precious life. And I could choose to spend it feeling terrible and guilty, or I could spend it trying to get to the bottom of this."

Max considers this for a moment as he looks around my parents' office.

"Do you think there's anything else in here?" he asks.

Without discussing it, the two of us begin searching the room. Max goes through boxes in the closet, and I look behind the furniture, under the couch.

Then, for the second time that day, I hear my dad's voice in the doorway.

"Lee!"

I push my mother's desk back where I'd found it, stand up quickly.

"Yes?"

"Are you looking for something?"

"A pump for the air mattress," I lie. My eyes dart across the room just in time to see Max hide something behind his back.

"It's in the hall closet," my dad says. "I think we're about to turn in, so you'd better clear out. I'm sure Sage wants to get some sleep."

Max and I go back out into the living room, where Harold is already snoring on the couch. This is a sight I'm used to. Even though Harold lives just downtown, he often prefers to stay up late and crash in our living room, or our attic, or even occasionally on our front porch. This half-feral habit is left over from the days when his band, the Little Thieves, was touring, hoarding their *per diems* and crowding together in one hotel room to save money.

"Come on," I say to Max. "We can go to my room."

"Don't stay up too late," my dad says, I guess because that's what parents are supposed to say, but why did it matter? It's summer, and I've been dumped and fired. There is nothing I need to be well rested for.

As soon as Max and I are in my room, I whisper, "What'd you find?"

Max reveals a VHS cassette labeled *The Dirty South Literati: Maya & Arthur's Engagement Party.*

"Do you know anybody with a working VCR?" he asks.

I shake my head. My parents are the kind of people who wear vintage clothing, shop at used record stores, and live in a creaky, hundred-year-old house, and not even *they* are retro enough to own a VCR.

Max lays the tape on the floor. Next to it, I place the poetry book and the passport.

Some stories you can research out of books. Others only take an interview or two to reveal themselves to you. But then there are stories that have to be chiseled out in pieces, reassembled like dinosaur bones.

Nineteen years ago, my father was getting ready to leave the country. My mother was writing love poems to another man, but those aren't the stories that happened. This one was. They got married and had me.

What I want to know is, why?

CHAPTER 8

Go Back to Being Us

A podcast loses a quarter of its audience within the first five minutes. You have to start strong and re-engage constantly. Vincent taught me that.

The introduction writes itself in my head while Max and I are sitting in my room. I imagine that I'm pitching the idea to Vincent for *Artists in Love*. I imagine showing him the passport, the tape, the poetry chapbook, and saying, *I just have to get to the bottom of this story.*

He'd nod seriously and ask, *Who will you interview first? What if they won't talk to you? Or worse, what if they do, and you find out something you don't want to know?*

And then I'd say, *I don't give a shit what I find, as long as it's the truth.*

I like imagining myself in a role like this. Not a heartbroken disaster and disappointment, but a fearless investigator tailing a story. Someone Vincent would respect.

Max is yawning, so I tell him he can have my bed, and instead of sleeping, I go up to the attic and make a list of interview subjects, a list of questions. I write three different scripts trying to explain exactly what it is that makes my parents so bad together, crumpling each of them up when they don't properly capture the dysfunction.

When that approach doesn't work, I pick up my mom's poetry chapbook, *Map Room Love Songs*, and start to page through. What surprises me the most is that they aren't love poems—not happy ones, anyway. A lot of the poems mention Greg by name, but they never turn out well. At the end, he's always leaving, and she can never hold on to him, so she writes another one, like if she keeps putting the same information in slightly different configurations, she might eventually arrive at a different conclusion.

There's one poem in the book that's not like the others, though. It's sillier. Happier. And while the other poems in the chapbook have titles like "Burn All Your Letters" and "Suffering Bastard," this one is just called:

GROSS
When I come home after my shift
you never ask how my day was.
Instead you ask,
"What was the grossest thing you had to touch all day?"

All day, I save up memories
of damp straw wrappers
wadded at the bottom of milkshake glasses,
already-chewed French fries,
a cold, runny egg yolk,
lipstick-smeared coffee cups—always fuchsia—
so I can turn them into a story for you.

One summer night you come home late,
caked in a dozen layers of sweat,
secondhand smoke, bar rags, and bleach.

"Can I be the grossest thing you touch all day?" you ask.

You're the only person I would have wanted to tell,
so I keep our story to myself.

"What was the grossest thing you had to touch all day?" It sounds like the way my dad would start a conversation. I wonder if he's the person she was writing to, the person she was keeping a secret while she's breaking her own heart on every other page, agonizing about her relationship with Greg. This poem is a ray of goofy sunshine compared to the rest. I can't decide whether this makes me feel better or worse.

At six in the morning, I finally stagger down from the attic and fall asleep on the air mattress in my parents' office, only to be awakened by Sage's phone alarm at eight. I cover my head with the sheet as Sage steps over me, and a few minutes later, I smell coffee and bacon.

I rub my eyes and go out to the kitchen, where Sage is standing at the stove, turning strips of bacon with a fork. There's a plate of croissants already laid out on the table and a bowl of freshly washed grapes.

"Dig in," they say. "Where's Max?"

"I couldn't sleep, so I let him have my bed."

"Poor kiddo. I'm sorry we're all crowded in here. That's probably the last thing you want right now."

I consider the alternative, my parents in separate bedrooms, not speaking to each other.

"I don't mind," I say.

My eyes sting, my body aches, and my ideas, which had sounded so shiny and exciting at four in the morning, now seem like a lot of work and a waste of time.

"Why are you up so early?" I ask Sage, who seems cheerful and industrious despite drinking a fair amount of bourbon the night before.

"I have tattoo appointments lined up all day at Trinity," Sage says. "I'm their guest artist."

"You're famous," I say.

They wave me off modestly. "It's just because I'm from somewhere else. Some people get very excited about that."

"When are you going to do my dad's tattoo?"

"I was thinking tonight, if he hasn't changed his mind."

"Right here in the house?"

"That's the plan."

Suddenly, the sound-engineer part of my brain engages. I imagine rigging up my mics, recording an interview with Sage and my dad with a tattoo needle buzzing in the background. I think there must be a way to do it, where it would add atmosphere without being annoying.

"Would you mind if I was there?" I find myself asking. "Like, if I talked to the two of you and recorded it while you're doing the tattoo? It's for something I'm working on, maybe. A story."

"What kind of story?"

"A love story," I say, then add, "I'm not sure exactly what it is yet."

"Ask your dad. If he's okay with it, then I'm okay with it."

The smells of Sage's cooking lure everyone else into the kitchen, and soon my dad and Harold and Max are gathered around the kitchen table, filling plates.

"Thanks for letting me sleep in your bed," Max says.

"Anytime," I reply.

My dad looks up from his breakfast, alarmed, like he's wondering what my mom would say about his parental judgment if she was here. I roll my eyes because he should know by now that it's not like that between Max and me. It's not just that we've been friends since we were little kids; it's that, in all that time, Max has liked guys, and only guys. During his family's last few visits to Memphis, Max had been dating some sweet, saintly boy named Niko, about whom Sage and Maggie would not shut up. I've seen pictures, so I remember the blonde French-crop haircut, the oxford shirts and crew-neck sweaters, the catalog-model aesthetic that Max seems to have fully abandoned now. I realize that no one has mentioned Niko's name once this visit, not even Max. Is Max recently heartbroken like I am, I wonder, and if so, why is he being so well-adjusted about it? What's his secret?

My phone buzzes, and I pick it up to see that I have three new texts from Vincent, in addition to the ones from last night. I don't want to know what they say, but also, I do—because it's Vincent, and I still want to know what he thinks about everything, in his beautiful, irresistible, long-winded texting prose. I would miss out on bacon to know what he's thinking.

"Excuse me," I say, and take my phone into my room,

where I sit down on my bed and scroll up through the long string of messages.

It's me again. That's not the note I want to end on. I hope you haven't read these yet. I hope you don't see anything I said. Just disregard it and skip to this part.

I love you and I don't know what to do. I wish you'd write me back and just say it was a mistake and it will never happen again, and that you'll come to DC with me, and we can go back to being us.

That's what I want. Say you'll come with me. I understand if you need time. I love you. I'll wait.

I understand why Lee Miller broke up with Man Ray. For him, the situation was perfect. He was an established artist at the height of his powers, with the most beautiful woman in Paris in his studio and on his arm. Without her, he was still Man Ray.

But as long as Lee Miller stayed with Man Ray, she'd always be in his shadow. People would think she only got the breaks she did because she was his lover, and she'd never be taken seriously as an artist in her own right.

I know how she felt, a little. Vincent was the one with the buttery radio voice on *Artists in Love*. I talked less during our shows because people didn't respond as well to my voice. I know this because they said it on the internet, frequently. The show was equally ours, but he wrote the words that made it beautiful. I added to them, edited them, made them sound beautiful, but the work I did was less visible, which made it seem more like his show than mine.

Come to DC with me, and we can go back to being us.

In his last texts, he wanted everything to change. Now

he doesn't want anything to change. Then again, what was wrong with that? Weren't we always happy together? And besides, it's not like I was doing anything else with my life here.

CHAPTER 9

Disappearing Act

My mom seems surprised to hear from me when I ask her to get on video chat, but I can also tell that I haven't caught her in the middle of a debauched New Orleans bender. She's dressed and wearing makeup, and unlike the adults at our house in Cooper-Young, she isn't visibly hungover. She shows me the view of the French Quarter from her room, and then Maggie pops on-screen for a moment to say hi and that she's on her way to the park and the art museum.

"How are things there?" she asks.

She knows, I think. She's using her witchy mom powers, the ones that let her hear the difference between when things are fine and when you're just saying that they are.

Then again, isn't that part of the reason I called her?

"I got fired from Java Cabana. Or not fired. Put on leave. There was some drama between Vincent and this other guy."

"What was Vincent doing there?"

"We'd sort of gotten back together, and he was being supportive."

"By getting you fired."

"Put on leave. Max was there. You can ask him."

"That's fine, Lee. I believe you. Who was the other guy?"

"Nobody. A rebound. A bad idea."

"Lee, do you need me to be there?" she asks, sounding worried. "Is everything really, actually okay?"

"Everything's okay. Mom, look, the other reason I wanted to talk was, you asked me what I was going to do with my one wild and precious life. And I was calling because I wanted to see if I could ask you some questions and record them for a story I'm working on."

"Have you slept?"

"Why did you dedicate a book of poetry to Greg Thurber?"

MAYA SWAN:

Can we start somewhere else, Lee?

LEE SWAN:

What's wrong with starting there?

MAYA:

You can't just lay on a big question like that all at once. It puts the person you're interviewing on edge. You have to work your way up to a question like that.

LEE:

Can you tell me about your first book, then?

MAYA:

Killing Time?

LEE:

No, your *first* first book. *Map Room Love Songs.* What was the Map Room?

MAYA:

A coffee shop. I used to write poetry there when I was in college.

LEE:

What kind of poetry did you write then? Is that a better work-your-way-up question?

MAYA:

Ha ha. You asked, so I'll tell you. At first, my friends and I, we were all even. We were all nobodies.

But then Harold's band got signed and went on tour, and Sage was invited to do their apprenticeship in Berlin, and Greg got into art school in Los Angeles. And I was staying in Memphis, waiting tables at a TGI Fridays.

So that was what my poetry was about: being terrified that I was being left behind, and I was never going to catch up.

LEE:

Why doesn't Greg ever come to visit us? It seems like all your other friends from college come back to Memphis all the time.

MAYA:

He always had a lot going on in LA. Maybe Memphis isn't that compelling to him anymore.

LEE:

Like, he's too good for you?

MAYA:

I wouldn't say that Greg ever made me feel like that.

LEE:

Well, you dedicated a book of poetry to him. How *did* he make you feel?

MAYA:

See? That's how you ask a question like that.

When we'd sit together at the Map Room, me writing, him sketching, he made me feel like what I was doing was real. Like maybe I wasn't going to wait tables at the TGI Fridays in Overton Square for the rest of my life.

LEE:

So the poems were about him?

MAYA:

Some of them were. I loved him.

LEE:

So if you were writing love poems at the Map Room with Greg, where does my dad come in?

MAYA:

The summer after graduation, we were all living together in that big house on Belvedere Street. Me, your dad, Greg, Maggie, Sage, and Harold. Your dad babysat for one of our professors' kids during the day, and every night, he came home and wrote his plays. Everybody else partied, tended bar, went to shows, kept crazy hours, but I always knew where to find your dad. His schedule never changed.

LEE:

So you ended up with him because he was *around*?

MAYA:

Doesn't it always start like that?

LEE:

Were you still in love with Greg then?

MAYA:

Greg was leaving for LA. There was no changing any of that.

LEE:

So instead of leaving Memphis with a man you loved, you stuck around and got together with Dad, and got pregnant pretty much immediately.

MAYA:

Pretty much.

LEE:

Do you wish you hadn't had me when you were so young?

MAYA:

Lee, my mother—your grandmother—died when I was twenty-eight years old.

LEE:

I remember.

MAYA:

Exactly. You *remember*. The two of you got five years with each other. I would never be anything but grateful for that.

My mom's eyes get red, the way they always do when she talks about my grandmother, who had raised her alone, who'd never had time to take up knitting or gardening or any grandmotherly hobbies, because all she ever did was work. She painted decorative finishes on the walls of all the new-money houses out in Germantown, the whitest and wealthiest Memphis suburb, where people stood in their actual *ballrooms* wearing sweatpants and haggling with her over the price. She'd take me with her sometimes, set me up in my Pack 'n Play in the corner while she went up on the scaffolding and sponged faux-leather texture on the ceilings.

When my grandmother got sick, my mom took over the business. She painted her way through her poetry degree at the University of Memphis. I wonder what Greg and his fancy art school friends thought of the kind of painting my mom and grandma did. Would he have looked down his nose at it, made fun of it?

"I should go, honey," my mom says. "Maggie's waiting on me."

She tells me that she loves me, and I thank her for talking to me, and we're about to hang up when suddenly—

MAN'S VOICE:
Maya, are you in there? Maya! Answer the door!

A man is pounding on the door of my mom's hotel room, calling her name.

My mother's head whips around.

"I'll be right there!" she says, and then she looks back at the camera, guilty and stunned.

"Who's that?" I ask.

"Nobody. Just a friend joining us for breakfast."

"He sounds pretty upset about it. Which friend?"

"He teaches at Tulane. He's showing us around today before the reading tonight, and we were supposed to get moving half an hour ago. Now, stop being suspicious. I love you."

LEE SWAN: (studio)
Talking to my mom reminds me of another one of her poems in Map Room Love Songs, one of the few that's not

about love, or Greg, or heartbreak, at least not the romantic kind. It's about wondering if you're going to be a waitress at TGI Fridays for the rest of your life.

I'll read it to you.

> DISAPPEARING ACT
> I always watch the kids at TGI Fridays.
> Not because I want one of my own,
> but because they know something I don't:
> how to get out of here.
>
> Like sideshow con artists,
> they wait for their moment, then
> spill something,
> break something,
> hit someone,
> cry.
>
> I'm apprenticing at the foot of miniature Houdinis,
> mastering the art of escape.
> And when their parents' lives come for me,
> I'll dislocate my shoulder,
> spit a piece of wire into the palm of my hand,
> pick the locks,
> and vanish.

When your mom writes a poem like that, it makes you feel like a padlock, a straitjacket, a length of chain.

As we hang up, I find myself wondering if she's pulling her disappearing act now, at last, after all these years.

I find myself wondering how many other things she'd lied to me about.

CHAPTER 10

An Unreliable Narrator of Your Own Life

I don't know what to say to you, I write to Vincent, then delete it.

Then: I don't know if I can do what you're asking me to do. And the next: I don't know what to do.

I don't send any of them.

There's nothing I can say that will make this neat and clean. I know that, but then my mind reels out this flight of fancy. I imagine finishing this podcast on my own, a work of such depth and sensitivity that Vincent would hear it and he'd know that I was an artist just like he was. He'd hear it and somehow that would be enough to magically resolve the problem of him being eight hundred miles away from me.

Of course, at the same time I'm telling myself this story and obsessing over my ex, the other lobe of my brain is writing the lead-in to the interview with my mom and cleaning up the audio, because, I think, *Fuck it. This is who I am. This is what I do. Let's ride this self-indulgent mine car out to the end of its rusty, broken track.*

I slip on the headphones and set myself up in front of the microphone to test my levels before I start to record the introduction, and it feels good. I can't control anything else about my life, but I know how to set up a pop filter, run the de-esser plug-in, and produce a clear and beautiful sound. I can take the interview with my mom, edit it together with my script, layer in some music. I might use an open-source piece, or one of the tracks Harold had given me to use, but I also keep a keyboard and sequencer in the attic because sometimes it's quicker to create a little melodic interlude myself than to search for a free one on the internet.

It feels weird to record the lead-in without anyone else around, knowing that Vincent isn't going to be there to listen to it, critique it, break it apart so we can build it up again better.

I trusted his ear. I trusted his taste. He was my *Object of Destruction*, keeping watch over me in my studio, letting me know if the work was any good. I'd never had anyone else like that in my life. I don't know if I ever will again.

If I could just move to DC and let us go back to being us, I think. *If I could just say it would never happen again.*

If I could just believe that was the real problem.

After I finish recording the lead-in to my mom's interview, I keep talking.

LEE SWAN:
Recently, I caught myself thinking, *When you've been kissing one guy exclusively for two years, you forget that other guys can be bad kissers.*

I may have been a little bit in denial when I used the word *exclusively*, because that would suggest that during the time Vincent and I were together, Vincent was the only person I was kissing.

There are a lot of ways to justify cheating. In movies, people say, *It didn't mean anything*, or *It was just the one time*, or *I never meant to hurt you*.

I justified it by telling myself at least I was discreet, and Vincent never found out I was hooking up with Claire after work.

But it wasn't just the one time. And it did start to mean something. And sometimes I wanted it so much, I almost didn't care if people got hurt.

There were other things I told myself. Like, if he didn't want to have sex with me, what did it matter? Why should he be jealous about something that he didn't even want?

Those are things you can tell yourself in the moment, but then afterward, you feel guilty for lying to people you love about who you are and what you've done. For lying to yourself.

Everybody thought Vincent and I had the perfect relationship. But I guess Vincent knew it wasn't perfect. And Claire knew it wasn't perfect. And deep down, I knew it wasn't perfect too.

I'd recorded myself before, but I'd never said anything so personal, not even when Vincent and I were breaking up. I almost delete it right away, but it feels honest and true. It seems important to keep it, as some sort of signpost to mark who I am in a post-Vincent world.

This part is just for me, I think.

Behind me, the top step of the pull-down attic staircase creaks, and I spin around to see who's there.

I don't know how long Max has been standing at the top of the stairs, but the look on his face suggests that he's heard a lot.

"What are you doing?" he asks.

"Nothing. Just messing around."

I could yell at Max for coming into my space, but ours is not that kind of friendship. We've known each other since we were eight. When I stayed at his house in Chicago, I walked in on him in the bathroom, squeezing pus from his zits or pulling his hand out of his pants. I was embarrassed, but this wasn't any different.

"What kind of messing around?"

"It's a true crime investigation," I say, then put on an old-timey radio announcer voice. "'Who drowned love in the bath-tub and made it look like an accident? You won't believe what the nanny is hiding!'"

However, my jokey deflection does not work on Max. He ignores it completely, doesn't even smile, and asks, "Are you making a podcast about breaking up with Vincent?"

I nearly throw my headphones at him.

"I'm heartbroken, but I'm not pathetic."

Max puts his hands up in self-defense. "I wouldn't blame you if you were. I've been dumped before. Whatever gets you through, right?"

"It's about my parents," I say. "That's what I'm doing. Investigating the story of how I never should have been born."

"That's an extreme position."

"Not particularly. Earlier today, my mom told me that she ended up with my dad because his schedule was easy to remember and everybody else left her for something better."

"Turn the mic back on."

"It doesn't work that way, Max. You don't 'turn the mic back on.'"

"Then hit record, or whatever shit it is you do."

MAX LOZADA:
What you need, Lee Swan, is an objective, impartial observer to prevent you from becoming an unreliable narrator of your own life. If your parents were so doomed, why did they stay together for almost twenty years?

LEE SWAN:
Because they're stubborn. Because it seemed like a lot of paperwork. Because of me.

MAX:
Still, you couldn't possibly have gotten the whole story in one conversation with your mom.

LEE:

You are probably right. Is that what you wanted to record? Me saying that you're probably right?

MAX:

No, I wanted to ask you again. What are you doing?

LEE:

I'm investigating the story of why my parents got together, and got married, and had me, when all the evidence I have suggests they shouldn't have.

MAX:

And why are you doing that?

LEE:

Because . . . because I want to know where they went wrong. Because I want to believe that love is possible, that it isn't something that's destined to rot or turn cold or end. Because I have to know whether they were doomed from the start.

A few hours later, Sage and my dad come home together with a bag full of Chinese takeout. Max and I head down to greet them, trying to look as though we haven't just been recording a podcast about my parents' horrible relationship.

My dad points at Max and asks, by way of a greeting, "If there was a reality show called *America's Next Top Carnivore,* which contestant would be the fan favorite?"

Max never has trouble keeping up with the questions that sprout in my dad's brain.

"Pit bull with a heart of gold. His name is Scraps, and he's looking for a second chance."

My dad clutches his heart and makes a tearful expression. "Scraps is gonna teach us all to love again."

I'm not sure why he's in such a good mood until he starts opening cartons while Max and I set the table, and he casually remarks, "So, I guess your mother was wrong. Greg is coming after all. He gets in later tonight."

Sage frowns. "I thought you wanted me to do your tattoo tonight."

"Why not? He won't be here until late. We can get these two night owls to go pick him up from the airport. Or he can spring for a cab. I'm sure he's good for it."

"I wonder why he decided to come," Sage says.

"To see us, of course! He said something came up, and he had to come out this way anyhow, so it all worked out."

"Uh-huh." Sage does not seem to share my dad's enthusiasm, and instead picks up their phone and sends a couple of texts as the rest of us load our plates with kung pao tofu and slippery shrimp.

"How was *your* day, Sage?" I ask, since no one else in the house had managed a normal greeting.

Sage puts down the phone and gives me a sad smile, then a hug.

"It's hard being here. I forget that sometimes."

At first, I think Sage is talking about our house, and like, sure, I get it, but I'm still about to get offended when they add, "I don't mean here. Or in this neighborhood. Or with all of you. You provide the context people seem to think they need to figure out how to interact with me. It's when I step outside that . . ."

I don't know if it's like this in every city, but sometimes it feels like Memphis has an unwritten book of rules. Some of them are dumb, like how if you're a guest in someone's house, you're not supposed to ask for anything that your host doesn't offer you. Not even if you're dying of thirst. Not even if there's no toilet paper in the bathroom. Some of the rules of Memphis are annoying, such as the way you're supposed to graciously accept the chivalry of guys opening doors for you, even if they're getting in your way, or slowing you down, or calling you a bitch while you walk past.

And some of the rules of Memphis just suck.

The rule that says it's more important to say *sir* or *ma'am* than it is not to misgender someone. The rules about where white and Black people go to school, where they live, where they go to church. The rules that say who belongs here and who doesn't, who is accepted at face value and who will be asked to explain themselves.

It's not written down anywhere. Even if your parents don't teach it to you—even if they teach you that it's wrong— you grow up knowing it. That's just how it is.

"Did something happen at Trinity today?" Dad asks.

"Something happens almost every day," Sage says. "And even if it doesn't, even if it's something little, it's stressful being on edge during every single interaction. Like, is this person going to be a dick? Even when nothing happens, my muscles are tensed up in a ball of knots all day."

"You're not the only one," Max points out. "It's not the same for me, obviously, but I know what it's like to have people look at you and decide they need to know exactly what you are."

"I know I'm not the only one, honey," Sage says.

I know exactly what Max and Sage are talking about because I've seen it happen. Most people who live in Memphis are either Black or white; there aren't a lot of Asian people here, and hardly any Filipino people. We'd be out somewhere, and Max would ask Sage or Maggie for some money for a Coke, and people's eyes would stay on him a moment too long, studying his skin tone, which was darker than either of theirs, trying to gender Sage, and I could see the questions on their faces: *Who are you, kid? What are you to them? How do the three of you belong together?*

And then sometimes, when it dawned on them that Maggie, Sage, and Max were a family, a queer family holding hands at the zoo or posing for a picture on Beale Street, I'd see the questions on their face curdle into judgment.

If I could see it, I didn't doubt that Max could feel it, their scrutiny of his race, his family, his sexuality.

What I don't understand is why Max gives Sage a dirty look when they call him honey, and why Sage looks away, turns to my dad, and says, "Well, we'd better get started on your tattoo."

An hour later, my dad is leaning over a chair back, his shoulder shaved clean and sterilized with alcohol, Sage is tracing the design with a stencil they'd drawn, and Max and I are gawking at the spectacle.

"Um, Sage," I say. "The thing I talked to you about this morning. Is it still okay if I record you?"

Sage turns to my dad. "Lee wants to interview us for something she's working on. Is that okay with you?"

"Sure. About what?" my dad asks warily, but I start recording as soon as he says *sure*.

CHAPTER 11

Some Slippery Fucking Logic

LEE:

The past. College. Your group of friends. Mom told me about the summer that all of you were living in the house on Belvedere.

SAGE STEELE:

Oh god, yeah. I was driving carriages downtown. Do you remember, Arthur, the nights when I finished too late to make it out to the stables? I'd drive the horses back to Midtown and keep them in our backyard overnight.

ARTHUR SWAN:

I don't really want to talk about the past. It's behind me. It's dead, Lee. Let it die.

LEE:

What about the future, then?

ARTHUR:

Well, I found some apartments today.

SAGE:

Did you sign anything?

ARTHUR:

I haven't even looked at them yet.

SAGE:

Is someone going with you?

ARTHUR:

God, Sage, I'm an adult.

SAGE:

Sometimes you're not great at seeing red flags.

ARTHUR:

Goddammit, I am a middle-aged man, shirtless and about to be divorced. This is a somewhat vulnerable position from which to have one's life scrutinized. Lee, would you please turn that thing off?

It's a terrible interview.

But the tattoo needle buzzing in the background sounds exactly as cool as I thought it would.

"What's going on with you and Sage?" I ask once Max and I retreat to the attic, surrendering the living room to Sage's makeshift tattoo parlor. "They're baring their soul at the dinner table, and you're shooting dirty looks?"

"What's going on with *you*, Lee Swan?"

He plops down in Vincent's chair, and I have to remind myself that it's not Vincent's chair anymore. It's just a chair.

"I think I've been more than forthcoming on the subject of my goddamn life," I say, sitting down next to him.

"I'm talking about what you said when you were recording yourself and you thought no one was listening. I'm talking about *Claire*, with her cute little freckles and nose ring," he says, adding teasingly, "You player."

I blush. "It's not like it was something I could talk to anyone about."

Max gives me a more serious look and a poke to my collarbone. "Then how come this is the first I'm hearing that you like girls?"

It would have been easier if he'd looked disgusted and judgmental about the cheating, but Max's face is open and smiling and expectant. He doesn't think I'm a terrible person. He's waiting to hear my side of the story, which makes me feel even more guilty.

"Max . . ." For almost a minute, I can't get any further than that. Every way I think about explaining what I've done only draws into sharp focus how much I've fucked up.

"Let me show you how to clean up this audio file," I say instead.

"I know what you're doing," he says.

I get up from my chair and turn off the air conditioner. It's miserably hot up here without it, but it's too loud to have it on while I'm recording or editing.

"Okay, I don't know what you're doing," Max says. "You know it's ninety degrees outside, right?"

"It'll stay cool long enough for us to do this."

I import the interview with Sage and my dad into my editing software. Max watches intently as I show him how to edit out the coughs, how to amplify the buzz of the tattoo needle at the beginning to set the scene, then fade it out so it doesn't distract from the interview. It's a comforting and familiar rhythm, one I know by heart. It calms me down.

Maybe Max knows this, and that's why he lets me spend a few minutes running my mouth about levels and ambient noise before he cuts me off mid-sentence and says, "Don't tell me you did it because you thought girls 'didn't count.'"

I know that this time he's not going to let me off the hook until I give him an answer.

"It wasn't like that," I say, turning away from the computer screen. "I could justify it to myself, like, well, I like girls, too. That's part of who I am, and that's not someone Vincent could be to me. And yes, maybe it crossed my mind that if I did get caught, maybe he wouldn't be as angry with me."

"That's some slippery fucking logic, Lee Swan."

I think he's going to turn his back on me and walk out of the room, but instead he says, "Do you want to know why Sage and I are fighting?"

"Sure," I say, grateful not to be talking about myself anymore.

"Because my sort-of girlfriend just broke up with me."

"Wait, your *girlfriend*?"

"Her name's Xochitl." He takes out his phone and shows me a picture of a girl with purple hair that's buzzed on the sides and long on top. She's wearing a leopard-print coat and a studded choker necklace, and her teeth are bared to reveal pair of Halloween vampire fangs; however, her eyes have a puckish smile and her arms are thrown wide, like she's about to hug whoever is taking her picture.

"Oh my," I say. She looks cool and fascinating and fun. She looks like someone I'd want to know, and I can tell right away why Max likes her.

"I don't know what it means or why it happened," Max says. "All I know is we started hanging out, and then I couldn't stop thinking about her, and now suddenly there are a few more constellations in my sexual universe."

"And you would like to develop an international space exploration program."

"Nobody's walked on the moon or anything, but yes. The problem is, Sage and Mom don't like her. They think all this is her doing." He gestures to his eyeliner, his piercings, his clothes.

"When did your parents get judgmental about style?"

Max rolls his eyes. "They think this isn't 'the real me.' Mom says I warped myself into a different person just to get her attention, and they made me come to Memphis because they said they didn't trust what I might get up to while they were out of town."

"They let you stay by yourself when you were dating Niko."

The saintly Niko, whom Max had been dating the last time I saw him. All Sage and Maggie could talk about was how talented and accomplished Niko was, what a fine young man, so good for Max.

"And they never had a problem with my presentation of self when it involved hanging out with bougie white people," Max says. "I tried to explain it to Xochitl, but she knew how Niko and I were when we were together, having cute little Friday-night dates and dinners at each other's houses. All sanctioned and approved of. She said it felt like I was keeping her off to the side, and I said I was still figuring some stuff out. So she said, 'I'm not your experiment,' and dumped me."

"I'm so sorry, Max. That's awful."

"And now she won't answer my texts, and Niko hates me. Sometimes I wish I could have been happy with what I had before I met her. Not that my life felt *right* before, but it was uncomplicated and mostly okay, and easier than . . . all this messiness."

"We are a couple of messy bisexuals."

"Speak for yourself. I didn't cheat on anyone. *You're* a messy bisexual. I'm an untidy queer."

"I'm sorry that you're stuck here in my attic with my bull-shit."

"Your attic is fine. Your bullshit is fine. But you know, Lee, what you did to Vincent . . . it's everything people say is shitty about us. That we can't make up our minds. That we can't be with one person. That we cheat."

"That's not fair," I say. I'm not trying to defend what I've done, but I also don't think I should be expected to model ideal bisexual behavior—whatever *that* is—at all times. When straight people cheat, they aren't failing the whole straight population. They are just failing one person.

And isn't that bad enough?

"I'm pretty tired," Max says, even though it's only nine o' clock, "and it's starting to get hot up here."

"You can take a nap in my room if you want. I'll wake you when it's time to pick up Greg from the airport."

"Could you maybe get him yourself?" I must seem like this hurts my feelings because his expression softens, and he says, "It's like Sage was talking about. It's exhausting being in a place where you don't quite know the rules."

I think about my editing chair and my computer and the way that working on an audio file centers me. That's my space and my comfort, and Max is five hundred miles away from his.

I think about the rules of Memphis, which I know like breathing but that Max has to improvise with every single interaction. No wonder he needs extra time to recharge.

"I'll sleep in the attic," I say. "Get your rest. I'll see you in the morning."

LEE SWAN: (studio)

The first time Claire and I hooked up, it was after an open mic at Java Cabana. The whole night had felt like a game we were playing, pushing each other to see how close we could come to the edge without going over. I touched her waist when I passed behind her at the register. She rubbed my shoulders while I worked the soundboard. And then, at the end of the night, I was in the storage closet putting away my gear, and I turned around and she was standing in the doorway, and it just happened.

I couldn't sleep that night. I thought about breaking up with Vincent, I thought about telling him everything.

But then, the next time I worked with Claire, we both acted like the whole thing had never happened. So I decided that instead of telling Vincent, I'd tell myself that it didn't mean anything and didn't matter, and for a while that worked.

Until the next time.

An hour later, I'm alone, texting my dad from the baggage claim.

The flight from Los Angeles, connecting through New Orleans, had already arrived; the passengers had all deplaned.

I hadn't seen Greg since I was eight, but I scan every face for some twinkle of familiarity. Thirty minutes later, there's just one big yellow suitcase left, wrapped in duct tape, abandoned by its owner and circling the Memphis airport baggage carousel.

My mom said that Greg wouldn't come, and my dad was so eager to point out that she was wrong, but there is one thing my mom is never wrong about, and that's knowing when people are going to disappoint you.

CHAPTER 12

Objects of Destruction

LEE: (studio)

My dad takes a vacation day, and the two of us go out to White Station to look at an apartment.

ARTHUR: (driving)

I can't live in a neighborhood called White Station. I mean, technically, it's named after a person, but it's a very strange coincidence that it just happens to be the first stop on the train out to White Flight Land.

Did you know that the founder of the Ku Klux Klan is still buried in a park downtown? They took down his statue, but they can't figure out what to do with his grave. I mean, if Hitler was buried there, would people be whining about historical preservation, or would they just yank his corpse out and toss it in the river?

LEE: (studio)

He's talkative, cheerful in his peculiar way.

The apartment we look at is in a modern complex, all metal and glass. The landlord shows us a place on the fourth floor with cream carpet and vertical blinds, two bedrooms, and a renovated kitchen.

ARTHUR: (sliding closed the balcony door)
It's within my budget, there's an extra bedroom, and I can walk to work.

LEE: (studio)
He doesn't sound happy about it, though, and he doesn't sign anything. We drive to the second place, a shotgun apartment back in Midtown.

There, the landlord immediately tells us ...

LANDLORD: (fumbling of keys in a lock)
This place is cursed. The last three couples who moved in here all split up within a year. Nasty breakups.

LEE: (studio)
My dad's face lights up at this news.

She tells us it was built in the 1920s for wealthy cotton brokers who used them as short-term rentals. The gentlemen would occupy the front rooms, and their servants would live in the back.

ARTHUR:

I do not have any servants.

LANDLORD:

Of course you don't. But you might be interested in this.

LEE: (studio)

We're standing in a tiny breakfast nook, in the part of the apartment that would have been for the servants, and there's a bookshelf built into the wall. The landlord walks up to it and pulls it open to reveal a hallway that leads all the way to the front.

ARTHUR:

A secret passageway?

LEE: (studio)

My dad will never choose the apartment with an extra bedroom that's within his budget and walking distance from work. He will sign a lease on the cursed fourplex with a secret passageway every time.

Maybe Sage would have pointed out all the red flags, but I don't have the heart to do it. When I called him from the Memphis airport baggage claim last night and told him that Greg wasn't on the flight, all he said was, "I see. Well, you'd better come on home."

He doesn't bring it up while we're apartment hunting

either, so on our way home from the cursed secret-passageway apartment, I finally ask him point-blank.

He shrugs and says, "Something probably came up."

"It *probably* came up? He still hasn't texted you to say where he is?"

"Haven't heard from him since yesterday."

"What if he's dead?"

"Well, if he was dead, someone would have texted me by now to let me know."

I can't stand how calm he's being.

After Dad and I get home, I find Max where I left him the night before, playing video games in my bedroom with the lights off and the air-conditioning on high, and it suddenly occurs to me that this is also a way to process a breakup. You didn't need to throw yourself into an artistic project or a frenzied mission. You could sleep a lot, or reorganize your bookshelf, or watch ten movies in a row.

"Do you want to go to Java Cabana with me?" I ask.

"Give me five minutes," he says. "I'm just finishing up the weapons system on this ship."

I love how Max plays video games. He'll never blow anything up with the ship he's designing, even though that's the point of the game. Instead he'll spend an hour naming it, carefully selecting its shields and outfitting the crew, giving them all names and elaborate science credentials.

He pats the spot on the floor next to him and says, "Talk to me while I'm playing. Tell me what happened last night. What happened when you picked up Greg?"

"Well, as you can see, he's not here."

I explain the rest of it while Max names his ship the USS *Kinsey*.

"What do you think happened?" he asks.

"That's why I want to go to Java Cabana," I say. "I want to get some perspective."

"Don't you have any other friends?" Max asks. "Like, regular, non-work friends?"

I start to answer his question with an indignant *Of course I do*, but then I catch myself. It was a question of what I had time for. Of course, I had nearly unlimited time for Vincent and for *Artists in Love*, but when I started to feel frustrated or pent up, I never talked to any of my friends about it. I didn't want them to know we weren't perfect. Instead I spent my limited free time flirting with Claire at Java Cabana. Claire, who didn't know me; Claire, who wasn't friends with my friends; Claire, who existed completely outside my supposedly perfect life.

I know the real answer to Max's question is *I used to*, or more accurately, *I used to, but I messed it up.*

Instead I tell him, "I have you. Besides, that's not important. What's important is getting to the bottom of a nineteen-year-old mystery."

Having been holed up in my bedroom for the past fifteen hours, Max does not protest further. We walk down the street, through the Cooper-Young District, right in the heart of Midtown, past all the restaurants and music venues, past Burke's Book Store, the comics shop, and the kickboxing studio.

When we arrive at Java Cabana, Claire is behind the counter, eyeing the gear bag I have over my shoulder.

"I thought you weren't supposed to be here," she says.

I'm somewhat taken aback. I know I'm not running sound for the open mic or the poetry slam or the shows, but it hadn't occurred to me that I might be Brent levels of banned.

"Trudy's not here, so I won't say anything if you won't," she says, and I feel better knowing she's at least partly on my side, that maybe she thought what had happened to me wasn't entirely fair.

"Max and I are working on something, and I wanted to ask if we could interview some people in the shop. Person-on-the-street kind of thing?"

"I don't know," Claire says, suddenly looking less on my side.

"Can we interview you, then?"

"I'm working."

"I'll do all the dishes if you talk to us," I say, looking at the sink behind us, overflowing with the blender containers for smoothies, which were such a pain in the ass to clean that the baristas left them to pile up until washing became unavoidable. "And wipe the tables."

Claire smirks at me but doesn't budge, holding out for a better offer.

"I'll clean the bathroom, too," I add, and Claire finally relents.

"Ask me anything."

The little bell above the door jingles, and I hear a voice behind me. "Oh hey, I wondered when I'd see you around here."

It's Risa, the girl with the guitar who played first at the last, disastrous open mic I'd hosted. The girl who'd had stage fright and sung with her eyes closed, even though she played the guitar with rock-star confidence. She gives me a grin, which I return even though I'm surprised she's concerned herself with my whereabouts.

"I know you're here a lot." I must look alarmed, because she quickly adds, "I promise I'm not following you around. I work at Burke's. I see you in here sometimes when I walk past. But anyhow, I wanted to say thank you for being so nice to me the other night. It helped a lot."

"You're a really good guitar player," I say. "And I liked your songs."

Behind the counter, I see Claire roll her eyes. Max gives her a look of commiseration, and in that moment, wins her over in a way that I never did.

"I've been writing nonstop since that night, so I'll have more to play for you next week," Risa says.

I stammer for a moment, trying to figure out a way to convey excitement about her songwriting without sharing that I've been fired and won't be there to hear it. Much to my surprise, Claire comes to my rescue.

"Lee's taking a couple weeks off from the open mic so she can focus on this new podcast she's producing."

"That's so cool," Risa says, looking at me with a respect that I in no way deserve. "What's it about?"

"It's about love," I say. "Making bad decisions about love."

Claire does not even try to conceal her snort of laughter.

Max extends his hand to her. "Max Lozada," he says. "Co-producer. Could we interview you?"

Now it's Risa's turn to look alarmed. It does sound awfully presumptuous and probably insulting to tell someone you want to interview them for a podcast about bad romantic decisions.

"We aren't going to ask you to talk about anything personal," I explain. "Basically, I'm going to tell you and Claire a very strange story about something that happened yesterday involving my mother's ex-boyfriend, and a book of poetry, and a missed flight, and a strange voice in the background on a video call, and I'm going to ask you what you think about it."

Both Risa and Claire look like they want to hear more, so while I wash the smoothie blenders and wipe tables, I fill in all the backstory, all the context, Greg's previous flake-outs, my mother's retreat to New Orleans, the man pounding on the door of her hotel room.

LEE SWAN:
So, my question to all of you is, what the hell is really going on?

RISA:
If I had to guess, I'd say that Greg is in New Orleans with your mom right now.

LEE:
Maybe she'd been planning to meet him there all along.

CLAIRE:
But we don't even know it was Greg outside her hotel room. It could have been some poetry professor from Tulane, just like your mom said it was.

MAX:

Then why didn't Greg show up at the Memphis airport last night?

CLAIRE:

He missed his connection.

LEE:

Then why did he ghost my dad?

CLAIRE:

He missed his connection, took it as a cosmic sign that he wasn't meant to come to Memphis.

RISA:

Or he intended to come, but your mom asked him to stay in New Orleans with her. Maybe it was very dramatic. She could have bought a cheap ticket to get through security, and met his plane at the gate and said, "Don't go, I need you."

MAX:

Are you okay, Lee? This is your family we're speculating about.

LEE:

Because I asked you to speculate. These are all really good theories.

MAX:

Okay, then let's go a step further. Let's say Greg gets off his plane in New Orleans. He's just flown from Los Angeles. He's tired, he only has a few minutes to catch his connection, but your mom is waiting at the gate, and he says, "What are you doing here?" and she says, "Lee is your kid."

CLAIRE:

Whoa.

RISA:

Whoa.

LEE:

That's ridiculous.

MAX:

Is it? They were all living together in the same house.

LEE:

They'd broken up.

CLAIRE:

And nobody in the world has ever hooked up with their ex.

MAX:

Certainly not Lee. Lee wouldn't know anything about that.

LEE:

Okay, fine. Maybe it's not ridiculous. Greg and my dad sort of look alike. Harold, too, like they're all on this white hipster continuum of willfully ungroomed to artfully disheveled.

This is why I wanted to talk to all of you for my podcast.

MAX:

Is that what this is? Your podcast? I thought you said you were just messing around.

LEE:

Our podcast, and no, I'm not messing around. Do we know anyone who has a VCR?

After we finish recording, Risa shakes her head in disbelief, then her arms, all the way down to her fingertips, like the story is stuck to her and she's trying to get it off.

"That was wild, y'all. If you ever need anyone to speculate further, you know where to find me."

"Maybe we'll come by Burke's sometime and interview you," I say, wishing I wasn't holding a mop and a bottle of toilet cleaner while I made plans with her.

"What's the name of your podcast?" she asks.

I haven't thought about that yet. I've barely allowed myself to think about it as something real, something I'm making, something that might someday find its way into the world. Something with a title.

"It's called *Objects of Destruction,*" Max says.

I start to glare at him, because really, in a creative partnership, you need to run those things by each other. You don't just go making big, disruptive decisions without a conversation. But I don't glare at him, because also, it's a good title.

"For now," Max adds with a smile.

"*Objects of Destruction,*" Risa says. "I like it."

CHAPTER 13

Dilettante Life

There are so many things I should have been honest about right from the beginning. Instead I hid them, and then I had to keep hiding everything.

I delete my reply to Vincent and try again.

I was worried you wouldn't love me if you knew who I really was. I thought I'd lose you if I told you the truth. But then I lost you anyway.

I delete that one too. It sounds like I'm making excuses for what I did.

It's so strange. We loved each other, and it felt very big, but the rooms where it happened were all very small, and there weren't very many of them.

It takes me half an hour to compose all these texts, and I don't send any of them.

Max and I are back from Java Cabana, sitting side by side on my bed with our backs against the headboard, legs outstretched, catching up on our correspondence. I don't know whether he's writing to Niko, or to Xochitl, or whether he's doing the same thing I am, writing drafts of texts and deleting them.

We hear the front door open and come out of the bedroom

to find Harold and Sage in the kitchen, stocking the fridge with ice, beer, and sodas.

"Where's Dad?" I ask.

"Grocery store," Harold says. "He has declared it a Cookout Night."

I feel a little teary-eyed at this news. My mom was the one who could infuse a trip to the dentist or an afternoon pulling weeds with something sparkling and magical. But it was my dad who invented all of our family rituals, routines, and feast days. At different points in my childhood, we'd had weekly Game Nights, Movie Nights, Museum Days, Outside Afternoons, Swimming Sundays. And from April through October, we had Cookout Night every chance we got. And this was probably one of the last ones we'd ever have together in this house.

That said, I am not one to let sentimentality interfere with an opportunity to get an interview. I look at Max, who understands what I'm thinking and runs to the bedroom for the digital recorder.

We corner Harold and Sage on the patio as they're installing a new propane tank on the grill. I want to tell them it's a waste of time, that Mom will never use it, that Dad is moving to a cursed fourplex with no room for a gas grill.

Harold shuffles his feet as he scrapes the grill clean, humming a tune to himself. It has no lyrics, but periodically, he chimes in with a doo-wop backup chorus part. Sage is hosing down the deck chairs, wiping off the filth of disuse. Ordinarily, we would have gotten the deck up to Cookout Night standards by this point in the summer, but I guess nobody had felt very festive these past few months.

"Sage, Uncle Harold, I was wondering if we could talk to you on the record."

Sage and Harold exchange a glance, as if they're working out the most prudent course of action, as friends, as family.

"You dad said he didn't want to talk about the past," Sage says.

"He let me record him the whole time we were apartment hunting," I say. "I just don't ask him to talk about the things he doesn't want to."

"What did you want to talk to us about?"

"A passport."

"Go ahead," Harold says, looking relieved. "That doesn't seem like so much."

LEE SWAN: (studio)
I show them my dad's unused passport. First they giggle at how young he looks, but then . . .

SAGE STEELE:
Did you know about this?

HAROLD WASSERMAN:
Not a clue what he was up to.

LEE:
So he didn't have any plans?

HAROLD:
He would have told me. Besides, your dad is the biggest homebody I know. Except maybe your mom.

LEE:
They had something in common?

SAGE:
Oh come on ... they have a lot in common. They're both writers ...

LEE:
Dad's an introvert, Mom's an extrovert. Dad likes theater, Mom likes movies. Mom yells, Dad gives the silent treatment.

SAGE:
I was going to say they both had dads who weren't around, moms who died when they were pretty young.

HAROLD:
And they have you in common, Lee. They have this house, and the people they filled it with, and the past twenty years. That's a lot to have in common with someone. I've never had that much in common with anyone in my life.

LEE: (studio)
If you ever want to feel like an asshole, launch a critical investigation of your parents' marriage. Learn that for every one of their bad habits, there's a tragic backstory. You start to feel sorry for the jerks.

Even if my parents' love story was about their shitty childhoods and thwarted dreams and me, somehow they managed to get almost twenty years out of it. It makes me wonder what Vincent's and my love story was really about after all.

When it happened, it felt like magic—someone who wanted to talk about art and ideas as much as I did. And when he said, "I've always wanted to have a podcast," I thought, *I have an attic and access to recording equipment, and I can figure out how to use it. I can make this happen for you. For us.*

I'm already beginning to see the shape of the first episode of *Objects of Destruction.* Even though I don't have the music in my head, I have the *idea* of it—something instrumental, sad and haunting. I introduce the poetry book, the passport. I'll record myself saying, "These are the clues to unlocking a mystery about how this all happened. These are artifacts of a love story I don't know how to tell. They are . . . *Objects of Destruction.*" And then the music, which has been building all this time, explodes into a theme song I haven't heard yet.

I'll read the poems and introduce each of the people who have descended upon my house and splice in the interview with my mom. Then, the first episode ends with the scene at Java Cabana, the cliffhanger that Greg might be my biological father.

I wish Vincent was here with me in the attic so I could ask him, *Does that sound right? What would you do next?*

While Man Ray was getting over his broken heart, he painted a giant canvas of Lee Miller's lips floating in the sky above the Paris Observatory. It took two years to finish, and each night he hung the unfinished canvas over his bed. This should be considered obsessive by nearly any metric. It is also one of the most iconic artworks of the twentieth century, so it was probably worth the suffering.

Max and I stay up late working on *Objects of Destruction*, and the next morning, we roll out of bed and go straight back upstairs. By noon, we've fallen into a comfortable rhythm, working side by side. While I edit and mix the segments we've already recorded, he searches for music clips we can use. He seems to have limitless patience for all of this, offering up his opinion on one cut versus another, making suggestions that I nearly always end up taking.

"What if we make that scene in Java Cabana a recurring segment?" he suggests. "Each episode, you bring all the evidence you've gathered to me and Claire and Risa, lay it all out, and we call it, 'What the Hell Is Really Going On?'"

"The next installment can be the fact that neither of my dad's two closest friends had any idea he was thinking about leaving the country right before I was born."

"I have some possible intro songs for you," he says, holding up his phone. I showed him some of the royalty-free music sites I sometimes used for *Artists in Love*. They're free, but you have to sift through thousands of songs by people you've never heard of, looking for something that captures exactly the feeling you're looking for. It can take hours of tedious searching just to fill a few seconds.

The first one he plays sounds like the instrumental music that would be playing in a hippie store that sells crystals and nutritional supplements. The second is catchy, but when we layer it onto my track, it's too flashy and distracting, so we throw it out.

"This is so annoying," Max says. "If I could play any instruments, I'd just write it myself."

The third song he's found isn't perfect, but we don't hate it, and for the moment, that's good enough for me. I mix it in, even though I can hear Vincent's voice in my head:

Lee, "good enough" isn't.

When I'm done, I notice that Max is lying patiently on the air mattress, combing through the free music databases, listening to one instrumental clip after another. Poor Max, I think. First his parents drag him to Memphis, and then I hold him captive in my attic.

"You know, Max," I say, "this is my weird deal. If there's some other way you'd rather spend your days, I would completely understand."

"I'm good," he says.

"Do you have something like this? Something that does for you whatever it is that this does for me?"

"This is it. I'm doing it."

"You didn't know how to use a digital recorder until yesterday."

"But now I do. I enjoy being a dilettante like that."

"Uh, Max, I don't think that word means what you think it means. Like, it is not a compliment. It means you're not a serious person."

"I know exactly what the word means, and I think it has a terrible and unearned reputation. Like you, Lee."

"Ha ha," I say, swatting him with the back of my hand.

"I like knowing a little bit about a lot of things. I like that I keep adding to my arsenal. It's an excellent way to be a person in the world, wandering around being fascinated by shit."

"And then moving on to the next thing."

I think about Max's litany of unrelated college majors, how easily he puts things down and picks up other things, and I wonder if he'll ever find one thing that holds his interest. Then again, I made all my college plans a year in advance and look where it got me.

"What of it?" he asks, sensing the criticism in my remark.

"If you just move on to the next thing, then what was the point?"

"So they can write on my tombstone, HERE LIES MAX, HE FOUND ALL OF THIS ENDLESSLY CAPTIVATING."

"What would mine say?"

"HERE LIES LEE. WE FINALLY GOT HER OUT OF THE ATTIC."

Even if Max said that he wanted to help me, I knew myself. I knew that if it was just me, I'd stay up here working for entire days. I'd steal the air mattress and sleep up here if I could. Just because that's how Vincent and I used to work didn't mean it was fair to hold a self-proclaimed dilettante to our unhealthy standards.

"Hey," I say, taking off the headphones, "I want to take you somewhere. Somewhere fun."

He perks up right away, and I immediately feel glad I suggested it. We brave the outdoors and walk to the Young Avenue Deli, where we order fried cheese and fried pickles and play pool. Then we walk to Goner Records and go through the bins of vinyl. I take him to the comic book shop and flip through issues of *Black Panther* and *Runaways,* and I remember that my friends and I used to come to these places all the time. But Vincent wasn't allowed to listen to secular music at his house, or have comics, and *Artists in Love* took up so much of our time. By the end of senior year, everyone I used to know had graduated, moved, switched schools, or stopped speaking to me, and Vincent was the only person left. By then, I was so focused on my future with him that I lost sight of everything else.

I buy a couple trades, to catch up on what I've missed, and then Max says, "Didn't Risa say she worked at Burke's?"

"She did."

"Let's go see if she's there."

I'm caught up in the buoyant spirit of the day, floating around Midtown with a belly full of fried pickles and a bag of comics and records slapping against my thigh. The strap of my sundress slips off my shoulder, and I leave it where it falls.

Tell me, what is it you plan to do with your one wild and precious life?

Would it be wrong if I answered, "Eat fried pickles and visit cute girls who work in bookshops?"

Risa is behind the register when we walk in, and she jumps up and down when she sees us.

"How's the investigation?" she asks.

"We're taking the afternoon off," Max explains. A customer approaches, and we step aside to let her help them. Risa's patient, even though the person can't remember the title of the book, or the author, or what it was about, only that a car runs off the road in a blizzard in the first scene and the cover is navy blue. I'm amazed as she leads them to exactly the right spot on the shelf and puts the book in their hands.

"Are you a witch?" I ask after she rings up the sale. "How did you do that?"

"That was an easy one. They talked about it on the *Today* show last week."

"What's your favorite section?" I ask.

"Music, of course."

"I'm kind of surprised you don't work at the record store," I say. "If you're this good with books, you must be a genius with music."

She blushes. "Musicians shouldn't work in record stores. Or at least I shouldn't. I need more variety in my life."

Max high-fives her and does a little dance while he sings, "Dilettante life! Best life!"

"Hey!" I say, rising to Risa's defense. "Most people still don't think that word is a compliment."

"I assure you, that is how I intended it," Max tells Risa. "We can't all be as focused as Lee."

"Speaking of," Risa says, "you never answered my question. How's the podcast?"

"Actually, I wanted to see when you were free," I say.

"Oh yeah?"

"Max had this idea for a recurring segment, like the thing we recorded the other day at Java Cabana. Would you be up for something like that?"

"My shift ends in fifteen minutes," Risa says, and excitement floods my senses. Not only do I get to hang out with her again—and soon—I can get back to work, too.

"Want to meet us at Java Cabana?" Max asks.

Suddenly, a twinge of worry creeps into my good feeling. It's open mic night, so there's a good chance Claire's there, and it's four in the afternoon, so there's also a chance that my manager, Trudy, is there. I don't want to mention this, since the last thing I want to explain to Risa is that I'm semi-banned and semi-fired due to boy drama.

"We'll meet you there in fifteen minutes, then!" I say.

Once Max and I are outside, I turn to him and say, "I'm going to run home for the recorder. Can you scope things out next door and text me if Trudy's there?"

"You couldn't take one goddamn afternoon off, could you, Swan?"

I roll my eyes at him. "Are you going to text me if she's there, or aren't you?"

"Of course I will."

I run back to my house, drop the bag of comics and records off in my room, and grab the recorder. There's a text from Max: **All clear, no Trudy.** My nerves subside, and I run back to Java Cabana thinking about the questions I'm going to ask instead of how I'm going to keep Risa from discovering that I'm a recently disgraced mess of a human being.

When I get there, Max has commandeered the quiet table in the corner, and Claire and Risa have joined him. We have the place pretty much to ourselves. Will, one of the part-time baristas, is covering the counter, wiping syrup bottles and cleaning the steam wand in a pot of water.

The scene is just how I want it, so I turn on the recorder before I even sit down. I want to capture the sound of chair legs scraping the tile, the hiss of the espresso machine, the sound of me taking my place at the table, setting down the recorder.

"We have a passport, issued to my dad six months before I was born. His two closest friends have no idea why he got it, or where he was planning to go. So. My question to you is, what the hell is really going on?"

I can already hear how it's going to sound in playback, and it's perfect.

Unfortunately, that's as far as we get.

CHAPTER 14

A Certain Amount of Reckless Abandon

I don't know how I feel about you being here."

That's what Trudy says when she sees me. Risa is the one facing the door—Risa, the only one who doesn't know that she ought to be tipping me off before Trudy is standing at our table, peering down her regal nose at me like I am a subject who has displeased her. I don't know what I was thinking, trying to maneuver around her. Not only was it a dick move, it was doomed to fail.

"Should I leave?"

"I didn't say that," Trudy says, though I can tell she is not finished with me yet. "Do you remember Steven St. Cloud?"

"Who?"

"Wire Mother."

I nod. Of course. Steve. The accountant in pleated khakis with a coffee can full of nails.

"His manager called. They're lining up a tour for the fall, and Steve wants you to run sound for him while his band is in town."

"They're playing here?"

"No, they want to play at a real club this time. One with Ticketmaster and twenty-one-and-up wristbands and stuff like that."

"Oh."

"So that's why I don't know how I feel about you being here. I guess there is a part of me that is feeling a little ungracious about it at the moment."

And I know what she means. I have lived my life surrounded by artists, some who get to do what they want to do for a living, and some who don't. In ten years, I could be Trudy, managing a coffee shop, booking acoustic singer-songwriters, busting my ass, and throwing everything I have at my dream. And if some recent high school graduate who didn't even take the job seriously enough not to fuck it up waltzed right into a legitimate, serious gig? If I was Trudy, I wouldn't be half as cool about it as she's being right now.

"What are you talking about? What's the recorder for?" Trudy asks, sitting down at the table with us.

"Passports. We're talking about whether my dad was planning to skip the country before I was born."

"Are you fucking kidding me?"

"Can we record you, and can you say that again?" Max asks. Trudy nods and Max starts recording.

TRUDY BOYD:

Are you fucking kidding me? Not only does your dad love being your dad, he's not a skip-the-country kind of guy. A move like that takes a certain amount of reckless abandon and adventurousness. Your dad orders the same black coffee every day within the same fifteen-minute window. Once, I offered him a shot of caramel syrup and he looked at me like I was trying to poison him.

RISA:

What if he had cold feet about becoming a dad? Maybe he panicked for a second and applied for the passport.

MAX:

Even if he did that, where was he going to go?

CLAIRE:

You said he used to be a nanny. Maybe one of the families he nannied for was traveling abroad and invited him to come along. Like an au pair.

MAX:

You always suggest the most reasonable, boring things. Don't you have any conspiracy theories in your soul?

CLAIRE:

Well, you're the one throwing around nonsense like "Greg is Lee's biological father." If that was true, doesn't the passport question become a moot point? Sorry, dude, but your conspiracy theories are at cross-purposes.

RISA:

She raises a good point, Max.

MAX:

Don't get me started on your conspiracy theories, Risa.

LEE:

Hey! Be nice to our esteemed panel. What's wrong with Risa's theories? For all we know, they're right.

MAX:

I'm just saying that if any of the rest of us suggested that your dad had cold feet about becoming a dad, you would not have been so chill about it.

LEE:

It's different coming from her.

MAX:

I see.

RISA:

What do you mean it's different?

MAX:

She means you're pretty, Risa.

LEE:

Max! I mean, you are.

RISA:

Aw, thank you. You're pretty too.

CLAIRE:

We're all goddamn pretty.

LEE:

Before we go, let's summarize our theories.

MAX:

My theory is Greg's your dad.

RISA:

And my theory is your dad panicked, but he changed his mind, and he's not answering your questions because he feels guilty about having had doubts.

LEE:

He should have had doubts! My dad's not great at noticing red flags.

TRUDY:

Speaking of . . .

Trudy knows her customers' habits. She knows my dad comes in at the same time every day, right after work, orders the same thing, and here he is. When he sees us sitting around the digital recorder, he gives me a cagey look, but Will the barista gets him his black coffee and he pays for it, then comes over and sits down with us.

ARTHUR:

The past is off-limits, but other than that, you can ask me anything.

LEE:

How are you?

ARTHUR: (laughs)

I've been better. But in other ways, this is the best I've been in a while.

LEE:

Knowing what you know now ... what's the point of it?

ARTHUR:

Of getting married?

LEE:

Of getting married, of falling in love, of mixing up your life with another person's. If it's just going to end, why bother?

ARTHUR:

Everything ends, Lee. Should we not watch movies because of the closing credits? Not go out with our friends because the evening will be over? Not enjoy our lives because some-day we'll die? There are people on this planet I've already seen for the last time. Every relationship I'll ever have will end. Even the one I have with you.

LEE:

That's dark, Dad.

ARTHUR:

It's dark, but I'm okay with it. Because I have to be.

LEE: (studio)

Everyone goes silent, and then he stands up like this is a nice, casual moment in the conversation to make his departure, and he says,

ARTHUR:

Welp, it was real good talking with you all. Lee, Max, come back to the house when you finish up here. I have a surprise for you.

After my dad leaves, Max goes to help Claire set up for the poetry open mic. I can hear him asking a lot of questions about the kinds of poems she writes, about the difference between a poetry slam and a poetry reading. I suspect he's half indulging his inner dilettante and half giving me a chance to talk to Risa alone.

"What inspired you to do this?" she asks me. We're sitting by ourselves at the table, our hands folded around coffee cups, which is the only thing keeping mine from trembling nervously while I try to talk to her.

Her hair is still doing that thing, where the piece that's tucked behind her ear curls forward around her earlobe. It's so cute, it totally kills me. But I also like how open she is, how willing to throw herself into the path of a situation like playing at an open mic or joining a table full of weirdos to speculate about the divorce of two people she doesn't know. She strikes me as a person who attacks life the same way she attacks chords—confident in her moves, not even looking down to make sure her fingers are landing in the right spot.

"I wanted to tell a story about love," I tell her. "Only not fake, not idealized. The way it really works."

"And what is the way it really works?"

"I haven't figured it out yet."

Suddenly, my pleasant jangle of crush nerves turns into something churning and anxious. Across the room, I see Max and Claire watching us. It's been months since the last time anything happened between her and me, and by the time it was over, I think we were both more relieved than anything. That's not what I'm worried about, not exactly.

I have a hard time concentrating on what Risa's saying. My eyes dart toward the door, like I half expect to see Ian and Vincent come ambling in together too. If Risa knew about all of them, about how I got fired, about my real reasons for making the podcast, about the feelings I still had for Vincent, would she want anything to do with me?

I could joke about it with Max, but I don't want Risa to think of me as a messy bisexual, a cheater, a liar.

Basically, all the things I am.

I wish I could be someone better for her.

"Are you all right, Lee?"

It's the first time I've heard her say my name. I like the way it sounds on her tongue, like being noticed and addressed by her, and so even though I'm thinking about all the reasons she's going to run away when she finds out what kind of person I am, I'm grinning like an idiot.

"You seemed like you went someplace for a moment."

"Sorry," I say. "I'm right here."

"I was just asking . . ." She pauses a moment, takes a too-big swig of her coffee, and immediately claps her hand over her lips, squealing before she spits the coffee back into the cup. It's too hot, and she gasps and fans her mouth, looking around the table frantically. I jump up and grab a glass of water from Will, run back to the table with it, and slide it into her grateful hands. She takes a sip and sighs with relief.

"You were saying?" I ask.

"Do you want to hang out sometime?" she asks.

I study her face, looking for a clue whether she's asking because she wants us to be friends, or whether she's asking me out. I always have this problem with girls. With guys, I can tell when they're attracted, but flirting with girls is always shrouded in so much nuance and subtext for me. Risa's being pretty direct, and I still don't know what's going on.

You could ask her, I think. *Or you could just answer the question she asked you, because either way, your answer would be the same.*

"I'd love to hang out."

"What's your number?"

I give it to her, and a few seconds later, my phone buzzes and I have a message from her, a string of kitties with heart eyes.

Have you been to Shangri-La Records? I type.

Don't ask stupid questions, Lee

I send her an eye roll emoji, then text, **Why did the hipster burn her tongue? Cuz she sipped her coffee before it was cool.**

She texts back a string of sobbing laughing faces, then

But I haven't been there with YOU

Max selects this moment to drift over. "Do you think we should go back to your house and see what your dad's surprise is?"

I do not think we should do this. I think we should stay here so I can keep texting with Risa while we're sitting across the table from each other, but Max starts drumming his fingertips impatiently on the tabletop, so I grudgingly text **Farewell** to Risa.

A block away from Java Cabana, Max says, "I guess I read that wrong."

"What do you mean?"

"I was getting woo-woo vibes from the two of you all afternoon, so I gave you some space. But when I looked over, you were both just fucking around on your phones."

"We're going to hang out sometime," I tell him.

"Like a date?"

"I'm not sure."

"Do you want it to be?" he asks.

"I just got out of a two-year relationship," I say.

"And no one has invited you to dive into another one."

"Shouldn't I still be in mourning, though?"

Max laughs. "Not you. You're a love junkie."

"What's that supposed to mean?"

We're walking up my street now, and I see Harold's car in the driveway.

"You're in love with love. Or lust."

"I'm a people person," I say.

"If you say so."

When we walk into the kitchen, my dad is cutting up a watermelon, Harold is seasoning the potato salad, Sage is opening a beer, and Greg Thurber is standing with his elbows on my kitchen counter like he belongs there, like he does it every day instead of once a decade. Like he hadn't made me wait for him at the airport, or gone silent when we tried to find him. Like he hadn't been in love with my mom.

He sees Max and me, gives us a big smile, and says, "Look who's here!"I want to march right up to him and ask, *So, are you my dad or what?*

But my mom is right. You can't start with questions like that. You have to put people at ease, work your way up to it. So I keep my accusations to myself. I don't even bitch about the airport. Instead I wave and smile and say,

"Yep, it's us! We've grown!"

CHAPTER 15

One Question

There are few things I hate more than the plot contrivance wherein people run around making one another deeply unhappy due to a misunderstanding that could have been cleared up by asking a simple question.

I refuse to fall prey to it in my own podcast.

It's not like I'm trying to access classified FBI records. The truth is one call away, and I can put the whole thing to bed with one question. I pick up my phone and call her, and when she picks up on the first ring, I do the thing she told me not to do. I don't work up to it with easier questions, I don't put her at ease, I don't even say hello.

LEE SWAN:
Mom, is Greg Thurber my biological dad?

LEE: (studio)
It is abrupt and inelegant, but it is direct. She doesn't say hello to me either. She doesn't ask how my heart is or gently correct my tactless interview style or ask me what I'm going to do with my one wild and precious life. She says,

MAYA SWAN:
I don't know.

LEE: (studio)
And I hang up on her.

CHAPTER 16

Someone Whose Life Is About to Change

Immediately my phone rings. I don't answer it. It rings again, so I turn it off, put it on my bedside table, and lie down on the floor.

My mom is a confessional poet. Up until now, this had always kind of amused me. Like, you got married and had me when you were twenty-three. What could you possibly have to confess?

And then a terrible thought occurs to me. What if this was the thing that had kicked off the whole divorce? My parents had never gotten along, but it never seemed like they'd actually do anything about it. I'd always imagined them grumpily cohabitating until they were eighty, avoiding each other around the house, lighting up only when their friends were around. But if the truth had finally come out after all these years, it might have been enough to set the wheels in motion.

I feel like I'm supposed to be angry with her. Is it weird that all I feel is sad?

Max knocks on my door, and I tell him to come in.

"What's going on?" he asks. "You took one look at Greg and disappeared in here."

I play back the call with my mom that I'd recorded.

"I'm not quite ready to face everyone yet," I say.

Max lies down on the floor next to me, propped up on his elbow. I can feel his eyes studying every contour of my face. I suppose he could be feeling some satisfaction at having his conspiracy theories proven right, but what he says to me is, "I don't see it."

"Don't see what?"

"Greg," he says. "I see your mom's eyebrows. Your dad's eyes. Your mom's nose. Your chin somewhere between the two. Your mouth is just . . . yours. But I don't see Greg in your face."

I swallow hard and take a deep breath, trying to stop my heart from racing. When someone looks right into the center of you, it's hard not to run out of the room. It's hard to sit there and take it, to let someone see you, especially when you're pretty sure that the center of you is a disaster.

I think about making a joke that he's not exactly a reliable paternity-testing apparatus, but I stop myself.

"What else do you see?"

"Someone whose life is about to change," he says.

"I suppose that's true."

"What do you see when you look at me?"

I try to see Max the way he's seeing me, right into the center, like I've locked onto his soul with a tractor beam. But when I open my mouth to speak, he looks away, and before I can say anything, he gets up from the floor and says, "Never mind. Are you ready to go out there?"

"Is something the matter?" I ask. I don't know what just happened, why Max changed his mind all of a sudden.

"I'm okay," he says. "It's just that lately, when people see who I really am, they end up being disappointed."

"Those people don't know what they're talking about," I say, but Max is already walking out the door.

LEE SWAN: (studio)
When we go back into the kitchen, there's a weird dynamic. Like Sage, Harold, and my dad are this unit, and Greg's not quite part of it. But also, they know what Max and I are doing. They know what we're going to ask Greg, and they want to protect him from us.

(the sound of footsteps ascending the attic steps)

Soon we have Greg in the attic, sitting in front of the mic with an agreeable and jolly look on his face. He seems to think what we're doing is very cute and charming.

I dislike him a little in that moment because he doesn't seem like a person who's ever suffered or struggled the way I know my parents and the rest of their friends have. He seems like one of those blithe assholes who floats along getting everything they want.

I don't like thinking that I might be related to him.

LEE:
So, Greg, you knew my parents in college. You knew them well. Were you surprised when you found out they'd gotten together?

GREG THURBER:

We all were. It happened so fast. One morning, they gathered us all around the dining room table, and out of nowhere, they announced they were getting married. We barely had enough time to throw together a wedding party for them.

LEE:

And nobody thought to ask, "Are you sure this is a good idea?"

GREG:

They seemed happy! Everybody else had their big plans and big news. Harold's band, Sage and Maggie going to Berlin. Me going to LA. This was Arthur and Maya's big news. We celebrated it like we'd celebrated everything else.

LEE:

Did anyone know that Mom was pregnant?

GREG:

By the time we found out about that, everyone had left town.

LEE: (studio)

There is a stack of Blackwing pencil boxes on the table next to my computer. Ten boxes, to be exact, one for all of my birthdays from the time I was nine until this year. Some of them are still full of pencils because how many could I conceivably go through in a year? But they smell nice, like cedar, and the boxes are very fancy, sturdy, slick cardboard lined with patterned paper. I use them to store my audio adapters, my splitters and couplers, and my guitar picks. The older ones are filled with my little-kid treasures—rocks I liked, feathers I'd plucked out of the grass in the backyard.

LEE:
Do you recognize these?

GREG:
Did I get you those?

LEE:
I have the cards, too. My dad joked that I could sell them to fund college. Is that true, by the way?

GREG:
I hoped you'd like them, but I doubt my little doodles would even cover your books.

MAX: (studio)
Last year, a pair of sketches by Los Angeles artist Greg Thurber fetched ten thousand dollars at auction.

LEE:
I've been wondering about them lately. Do you remember when you started sending them to me?

GREG:

I don't think so.

LEE:

Sage and Maggie had just adopted Max, and the three of them came to our house.

MAX:

Technically, the adoption didn't happen for another two years. But they'd just gotten custody of me.

LEE:

The party at our house was a really big deal.

MAX:

It was really important to my parents that everyone was here. It was a "Hey Everybody, This Is Max and He's Part of Our Crew Now" party.

GREG:

I remember now.

MAX:

You spent the whole weekend up in the attic with us, drawing pictures. I barely saw you with any of the grown-ups, aka your friends, that weekend.

LEE:

I heard them talk about you all the time, but that was the

first time I remember you coming to our house.

GREG:
I guess it was. I missed out on a lot of stuff in everyone's lives. Such as the two of you.

MAX:
But the Blackwing pencils and birthday cards. You only send them to Lee.

GREG: (nervous laugh)
I don't know when your birthday is.

MAX:
It's May twenty-third. But that's not the point.

LEE:
What we're getting at is, well, we wanted to know whether there was some reason . . .

GREG:
Have you talked to your parents about this, Lee?

LEE:
I'm asking because I think you do remember why you sent me those pencils and cards. And I wanted to ask what was going through your head that weekend, when you came to our house and met Max and me.

GREG:

I'm … I'm at a loss. I think I'm on your dad's side, Lee. Maybe I'd rather not talk about the past.

LEE:

But that's all any of you talk about! All your adventures, how wild you were, crazy shit you did.

GREG:

That doesn't mean that I want to talk about it with you.

CHAPTER 17

Another One Waiting to Take Its Place

After Greg retreats down the attic steps, Max and I plan our next moves, which are few. When you're interviewing people, you can't force things. You can't go back over and over again until you wear them down. You can't bully someone into talking to you. I mean, you can. One can. But I choose not to.

"I don't know what to do next," I tell Max. "Maybe there's nothing to do. Maybe this isn't a story I can figure out."

Max sits down next to me on the air mattress and gives my hand a comforting squeeze.

"It makes me sad, though," he says. "*Objects of Destruction*. It sounds like it should exist."

"Maybe it was only ever an *Object to Be Destroyed*. Make it, get it out of your system, and then smash it to bits. You get over yourself."

Max chuckles. "Who's this 'you' you're speaking of?"

"The royal 'you,'" I say indignantly. "Anyhow, how do *you* deal with heartbreak?"

"I keep busy," Max says. "Look for something else to be interested in, whatever keeps me out of my own head."

I think about Vincent, specifically about his Shure SM7B

studio-quality microphone. I wonder if he'll think about me when he packs it to take to Washington, DC, the way we went to Yarbrough's Music together every week to visit it while he was saving up the money to buy it. We called it our puppy, and then when he bought it, we named it Puppy. Sometimes he'd leave Puppy at my house over the weekend, then text late at night, **Give Puppy a good-night kiss from me. Save one for yourself, too.**

I want to shake myself out of memories like that before they get any realer, any more raw, but what's the point? There's always another one waiting to take its place.

I put my head on Max's shoulder and sigh.

"Nothing keeps me out of my own head."

"You two sure know how to kill a party," Sage says when Max and I come down from the attic a few minutes later.

"We won't bother you anymore tonight," I tell Sage. "Will you tell them that when you go back outside? Tell them I'm putting the recorder away."

Sage looks surprised. "Wanting to know things isn't wrong, Lee."

"I know."

"And you're allowed to ask questions."

Beside me, Max has the same politely antsy look on his face that he did this afternoon before I took him out for fried pickles. He has little patience for Sage right now, especially when they're being wise and understanding with someone who's not him.

"Do you feel like doing something?" Max asks me suddenly.

I feel guilty about it, but I don't think I can set foot in Java

Cabana tonight without it feeling like failure on two fronts.

"I'm going to go to bed," I say. "I'm sorry. You should go out. Do something fun."

He looks at the clock on the microwave and says, "I told Claire I might stop by the poetry open mic."

"Don't stay out too late," Sage says.

Max glares at them, and I realize that working on *Objects of Destruction* with me hasn't just distracted him from his breakups—it's allowed him to keep his distance from Sage.

"I don't need your permission," he says.

"And I don't need your attitude."

"Cool."

"It isn't cool."

Max bites the back of his hand and stifles a frustrated sigh, then shakes his head and marches out the front door in his postapocalyptic-rogue-from-the-club wear.

Sage stares after him, at the door he's slammed shut.

"And that's what I get for being nice," they say to no one in particular. I mean, I suppose it's for my benefit since I'm the only one standing in the kitchen.

"What's going on with you two?" I ask. I feel like a traitor asking, for not automatically accepting Max's version of events. But Sage has always talked to me like I was a person with potentially interesting things to say, more than almost any of my parents' friends. They treat me like a fully formed human, and a person like that is worth giving the benefit of the doubt.

"Having a kid is crazy hard and deeply weird," Sage says.

"You're lucky to have Max," I say because I can't not

defend him, and also because it has the virtue of being true.

"I know I am. I wouldn't choose another kid on the planet if I could, no offense."

"None taken."

"When he was little, I thought, well, I'll just love him and that'll be enough. But it's not. That's what I know now, that you can love someone more than your own life and still fail them as a parent."

I wonder if this is how my mom feels right now, if she's sitting in her New Orleans hotel wondering if what's happened this week cancels out eighteen years of being a good parent. It wasn't her fault. When she made her plans, she thought I'd be up in the attic with Vincent, in love and too busy to notice she was gone. I could have told her that I needed her; I could have asked her to stay.

But I think, really, I wanted her to *know* that I needed her and stay without being asked.

"What do you think Max wants you to do?" I ask.

"Right now? I think he wants me to leave him alone," Sage says.

Maybe humans aren't made to experience love, I think. We never evolved the kind of telepathy it seems to require.

CHAPTER 18

The Rush of What Comes Next

Staring at my bedroom ceiling, I continue this trend of cheerful and life-affirming thoughts.

I begin to second-guess everything I've been doing for the past three days. What if I'm telling the wrong story, from the wrong angle? What if the only thing I have to show for it is a pile of interviews with people who do not want to talk to me? And why should they? Just because I'm a melodramatic attention whore who breaks up with her boyfriend on a podcast doesn't mean everybody wants to dredge up their lives in public. I remember what my mom said, how the last episode of *Artists in Love* seemed like a lot of my heart to spill out on the pavement.

When a confessional poet tells you that you overshared, it's time to reevaluate your life choices.

I never doubted myself like this when I was working with Vincent. Realizing this makes me miss him all over again, fresh and visceral as if I'd just lost him this minute. I miss all of our old rhythms, the way we planned stories, the things we argued about. I could talk to him about art and life and love, and he never treated me like I was being too serious or pretentious. He loved those things about me. I loved being loved for those things.

What if I never had that again with anyone?

I get out of bed and walk out to the living room, to the spot where I was standing when Vincent told me that life would be intolerable without me.

I could still have everything I wanted. I could write him back. I could take my one wild and precious life to Washington, DC, with someone I loved. What was so bad about that?

In the backyard, I hear my dad and his friends talking, listening to music on the outdoor speaker system that Harold installed for us. I know I could go out there and join them. Sage would give me a hug, and Harold would let me pick the music, and my dad would find little ways to include me in the conversation.

Instead I go out the front door and get in the car. And because I'm me, because I'm not happy unless I'm having it both ways, I bring my recorder with me.

LEE: (in the car)
Don't judge me.

It's eight p.m. on a Sunday night, and I'm parked across the street from my ex-boyfriend's house.

Don't judge me, because you never know when the universe will conspire to make you the sad girl parked across the street from your ex-boyfriend's house, trying to decide what you're going to do about it.

If I texted him right now, I'd say, *I'm parked outside. Come on, let's go someplace.*

Maybe he'd come out. Maybe he wouldn't. But either way, I'd have that nervy, electric buzz running through me while I waited to find out what was going to happen.

Maybe that's what Max meant when he called me a love junkie.

What if I don't want love? What if I just want the rush of what comes next?

Suddenly, the front door opens and people stream out of Vincent's house. I'd forgotten that Vincent's parents always had people from church over at their house on Sunday nights after evening service. When they were younger, they were missionaries. That's how they met, actually. Vincent's mom, a white lady from Germantown, Memphis's most affluent suburb, went to Kenya to teach at a Christian school. Vincent's dad, who's Kenyan, was teaching there too, and I don't know, their eyes met across the lunchroom; they brushed fingers while they were reaching for the same piece of chalk. They never talked about how they fell in love, only that it was God's will that they did. They didn't act lovey-dovey around each other. They didn't kiss hello or hold hands in public. However, they interacted like they were two gears in a clockwork that kept perfect time, a perfectly aligned team.

Vincent says they talked about staying in Nairobi, but

his mom got homesick, and his dad was curious to see what Memphis was like. He'd been to Boston and New York, but Memphis wasn't rich or glitzy or cosmopolitan. There was work to be done in Memphis; they prayed about it and decided together. And now they're church leaders. His dad directs the choir. His mom is a deacon. It's a nondenominational Pentecostal church that's fairly integrated by Memphis standards. Like, it's not a white church attended by five Black families who are in every single picture on the website, or a Black church with a couple of white members who never shut up about how they go to Black church because it's so *authentic* and *real.* Vincent's church actually looks more or less like Memphis does, all in one place. However, it's also the kind of church that says marriage exists between one man and one woman right on the home page so nobody misses it.

I've never really understood how Vincent wraps his head around it. He doesn't agree with it, but he never speaks up or stays home or finds another church to attend. He just keeps going, like he doesn't have any choice in the matter.

Vincent was homeschooled until he was in tenth grade, when he begged his parents to let him go to public school. He told me that it took six months to convince them. As far as I could tell, he'd never confronted them about anything since. It was almost like he'd used up all his stamina for teenage rebellion on that one argument, and spent the rest of high school trying to prove to them that they hadn't made a mistake.

I realize that I don't even know why he fought them so hard to go to public school. I think I assumed he felt like I did, that it would be stifling and boring to have your parents be your teachers. Maybe he had other reasons, though.

He still went to church and youth group every week. He still sat on the couch with them every week when they had people over to pray for missionaries, the sick, the suffering, and the sinful. And now, at the scandalous hour of eight p.m., the party was breaking up. I see his parents standing in the doorway, waving to their guests. I duck, hoping they don't recognize my parents' car—a ridiculous hope, since they've seen it a million times, and it's plastered in bumper stickers that say RESIST HATE and MIDTOWN IS MEMPHIS, and it really needs to be washed.

One of the church couples is parked behind me, and as they walk to their car, they make eye contact with me while I'm slouched behind the steering wheel like some kind of perv. The man scowls while the woman whispers something in his ear, and they both cringe. That's when I realize, they know who I am, and it's very likely they've spent the evening praying for their friends' son to be delivered from me and deposited safely in Washington, DC, far from my corrupting influence.

I'm sure their prayers seem rather well justified now.

I don't start the engine and drive off right that moment because that would be admitting guilt. There is no law against sitting in your car for five minutes after you park it. Maybe I was thinking. Maybe I was praying!

The woman shakes her head at me and I look away. A few seconds later, their headlights come on behind me and they drive off.

I'm too mortified to text Vincent now. I doubt his parents would even let him come outside if I did.

And with that thought, I have a reckoning so sudden and stark that I have to remind myself to breathe. I lose track of where I am, why I came here, as I reach for the recorder and press the button.

LEE: (in the car)
He was never going to get an apartment in Memphis with me. His parents never would have let him do that. And even though he's eighteen and it's not up to them, he never would have gone against their wishes.

The plans he made with me were just a fantasy. Maybe he wanted them to be true; maybe he liked the idea of them so much that he couldn't help talking about them.

But either way, our future was a figment of his imagination.

(in the background, a phone pings)

It's a pretty low moment, and I don't know how I would have gathered up the dignity to flee the scene had I not gotten a text from Risa that says, Meet me in front of Burke's after you get off work. Bring the videotape.

CHAPTER 19

Cult Flicks & Bizarre Oddities

I text her back right away, and ten minutes later, she's sitting next to me in the car.

"You got here quick," she says, and I hope I don't look too eager.

"Is that okay?" I ask. I mean, I am eager. Eager to see her. Eager to be here feeling curious and excited, instead of parked in front of Vincent's house feeling ashamed and terrible.

"Of course it's okay."

It's not a long drive to the other side of Midtown, but we talk about music almost the entire way. It's amazing the amount of space this conversation can fill:

"Have you heard _____?"

"Yes! I love _____. Let me tell you why."

or

"No, I've never heard _____."

"Let me play _____ for you. Let me tell you everything about _____."

I bet there are people who go years and never get around to talking about anything else. We go back and forth, trading music, Risa DJing on her phone while I drive. She knows a lot more than I do, and her stories about who recorded what, and where, and with whom, and how they got that sound, come bubbling up one after the other.

She's wearing a black T-shirt with the sleeves cut off and boots that lace halfway up her shins with a short skirt. I wish I was wearing something edgier than a floral sundress, but at least I like the way my shoulders look in it.

"Turn right on Cleveland," Risa says, and a few blocks later, she tells me to park in front of a long, low storefront with the words BLACK LODGE stenciled in red above the door.

I know this place, or at least I know of it. It's a video store, probably the last one in Memphis. I've heard my parents talk about it, but always in the past tense. It was a place where they used to go rent movies together, back when people still did that.

"I thought this place closed down," I say.

"It did," Risa said. "But they reopened a couple of years ago."

I'm surprised my parents haven't mentioned this. It's exactly the kind of retro, indie Memphis-weirdo stuff they live for. Although I guess it's been more than a couple of years since my parents wanted to go out and rent movies together.

When we go inside, it feels like traveling twenty years back in time. There are racks and racks of DVDs labeled with headings like CULT FLICKS & BIZARRE ODDITIES and GANGSTERS, SPIES, & FILM NOIR, and posters advertising the Time Warp Drive-In and Memphis: QueerAF! and the Pandemonium Cinema Showcase.

I'm gawking down the aisles, at the walls, at the movie playing on the big projection screen at the back of the store, but Risa walks up to the counter like she's been here a hundred times, and I hurry to catch up with her.

"Hi, I called earlier about the VCR," she says to the clerk.

"Risa from Burke's," he says, smiling with recognition. "And your friend with the podcast. I'm Matt. Come right this way."

I feel like it's the 1920s, and Risa's just whispered the secret words to get us inside the speakeasy. Matt leads us into a back room with an old television and VCR, and a tabletop covered with dozens of old VHS cassettes.

"We use this to convert old movies that were never released digitally or on DVD," he explains, then asks, "What's your podcast?"

"It's new. I haven't put it up anywhere," I say. I'm about to leave it there, but I feel emboldened by the special treatment, Risa and I being let into the off-limits area and given access to gear like we're legitimate creators.

I add, "But I used to do this podcast called *Artists in Love*."

"No kidding!" Matt says. "I've heard of that one. Didn't they write something about you in the *Flyer*?"

"It wasn't much," I say, looking at my feet.

Earlier this year there'd been an article in the free weekly called "The Fifteen Best Memphis Podcasts to Listen to Right Now (Plus Two More)." Vincent and I hadn't been in the top fifteen—we were part of the two more, an honorable-mention section at the end where they'd called us "passionate young up-and-comers." Vincent had been annoyed by it. He didn't want to be recognized for our potential, he wanted to be recognized for what we'd already done.

"That's so cool," he says. "After I get you two set up back here, I'm going to have to go check that out."

I'm about to protest and tell him he doesn't have to do that, but then I notice the bemused grin that Risa's giving me. It's a grin that says *Get out of your own way, Lee Swan*.

And so I just say thanks and hand him the videotape.

Matt opens the cartridge to inspect the tape and studies the label for a minute before popping it into the VCR.

"The Dirty South Literati," he says. "What does that mean?"

"We don't know," Risa says.

"Well, I don't want to spoil the surprise for myself," he says, then gets up to go back to the checkout counter. "Let me know when y'all put this up somewhere, okay? I'd love to hear it."

"He's nice," I tell Risa.

"Yeah," Risa says. "He comes into Burke's sometimes, and I come here to see shows. Midtown retail people stick together."

That might be part of it, I think, but I think it goes deeper than retail solidarity. I think it's because they're both part of the art-weirdo Memphis underground. This place is part of it, and Java Cabana is part of it, and so is Burke's Bookstore and Goner Records, and Risa and I are part of it too. I've always known there was a Memphis like that outside my attic, but it seemed like such an exclusive club, full of people who were older and cooler and more talented than I was. This is the first time it's ever occurred to me that I might belong to it, that the people in that world might look at me and think, *She's one of us.*

I remember the other day when Risa asked me what inspired me to make my podcast. Suddenly, I want to ask her the same kinds of questions. I want to know how she got to the art-weirdo Memphis underground too. What are the places she's been to, who are the people she's met? Now that she's here, what does she plan to do next?

"How'd you get into all this?" I ask.

"This?" she asks, motioning to the video store workroom.

"Not my thing," I explain. "Your thing. Your music."

"Sometimes it feels like the only thing I think about," she says. "Making a record, signing to Matador Records, going on tour, playing shows. Having this be what I do with my life."

When she's describing it, she starts off very businesslike and goal-oriented, but when she gets to the last part, there's a passionate quaver in her voice, and I see her eyes go someplace else, someplace familiar yet far away, like a beautiful dream.

"I want to make a record that reaches out into the world and makes people feel something real and heartbreaking and true. I want my music to make people feel less alone. I want them to know that the way it feels to them is how it feels to me, too. I want us all to feel less alone."

I'm big-eyed and clutching my knees, hanging on every word. She's speaking my language. And then she comes back, and the room feels charged with her words, like there's a kind of energy crackling all around us.

"Yes," I say, and even though I want to say more, I don't want to add a single thing to what she's said because it was perfect.

"Are you ready to do this?" she asks.

"Yes," I say, and I press the play button.

All her ideas make me want to say yes.

CHAPTER 20

Don't Tell Me What I'll Regret

OBJECTS OF DESTRUCTION, EPISODE #2: "The Dirty South Literati: Maya & Arthur's Engagement Party"

LEE SWAN: (studio)

I've heard my parents and their friends talk about the big house on Belvedere, and what strikes me right away is that it's not big.

In the grainy video, young Greg has spiky black hair and a goatee and is wearing sunglasses even though they're indoors. I squint, looking for any sign of a family resemblance, my features in his, but too much of his face is covered. He stands in front of the camera, and everyone else is gathered around him in a semicircle. I can see Maggie and Sage sitting together on one of the couches. Maggie has her legs thrown across Sage's lap, her arms thrown around their neck. Sage is wearing a flannel shirt with the sleeves cut off, and I can see the cereal-box shamrock tattoo all by itself on their arm.

There are a couple of people I don't recognize, and then, of course, my parents. Dad is sitting in an armchair, and

Mom is on the floor in front of him, sitting on a cushion. He's rubbing her shoulders and she's smiling a little half smile, her eyes closed. The only person I don't see is Harold, which means he's probably the person taping everything.

Greg takes off his shoe and pounds the coffee table with it.

(pounding sound in background)

GREG THURBER: (video recording)
I call to order this meeting, this gathering, this soiree, this esteemed salon. The reason we're here one last time before we scatter to the four winds, is to celebrate Maya and Arthur, who are getting hitched. I need a drink. We should all have a drink.

LEE SWAN: (studio)
The video cuts out for a moment, and when it resumes, everyone is holding a glass of champagne, though only my parents have glass champagne flutes. Everyone else is lifting a red Solo cup.

GREG: (video recording)
Look, I don't know what love is, but I think it has something to do with staring down the barrel of the rest of your life and saying, "I want to face this unceasing maelstrom of drudgery and obligation with you."

LEE: (studio)
Everyone in the room is frozen in discomfort, like they've all just realized letting Greg give this toast was a terrible idea. From behind the camera, Harold breaks the tension.

HAROLD WASSERMAN: (video recording)
You bleak motherfucker, this is supposed to be a party.

GREG: (video recording)
Give me a second, Harold. I'm about to land the plane. What I'm saying, Arthur and Maya, is we're counting on you. Show us how this shit is supposed to work, okay?

To Arthur and Maya.

LEE: (studio)
Everyone in the room lifts their glasses and repeats it after him. My mom touches the glass to her lips, but doesn't tip it back, and I think, *Holy shit. She's pregnant with me in this video. I'm on this VHS tape.*

The room starts to break up into small pockets of chitchat. Greg pours himself another glass of champagne and drinks it in a single gulp. He walks out of the frame, and I think that must be the end of the tape, but it isn't.

A moment later, Greg comes flying back into the center of the room until he's staring down at my mom, who's still sitting on her cushion in the middle of the floor. She looks up at him and he says,

GREG: (video recording)
Maya, don't stay here in this mosquito-infested shithole. Don't marry this guy. Your life could be big, but you're making it small, and in twenty years, you'll be wondering why you didn't want something better for yourself. Come with me to LA. If you stay here, if you do this, you'll regret it.

LEE: (studio)
The room goes silent, as everybody in the video waits to see what's going to happen next.

My dad doesn't react at all. He looks like he's giving up, or worse, like he's secretly agreeing with Greg and he's just waiting for my mom to walk out the door with him.

He doesn't speak up. He doesn't fight for her. He doesn't tell Greg to fuck off.

My mom does that for herself.

(sound of a thump, then a crash, chairs being pushed back, a clamor of indistinct voices)

HAROLD: (video recording)
Maya! Wait!

LEE: (studio)
The next thing that happens in the video is that my pregnant mom leaps to her feet and flips over the coffee table. Everything goes flying—the red Solo cups and coasters and ashtrays.

She makes a lunge for Greg, but then Harold runs out from behind the camera tripod and throws his arms around her and holds her still.

This calms her, but only for a second.

When people say things are being recorded for posterity, they don't usually mean it literally. I'm the posterity. I get to see the moment in the video when my mom breaks free from Harold's grasp, sticks her finger in Greg's face, and says,

MAYA SWAN: (video recording)
Don't tell me what I'll regret.

LEE: (studio)
Okay, I think, this time it's really the end.

Greg leaves, and my mom asks everyone else to give her a minute. They all go outside to smoke on the front porch, and my mom starts tidying up the glasses and plates. She doesn't know the camera is still running when she sinks down into a chair and buries her head in her hands.

Then I hear the slam of a screen door, and then Harold's there. He sits next to her, takes her hand, and gives it a squeeze.

HAROLD: (video recording)
Are you okay?

MAYA: (video recording)
Yep.

LEE: (studio)
She's not okay. He's not okay. I can hear in their voices an iceberg of unspoken things. This isn't a friendly check-in. It isn't commiseration. It isn't about Greg, and nobody is okay.

HAROLD: (video recording)
Are you sure this is what you want?

LEE: (studio)
My mom nods, but she won't look at him. They're both crying a little bit, their voices cracking when they talk to each other.

HAROLD: (video recording)
Are we still friends?

MAYA: (video recording)
Of course we are.

HAROLD:
What about everything else?

MAYA:
We act like it never happened.

HAROLD:
Okay.

LEE: (studio)
One summer night you come home late,
caked in a dozen layers of sweat,
secondhand smoke, bar rags, and bleach.

I thought that poem was about my dad, but nannies don't
come home smelling like those things.

Harold takes her face in his hands, pulls it close to his,
and kisses her once on the lips and once on the forehead.
She rests her head on his shoulder, but only for a second
because the screen door opens again.

In the video, I see my mom and Harold jerk upright, pull
apart, and wipe their cheeks with the backs of their hands
before my dad appears and sits down by her other side.

ARTHUR: (video recording)
Oh sweetie, don't let him get to you.

LEE: (studio)

And I realize my dad thinks she's crying about Greg.

You're the only person I would have wanted to tell,
so I keep our story to myself.

That's how my mom ended the poem she wrote about Harold. She wrote what she meant, and she kept her word.

CHAPTER 21

Bi Girls to Watch Out For

People think they want the truth, but they don't. What people really want is a story that sounds like it *could* be the truth, something that slaps a bow on the whole thing and lets them walk away feeling satisfied.

When I say *people*, I mean me.

If the point of *Objects of Destruction* was to figure out why my parents ended up together, and the obvious answer was me, the story I'd been hoping to find had some feeling in it, some passion, some spark. Some hope.

Instead I found my dad, passport in his hand, and ambivalent about the whole thing. I found my mom crying at her own engagement party, settling for the only guy who wasn't leaving.

This is the kind of story where even if I dig up all the pieces, nothing could put them back together.

It's like Greg Thurber said. Love is just an unceasing maelstrom of drudgery and obligation. It's a fantasy; it's a figment of your imagination; it's a story with the same shitty ending every time.

Nobody wants that kind of truth.

"Huh," I say. I lean forward and eject the tape, but I don't take it out of the VCR. I sit there, staring at its peeling paper label and half wishing I hadn't watched it.

Risa cups her hand over the back of my hand. "Are you okay?"

I'm not sure how to answer the question.

"Do you want to go to my house?" she asks.

That one's easier.

Risa lives in a neighborhood in Memphis called Sherwood Forest, where all the streets are named after characters from Robin Hood. Her house is on Maid Marian Lane, on a block of redbrick houses, each one almost identical with white shutters, carports, and concrete steps.

When we go inside, everything smells like flowers, real ones, not air freshener. There's a vase or a pot on nearly every table I see. The couch has a floral print, and even the walls are covered with sprigs of dried lavender and heather.

I was quiet in the car most of the way here, but I feel better as soon as I set foot inside. It's hard not to feel at least a little bit of fascination and delight when you're in Sherwood Forest.

"You can leave your shoes here," Risa says, pointing to a pile of no fewer than a dozen pairs of sandals, boots, wedges, and stiletto heels.

"Does someone in your family have a shoe problem?" I ask.

"The boots are my aunt's. The sandals are my mom's. They share the heels."

I look around for some sign of them, but the house seems to be empty except for us. I follow Risa to the kitchen, and she fills the room with conspiratorial small talk while she gets glasses down from the cupboard.

"They both had dates tonight," she says. "You should have seen them two hours ago. They were doing their eyebrows and saying judgmental things about each other's outfits. And then they started saying judgmental things about *my* outfit, and I was, like, leave me out of your straight-lady psychodrama."

So she is queer, I think.

"Their dates were named Bear and Bragg. They probably showed up wearing Grizzlies jerseys." She seems like she's winding up for another rant, then catches herself and giggles. "But I'm rambling and you didn't come here to talk about my mom's love life."

"You're not rambling," I say. "Or if you are, it's endearing."

She hands me a glass of water. "This might be an odd thing to say given the circumstances, but I'm glad you came over. Are you feeling better about the video?"

"It was a lot to take in," I said, "but I can take it."

I think about what we saw on the video, how raw and confusing it was, how private and sad. *Am I okay?* I wonder. *Or has it not sunk in yet?*

It must show on my face because Risa puts her glass on the countertop and takes me by the shoulders.

"You know, it's okay if you're not okay," she says.

Her hands feel like they're grounding me, pulling me out of my head and back into the rest of my body—pulling me back here with her.

"I don't know if it's the right time, but I have something to show you," Risa says tentatively. "It's for *Objects of Destruction.*"

"What is it?"

"Something I made."

"Then I definitely want to see it," I say.

For a second, she hesitates like she's going to change her mind and take it back, but then she says, "Okay, then. Follow me."

She leads me down the hallway to her room, which is an explosion of cables, stereo equipment, and gear. There's a knee-high practice amp by the bed, next to a guitar stand with an electric and an acoustic propped up on it. When I see her desk, my heart leaps because I see the makeshift home studio setup, not dissimilar to my own.

I'm struck by a desire to be as bold as she is, asking for my number, sending me songs.

"When you said you wanted to hang out, did you mean as friends, or like a date?" I ask.

"I know you date guys," she says. I can't read the expression on her face, can't tell whether she's hanging back because she doesn't want to lead me on, or because she thinks I'm straight.

"Not exclusively," I say, eager to set the record straight.

"I also know you're not terribly exclusive," she says, and my face burns.

"How do you . . . ?" I'd always prided myself on never getting caught, but I don't finish asking my question because as soon as the words leave my mouth, it occurs to me that it's nothing to be proud of.

"Lesbian whisper network," Risa says. "Bi girls to watch out for."

I feel like I should defend myself, but Risa isn't looking at me like I'm a bi girl to watch out for. Whatever she thinks about my reputation, at least in this moment, she seems to be smiling about it. So I decide not to make a big deal out of it either.

"For what it's worth, I think my cheating days are over," I say.

"You're embracing monogamy?"

"I'm embracing honesty."

She takes the chair at her workstation and motions for me to sit on the bed as she picks up a pair of headphones.

"Well, then I'd like your honest opinion of this piece," she says. "It's the theme music for *Objects of Destruction*. Or at least I'd like it to be."

She slips the headphones over my ears and hits play, and immediately, I'm in love. It sounds like the song of an old music box that you might find tucked away in an attic, creaky and haunted. And then the chords turn shimmery, like shards of glass catching sunlight one by one. There are gentle, winding lengths of it, perfect for layering under a monologue, or nesting between segments. There's a spot that builds and explodes, just the way I'd imagined it.

She doesn't watch me, doesn't listen along. Instead she follows the sound waves on the computer screen, and only when it's over does she look at me.

I'm so thrilled that she made something for me, thrilled by the fact of her, her home recording studio, her house full of flowers on Maid Marian Lane.

"It's like you pulled the ghost of a song out of my brain and made it real."

"Then you like it?" she asks.

"It's perfect," I say. "It's exactly what I wanted."

We're both still, and I can tell there's something other than the song hanging in the air between us. I feel like I should break it.

I feel like I should lean over and kiss her to break it.

The only reason I don't is because I'm thinking about what happens after.

I'm thinking about the second time that Claire and I hooked up. It was a month after the night in the storage closet, long enough that my conscience had begun to ease up, and instead of feeling guilty about what had happened, it almost seemed like it hadn't happened at all.

But then Claire and I worked another closing shift, and it was just her and me in the shop, and I felt this prickly, rangy energy coursing through my body, and when she asked, "Do you want to see if there's anything interesting in the storage closet?" I followed her.

There's something about the moment you decide to hook up with someone, especially when it's accompanied by a little voice that asks, "Is this a good idea?" It's so hot to push that voice aside and lose yourself in a bad idea, in someone's kiss, and let the momentum carry you as far as it will.

Every time I cheated on Vincent, there was a moment when I realized it was a bad idea and did it anyway.

Not that hooking up with Risa would be the same thing. I wasn't sneaking around. I wasn't lying to anyone. But my emotions had been jacked up all night, from the interview with Greg, to getting caught outside Vincent's house, to watching the videotape of my parents unhappy at their own engagement party. It would have felt good to obliterate those difficult, twisted-up feelings and replace them with something nice. That was what held me back: Did I like *her*, or did I just like getting lost in someone who wasn't me?

"You look like you're having some thoughts," Risa says.

"I want to kiss you," I say. "But I shouldn't. I'm a flaming wreck of a human being right now."

Risa laughs. "How bad could you possibly be?"

"When you texted, I was sitting in a parked car outside my ex-boyfriend's house having an existential crisis."

Risa stops laughing and her face turns serious. She doesn't say anything, so in the spirit of honesty, I decide to keep going.

"'Taking time off' from Java Cabana to work on my podcast was not my idea. My boss pretty much fired me because my ex got into a fight with the guy I hooked up with the night after we broke up."

I decide I'm going to keep talking until Risa says something, or tells me to stop, or kicks me out.

"I cheated on him, more than once, with Claire from work. My parents are splitting up, I don't know what to do with my life. I don't know what love is or if it exists. I thought I understood love, I thought I had my life figured out. I liked that feeling, and now it's gone."

At first, she doesn't say anything. There's a loose thread on the edge of her bedspread, and she picks it up and starts to pull at it, slowly unraveling the hem until the thread gets stuck and goes taut. She glances up at me, like, *I'll be right with you, but first I need to see what happens with this bedspread,* and then winds the thread around her fingertip and yanks it until it snaps.

As she unwinds the thread from her fingertip, she looks up at me and gives me a grin that might be pitying or exasperated, or that might be kind.

"Thank you for telling me all of that," she says.

"Thanks for not telling me to get the hell out of your house."

Risa gets up from her chair and sits next to me on the bed. She puts her hand on top of mine and says, "I appreciate your honesty, but just because you're a flaming wreck of a human being doesn't mean you can't have nice things."

"What do you mean?" I ask, and instead of answering, Risa leans over and kisses me.

It's not a shy kiss, or a soft one. Risa kisses like she plays the guitar, like she has one chance to deliver an urgent message. She kisses in a way that makes me think, in the middle of kissing her, that if I hadn't done this, I'd walk around for the rest of my life with some kind of regret whose origins I could never entirely place.

My fingertips explore her jawline, her neck, the tendril of hair that cradles her earlobe. It is the opposite of my disappointing parking-lot hookup with Ian, the opposite of my furtive cheating with Claire. It's like I just picked a lock, threw open the door, and what came tumbling out was the rest of me.

The next thing I know, she's pulling off her T-shirt and throwing it over the back of the desk chair. Inspired by her daring, I do the same thing with my sundress, and then we're on our knees, facing each other on her bed. I reach for her again, and when we kiss this time, I feel her hands run down my sides and land at the small of my back.

She pulls away and looks me up and down. Before I have a chance to feel self-conscious about being on her bed in my bra and underwear in unflattering, bright overhead lights, she says, "You look so pretty."

"*You* look so pretty," I say, admiring her.

I love the way she's looking at me, the way she's admiring me. It puts me at ease, lets me know that whatever my body looks like, whatever effect the lighting is having, it's good.

Don't get me wrong, I'm also terrified.

Because I know what it's like to be touched by people who are bad at it, or lazy, or indifferent. While I'm touching her, the part of me that isn't melting with pleasure is frozen in fear that I'm not doing it right.

We lie down and kiss some more, our arms wrapped around each other, our bellies pressed together. It's languid and dreamy, and I can't remember the last time I felt so good. If Risa told me I could stay with her exactly like this, for the rest of the night, I would do it in a heartbeat.

But then I wonder, should I be doing something else? Does she want me to go further? I feel good about everything we've done so far, but I can feel the anxiety building inside me about where it's all heading.

I pull away for a moment and look into her eyes. On the pillow, our faces are so close I can count her eyelashes. Near the foot of the bed, our toes touch.

"How are you doing?" she asks. "Is this okay?"

I think about the way I felt the mornings after I'd hooked

up with Ian, with Claire. I'm pretty sure right now that when I wake up tomorrow morning, I'm not going to feel regret about anything that's happened between Risa and me. But given the tumultuous quality of my life, I know better than to make predictions about how I'm going to feel about anything.

"It's very okay," I say. "How about you? What would you like to happen?"

"I'd like to keep doing this," she says, then adds, "but we should probably stop. I don't know what time my mom and aunt are getting home from their dates. And besides, this is a lot."

"I'm glad it happened, though," I say.

"So am I."

As I put my bra and sundress back on, I think about the joyless and cruel conversations Claire and I started to have after the second time, conversations like: *this didn't mean anything; this won't happen again; don't tell my boyfriend.*

"So, what happens next?" Risa asks.

"I don't know," I say, "but I like the honesty thing. Can we keep doing that?"

"Like letting me know if you drive past your ex's house?"

"I'm going to try not to do that again."

"I like that you didn't promise you wouldn't. Very honest."

"I know myself. I'm weak. Some people have even called me a bi girl to watch out for."

Risa rolls her eyes at me. "You're lucky you're cute."

I don't know what's gotten into me, all this giddy nonsense. If I'm not careful, I'm going to piss her off.

"I'm sorry. I'm being weird," I say.

"You are worth the weirdness," she says. And I kiss her

again, kiss her until we hear her aunt's car pull up outside, and she walks me to the foyer so I can put on my shoes and exchange awkward family introductions with a woman whose lipstick and hair are as tousled as ours.

I'm looking for the problem, for the thing I'm going to feel rotten about tomorrow, and I can't find it. But maybe, I think, instead of looking for things to feel guilty about, I could just feel happy.

I'm a flaming wreck of a human being, I think, but I am worth the weirdness.

CHAPTER 22

Never Just One Thing

There's this movie cliché where people fall into a deep and immediate slumber after fooling around. I don't know what that's about because when I get home from Risa's house, I'm too wired to sleep. It's after midnight and Max is already in my bed when I come home, his snoring drowned out by the air conditioner. I go up to the attic so I can sit for a minute with everything that happened tonight. It started with me antagonizing the man who might be my biological father, and ended here, my lips swollen from kissing, my heart racing every time I catch the scent of her still clinging to my skin.

I can't wait to hear how Risa's song sounds in the mix. She's given me so much to work with—dreamy synth parts, electric guitar riffs. It doesn't sound like noodling, though. It's a composition with a theme it keeps returning to. When I get this done, I think, I'll have her over and she and Max and I can listen to it together, this thing we made.

When I finally go downstairs, it's almost three in the morning, and I almost have a rough mix of the first episode. I love my house around this time when it's a still, tiny kingdom with a population of only me. Except tonight, it's not only

me. My dad is sitting at the kitchen table, writing in his notebook. He looks up and waggles his fingers at me in a sheepish,
we're-both-up-too-late kind of wave. I join him at the table,
knowing I'm not going to get a lecture about staying up too
late. We don't do that at my house.

"What are you writing?" I ask.

He shakes his head and closes the notebook.

"Nothing important," he says. "How about you? What
were you working on?"

"Just messing around," I say.

"Are you getting enough sleep, Lee?" he asks. "It's important to sleep when you're under stress."

"Said the man who was up at three a.m."

"What did you and Max say to Greg earlier?" he asks. "He
looked queasy when he came down from the attic."

"The same questions I've been asking the rest of you.
Don't worry. Greg didn't answer them either. Your secrets are
safe."

My dad folds his hands on the table and gives me an exasperated look.

"Lee, honey," he says. "I don't know how to talk to you
about any of this."

"It's your story," I say. "You can talk about it any way you
want."

"That's the problem," he says. "If I decide on one way to
tell you, then the story becomes one thing, and the story of me
and your mother was never just one thing. Not ever."

"I know that."

"No, I don't think you do."

"It's late," I say. "I should try to get some sleep."

I'm getting up from the table when he says, "One more thing, Lee. I don't want to get in the middle, but I think you should call your mom."

"If you don't want to be in the middle, don't say things like that."

Correspondence from People I Don't Want to Talk to, Three a.m. Edition:

Voicemail from my mother: *Lee, I'm sorry. I should have told you that in person, not over the phone. I'm sorry I'm not there right now. I miss you. Call me when you're ready.*

And then another: *Actually, call me even if you're not ready.*

And a text from Vincent: I wish you'd write back instead of sitting outside my house. I know you need time, but your silence is becoming very loud.

CHAPTER 23

Conspiracy Theory

I don't call my mom. I don't text Vincent. I sleep until two in the afternoon, eat a bowl of potato salad and a hot dog, and once I realize there's no remaining trace of Risa's scent on my skin, I shower. It seems like days since I was in her bed, even though it's only been hours. Between the conversation with my dad and the messages from my mom and Vincent, all my human communication between the hours of three and three fifteen was sufficiently unpleasant to snuff out the good feelings I'd been carrying around. And then there was the fact that I'd texted her this when I got home:

I had such a good time with you. Thank you for my song, and my kisses, and for being you.

It's been fourteen hours, and she still hasn't written back.

I go back up to the attic and play back the rough mix of *Objects of Destruction* with her song layered in. I make a note of the transitions that need work, gaps in the story, the places where my attention starts to wander. I've been at it for a couple of hours when Max comes up the stairs.

"Where've you been?" I ask.

"I could ask you the same question," he says. "I thought you were going to bed early last night."

"I exercised some questionable judgment," I say.

"You got back together with Vincent?"

My mouth drops open in mock outrage.

"I did not," I say, neglecting to mention that I'd merely been apprehended lurking outside his house. I wonder what would have happened if Vincent had come outside instead of his parents' friends? What if Risa hadn't texted and invited me over? It's not the wildest thing in the world for Max to suggest. He knows me. He knows what I'm capable of.

"Risa found me a VCR," I say. "And she wrote us a song."

I offer the headphones to Max, but before he takes them, he pauses, scrutinizing my face.

"And?" he asks with an impish grin.

"And what?"

"You're glowing."

"Because I just got out of the shower."

"Because you're happy."

Max takes the headphones from me and puts them on.

"I'm glad you had a good date, Lee," he says.

He closes his eyes as the music starts. Five minutes later, he hasn't opened them, hasn't moved. He listens to the song by itself, then listens to our intro with the music layered in. When it's over, he slips the headphones off and says, "This is too good not to finish."

His words give me goose bumps, the kind of creative shiver that tells you to follow it like a divining rod, not to stop, not to wander off course, but to keep going, keep moving, keep following that feeling.

I haven't felt like this since the very beginning of *Artists in Love*, when Vincent told me I was his muse and his inspiration, and I believed he was mine too.

"So then let's finish it," I say.

Max stands up and reaches out his hand to help me up. "I'm one step ahead of you there. Harold's expecting us at his apartment in half an hour for an interview, so let's get in the car and you can tell me everything about the tape on the way there."

"Why are we going to interview Harold again?"

"Because Harold's the key to all of this."

Max doesn't understand why I look so surprised when he says this. He hasn't seen the video for himself. He doesn't know what I know, and yet still, somehow he knows.

"It's my conspiracy theory," he says.

I've only been to Harold's apartment a few times before, usually when my dad is stopping by to return a record or a casserole dish. It's in a building that used to be a warehouse, and all the apartments are big open rooms with concrete floors and exposed brick walls. Harold has lived here for as long as I can remember, even though it's sometimes seemed more like he lived with us.

On the way there, I tell Max what Risa and I saw on the Dirty South Literati VHS cassette. I pepper in all the little contemptible details about Greg's goatee and indoor sunglasses. Max slaps the dashboard and cackles when I tell him how my mom flipped the coffee table and told him off. But when I get to the part about Harold and my mom, his face turns serious.

"You said you wanted to know whether your parents were

doomed from the start," he says as we pull into the underground parking structure for Harold's warehouse apartment building. "I guess you have your answer."

"I do," I say. "Turns out, if you have a choice between the life you'll regret and the life you won't, you can't trust love to help you pick. It's like my dad said. It ends. It always ends, and no matter what you choose, you end up regretting it."

"That's a depressing answer."

I take the key out of the ignition, but neither of us unbuckles our seat belt. After a moment, I say, "What about your conspiracy theory? You said Harold was the key to all of it."

"When lions are hunting wildebeest, they don't take on the whole herd. They separate one out. They get him alone," Max says. "Not that I'm calling Harold the weak member of the herd."

I know what he means. Harold doesn't have Sage's protective streak. He won't dismiss us as nosy kids like Greg did. He doesn't have my dad's stubborn will. If we get him alone, Harold will crack. He will tell us anything we ask him.

"Now I feel like a dick for taking advantage of him," Max says.

"We're not predators, Max," I say, and I unbuckle my seat belt. Max does the same, and we get out of the car, walk through the parking garage to the elevator. It's the same one that was there when it was still a warehouse, big enough to transport a grand piano. We take it up to the third floor, and I walk down the long concrete hallway with purpose.

I don't want to pry out Harold's secrets. I don't need him to solve any mysteries.

I want to ask him what he regrets.

Harold answers the door still in his work clothes: jeans, a button-down shirt rolled up at the sleeves and untucked, and a pair of Doc Martens boots. The only other clothes Harold owns are T-shirts with band names on them.

"Come in," he says, peering into the hallway with some furtiveness, like Max and I are drug dealers or something.

Inside Harold's apartment, it looks like he never finished moving in, or like he didn't intend to stay. The television and stereo are set up on milk crates, and the rest of the furniture is minimal—bed in the corner, one table, two chairs, a sofa. You could never have a cookout here. I can't even imagine Harold inviting someone over to dinner.

The one thing that looks cared for, that makes it look like Harold has lived here for more than two months, is the home studio built into the corner.

It reminds me of Risa's, and I wish she was here to see it. She'd flip out. In addition to the rack of guitars, Harold has a mandolin, a banjo, a dulcimer. He has an amp that he built himself, a bass guitar rig, a small drum kit. This is why Harold lives in this space. The concrete walls are two feet thick already, and he's soundproofed everything. He plays in pit orchestras for a lot of local theater productions and records local bands, usually the ones who can't afford to record anywhere else. About once every three years, Harold puts out a record of his own, and once or twice a decade, he plays a show.

"What did you want to ask me about?" he asks.

Max unzips his backpack and pulls out the VHS tape

labeled *The Dirty South Literati: Maya & Arthur's Engagement Party* and hands it to Harold.

"Where did you get this?"

"We found it in Mom and Dad's office," I say.

"Why would they still have this?" he asks, turning it over in his hands. "Have you watched it?"

I nod. Harold's face turns ashen, and I can tell he already knows what's on the tape, knows what I've seen. Still, he offers us the chairs at his kitchen table and takes a seat on the arm of the sofa.

"I thought your parents would have thrown it away by now," he says.

"Have they watched it?" I ask.

Harold gives me a stricken look and nods. "What do you want to know?" he asks.

Don't start with the big questions, I think. *Work up to them. Put him at ease.*

LEE SWAN:

Why did you call yourselves "literati"?

HAROLD WASSERMAN:

It was your mom's idea. We were always talking about these famous groups of artists like the Algonquin Round Table, and your mom said, "They didn't know they were famous and historical. They were just friends, talking about interesting stuff and showing off for each other." She said, "Let's call ourselves something, and then someday, when people talk about famous literary circles, they'll talk about ours."

MAX LOZADA:

Did you really just sit around talking about art?

HAROLD:

We didn't just talk about it. We made it. Music, poetry, theater, paintings.

LEE:

Do you think my parents should have gotten married?

HAROLD:

Uh ...

LEE:

Did they love each other?

HAROLD:

Where did you find the VCR?

LEE:

The Black Lodge.

HAROLD:

Love that place. I mean, you think you can watch anything you want to, but you can't. *Pink Flamingos, Better Off Dead, Wild at Heart.* A lot of those classics you can't even get online ...

LEE:
Uncle Harold.

HAROLD:
I've had a long time to think about those questions, Lee, and here's what I've come up with.

About fifteen years ago, my music career kind of blew up in my face. My band got dropped by our record label while we were on tour; then we had a fight and broke up on the drive back to Memphis. When we got home, I was having some pretty dark thoughts about wasting my life and having nothing to show for it.

But the next night, your mom and dad had me over for dinner. You were probably about four, and your parents grilled steaks and baked a pie, and after dinner, your mom gave me this scrapbook that your family had made for me. In it was every article, every blog post, all the photographs where we looked famous and cool, all the nicest things everyone ever said about us. You colored in the borders and put stickers on all the pages.

And when I saw all that stuff together in one place, I thought, this is what family does. What they're supposed to do, when it's all working the way it's supposed to.

I know it's a mess, Lee, but when I think of your parents

together, that's the part I think about. There was always a lot of love in your house. Your parents knew how to make other people feel loved.

LEE:
Then why couldn't they make each other feel that way?

LEE: (studio)
Harold knows my parents better than anyone else in the world, but when he tells me that he doesn't know, he looks so sad that I don't want to ask him anything else. Besides, I already know the answer.

He made his choice. He chose both of them. He chose their friendship, their house full of love. He chose them as his family. And now that was over.

Harold looks like he regrets everything.

CHAPTER 24

Memphis May Not Always Love You Back

Risa still hasn't texted when we leave Harold's apartment. It's early evening now. Twenty hours since I texted her. Immediately, my mind leaps to the most dire conclusions: last night meant nothing to her, or worse, she already regrets it. I shouldn't have texted her so quickly, and I definitely shouldn't have been so cheesy. She probably thinks I'm needy or clingy, or one of those people who says "I love you" creepily early in relationships.

Max is quiet too, in the elevator down to the lobby. When we're back in the car, I ask him, "Is everything okay? You seem like you have something on your mind."

"I'm just thinking about Harold. He looked so sad," Max says.

We pull out of the parking garage, and soon the riverfront loft apartments and touristy pedestrian malls fall away, and we're in the neighborhood between Downtown and Midtown. I don't know its name, only that everybody says you shouldn't walk in it, and if you ask why, they say "Because of the crime" in this sort of nebulous way that probably means something else.

There's no one on the sidewalks, though, so I guess it's

just one of those rules of Memphis that people follow whether there's any truth to it or not.

Max looks out the window at the empty storefronts, the parks without a single person in them.

"Why do you want to stay here?" he asks.

I can feel the judgment in his question, and suddenly want to rush to the defense of my city.

"It's not like anyplace else," I say. "It feels right to me. It has good energy."

"Does it?" Max gestures out the window toward a row of cinder-block storefronts: a liquor store, a check-cashing place, and a bail bondsman.

"Like you don't have that in Chicago."

"Have you ever noticed how much poverty there is here?" he asks.

"There's poverty in Chicago."

Max sighs. "I'm not trying to defend Chicago. I'm asking you why you want to live in a city with this much crime and poverty and segregation and backward-ass Southern non-sense."

"Because that's not all Memphis is," I say. "Every time I see anything about Memphis on TV, it's about police and gangs and guns, like those are the only stories people want to tell. What about the art and music? What about the fact that a city this weird and wonderful is stuffed into a corner of Tennessee? Those are good stories too."

"And what about Vincent?" Max continues. "How does he feel about living in a city that's mostly Black, but white people run most of the shit in it?"

In that moment, I feel a little less idealistic about my inclusive artsy vision of Memphis. I know that what Max is talking about is true. But at the same time, I don't want to concede all the good things about my city, the things that feel different than any other place in the South, the parts that fight back when anyone tries to push their backward-ass Southern nonsense on us.

"What about Stax Records? Sun Studios? The Vollintine-Evergreen neighborhood?" I say. "What about all the places in my city where Black and white people stood together and refused to let segregation get a foothold?"

"Good for them," Max says. "What'd you have to do with it?"

"That's what I care about doing too," I say. "I mean, my family lives in Midtown. Vincent was my boyfriend for two years. I went to public school with, like, six other white kids."

Max's sigh stops me from going any further. While we're stopped at the red light at Union and McLean, he takes off his sunglasses and puts his hand on my shoulder.

"I say this with love, Lee Swan, but there are no white girl merit badges for attending public school. Or falling in love with a brown boy. Or living in an integrated neighborhood. You're going to have to try a little harder than that."

"How?" I ask.

"For starters, you could understand that just because you know the situation is messed up doesn't mean you know what any of this is like for Vincent."

"The other day, Vincent told me he felt like he was the wrong kind of Black for Memphis," I say.

"How can you be the wrong kind of Black for anywhere?"

"I don't know."

"Well, maybe you should have asked him what he meant when he said that instead of nodding your head like you already understood what he was talking about."

I think about my defense of Memphis, how thin and insufficient it seems. I hadn't even answered Max's question: How does Vincent feel about living here? Two years we'd been together, and I didn't know.

We'd expressed broadly progressive ideas to each other, almost like we were trying to signal some sort of reassurance: *I'm not* that *kind of Christian. I'm not* that *kind of white person.*

I knew what he believed and how he felt about art, love, and the universe, but the real-life things—how he felt about having a white mom and a Kenyan dad, and how he felt moving through the halls of our school as a biracial person, or when he filled out that application to Howard University— never seemed to come up between us. Or at least I never asked, and he never volunteered. It was like we wanted to prove that the differences between us didn't matter, so we started to act like they didn't exist.

Max and I both go quiet as we drive down Cooper Avenue, past the antique shops and diners, but when we drive under the train tracks, the semiofficial beginning of my neighborhood, he turns to me and says,

"Another thing . . ." Like he's been thinking about it this whole time.

"Another thing?"

"Another thing."

"Give it to me," I say.

"You haven't really lived as an out queer person here. You don't know what that's like."

"So?"

"So you may love Memphis, but Memphis may not always love you back."

I know the rules of Memphis enough to know he's right, but still, I can't help thinking, *What if it could?*

I don't say this out loud. It would sound as naive and clueless as the ways I'd tried to defend Memphis on our drive from Downtown.

But I know I'm onto something, maybe something from the appendix to the rules of Memphis, the revised edition. Something that's worth defending.

Sometimes you live in a place, and you can tell people are happy with things the way they are, even if no one is actually very happy. A lot of the South is like that. But I don't think people in Memphis are happy with the way things are. People in Memphis know we all deserve better.

If that's how you feel, why'd you spend the last two years in the closet? Did you think Memphis would love you back if you lied to it?

Or maybe I am just being naive and clueless.

We pull into the driveway, and when we get out of the car, I see that for the first time in days, no adults are sitting on the porch. I look at Max, then back at the porch, and we both make a beeline for the swing, like if we hesitated a second more, some forlorn grown-up would come out the front door and snatch it from us.

It's a good front porch swing. I should know—I've been

swinging in it for over a decade. We get into a nice summer-evening rhythm on it, watching the fireflies, listening to the kids two houses down playing in the yard.

"What did you think about Harold's interview?" I ask.

"The things he said about your family were sweet," he says. "Or at least they were sweet if you can look past the sad parts."

"It made me realize how lonely his life is," I say.

Max nods. "It made me think, what if I end up like that? What if I'm this sad, lonely person who's on the periphery of everyone else's life?"

"That's not fair," I say. "That's not who Harold is. He's my family."

Then I realize it doesn't matter what Harold is because Max is talking about himself. This is what Max is scared of. I meet his eyes and when he tries to look away, I reach out, touch his chin until we are face-to-face. I look into the center of him, the way he did to me, the way that made me want to run out of the room. And this time, he lets me.

I see a person of tremendous goodness. A person who'd been pitched into my shitshow household and met us where we were.

I see a person who needs to be able to trust that the people in his life are going to stick around. That their love for him doesn't hinge on him dating sweet, saintly gay boys. Or being one.

I see a person who moves through this world, this life, finding all of it endlessly captivating.

"I love every version of you I've ever met," I say. "I love

them all. You are too lovable to be on the periphery of anyone's life."

I'm still holding his chin when my phone buzzes. I glance
down because I want to see if it's Risa.

It isn't.

Max pulls free from my distracted touch.

"Who's that?" he asks.

"Vincent," I say, and then I pick up the phone, and I read
his messages, and all the air goes out of me.

Vincent, who knows me. Who knows how my heart works,
and how to crack it wide open.

There are so many things he doesn't know about me, but
he knows what to say to make me put aside whatever it is I'm
in the middle of doing and go to him.

He's sent me a message that reads, **My heart is a ruin.**

And a Lee Miller photograph.

It's one she took when she was living in England, during
World War II. The Nazis were bombing London, and she was
out in the thick of it with her camera. The photograph is called
"Nonconformist Chapel"—it's a bombed church, its doorway
filled to the top with rubble, chunks of brick and plaster spilling out into the street.

I've always loved this photograph. I love that even in the
middle of a war zone, Lee Miller could see art. And the title
reminds me of Vincent. I know his faith is important to him,
even though he doesn't talk about it in the same way his parents do. He doesn't agree with a lot of things his church stands
for, doesn't believe in their version of hell or sin or damnation.
He's his own tiny nonconformist chapel.

And right now, he is a ruin.

Beneath that he writes, **Please come over as soon as you can. It's important. I have something to show you.**

I give Max a pleading look. I know I should stay here on the front porch swing with him; I should be a good friend.

"Go," he says. "You'll be miserable if you don't."

"Thank you for understanding."

"I didn't say I understood it. I just know better than to stop you."

"You're a good friend."

"I know I am," Max says. "I'm such a good friend that I won't even tell you that you're making a mistake."

I'm about to be indignant, to remind Max that he'd *just* said I'd be miserable if I didn't go. But then I remember what I told him on the drive to Harold's: *no matter what you choose, you end up regretting it.*

I get my car keys and prepare to be miserable either way.

CHAPTER 25

Boyfriend Stuff

This is stupid, I think, looking at my phone and banging my head against the car headrest.

Fifteen minutes ago, I texted the following to Vincent: I'm outside.

And since then, nothing.

If I had any self-respect, I would have left by now. But instead, I'm manufacturing reasons he hasn't replied. He was talking to his parents, he was in the shower.

When someone makes a dramatic post-breakup gesture like this, you're not actually supposed to take them up on it. The whole point of those gestures is that you get to say a lot of over-the-top bullshit and nobody calls your bluff on it, and that's how you get it out of your system.

And then I see him, framed in the porch light. He peers out into the darkness, and I see him lay eyes on my car, and I realize, oh shit, I didn't take the hint, and now he has to come out here and let me down easy. He descends the steps, looks both ways before he crosses the street even though the only traffic on this block after six is generated by people going to church or bible study. Then he's standing by my car. Sheepishly, I roll down the window and brace myself for whatever it is he's about to say.

"You came."

I clear my throat. "I missed you."

"I missed you too," he says, and then he looks over his shoulder like he's afraid of being spotted. "Can you come around to the backyard? I want to show you something."

I get out of the car and follow him around the side of his house. I notice how he tiptoes across the gravel. It's almost nine, which means his parents are getting ready for bed. Vincent's parents sleep like they're hosting a middle school lock-in at all times. I've never been inside their house this late at night. I've never been in Vincent's bedroom. I've never been in his backyard before.

It's so dark I can't see much of it now, but I suspect that someone in the family is a gardener. I can smell jasmine and rosemary, roses and lavender. He leads me toward the back corner of the yard, where I can just make out a tent, hidden from view by the low-hanging limbs of an oak tree draped with Spanish moss.

"I'm sorry I kept you waiting," he whispers, unzipping the tent and gesturing for me to go inside. "I was waiting for my parents to go to bed. I didn't think you'd get here so fast. Honestly, I wasn't sure if you'd come at all."

"Well, here I am."

"And I'm glad you are."

Once we're inside, he turns on the flashlights he's positioned in each corner of the tent, aimed up at the domed ceiling, and I can see pictures taped to the walls. When I lean in close and squint, I see a picture of a red Victorian house with turrets and bay windows and a front porch.

"That's the house I'm renting this summer," Vincent says, and as I'm wondering how much money NPR is going to pay him exactly, he adds, "Well, one bedroom of it."

We're on our knees in the tent so our heads don't bump the ceiling. I pivot and see photographs of a coffee shop, a park with a fountain in it, the pandas at the National Zoo.

"All of this is in my neighborhood," he says.

I turn to the third wall, which Vincent has covered with prints of art by Elaine de Kooning, Diego Rivera, Georgia O'Keefe, Jasper Johns—there were over a dozen of them, all artists we'd talked about on *Artists in Love*.

"Those are in the National Portrait Gallery. That one's at the National Gallery. The Museum of American Art. The Hirshhorn."

I can tell how excited he is, like if he could, he'd leap straight out of the tent and into that life. And I understand it too. It seems so much bigger than his life here.

"Are you trying to make me jealous?" I say, joking.

"I wanted to show you this could be your life," Vincent says. "I know you love Memphis, but I wondered if you could see yourself in D.C."

"With you," I say.

"With me."

"Vincent," I start to say, but he cuts me off before I can continue.

"I know what you're worried about. That's the other reason I wanted to see you."

He puts his arms around my waist and pulls me close to him. No matter what happened the night before with no-texting

Risa, it's hard to fight the allure of someone who's spent two years learning how to hold you in ways that make you melt, who has compensated for hardline abstinence by giving you transcendent cuddles and otherworldly snuggles and back rubs that make you levitate with pleasure.

"Is this okay?" he asks.

"Yes," I say, folding myself into his arms.

After an indeterminate amount of time, he pulls away. His lips are parted, and I can feel his heart thumping against my chest when he says, "I've thought about it a lot, Lee. I want to feel ready to do . . . boyfriend stuff with you."

Even with Vincent's soft caresses, his strong arms, the solidness of his shoulders, a tremendous amount of sexiness contained within a single human being, it is decidedly unsexy to hear the person you're kissing refer to sex as "boyfriend stuff."

I think about all the times early on in our relationship when we'd been kissing and I'd let my hand drift up his thigh. How he'd always pick it up and set it down off to the side, like it was a pet turtle that had gotten out of its terrarium. I remember one night, he invited me over for dinner because his parents had insisted that they had to meet me if he was going to be spending time over at my house to work on the podcast. Afterward, his parents sat us down on the couch in the living room—the nice room where nobody ever sat—and talked to us about the importance of remaining pure. Vincent's mom told me that giving your virtue away was like a piece of bubble gum that everybody in the school had chewed.

"If someone handed you that piece of gum at the end,

would you want to put it in your mouth?" she asked me, cocking her head to the side as she awaited my answer. And there was only one acceptable answer.

"No, ma'am."

If she wasn't my boyfriend's mom, I might have laughed, but I was too shaken to laugh. I knew she thought of me as that piece of chewed-up gum. I wasn't what they wanted for their son. They wanted a good girl for him. A church girl. A modest girl.

After that night, I only ever dropped him off or picked him up. He never invited me inside. I'm not even sure if he told them I was his girlfriend.

"What changed?" I ask. "Why do you want it now when you didn't before?"

"Because I want to be with you," he says.

And then, to show me how serious he is, Vincent strips off his T-shirt and tosses it to the side. He's never done this before. I've never even seen him in a bathing suit.

He looks down at the shirt, like he's rethinking the whole thing, and then he looks back up at me and gives me a grin that's sheepish and silly and entirely endearing.

We can fix this, I think. *We love each other. We respect each other.*

I take off my shirt and unhook my bra so we're equally naked. It's almost like Lee Miller's topless picnic, I think, and stifle a giggle. Vincent looks like he's about to pass out. His eyes get big, and then he whispers "Wow" like I've presented him with Disneyland and fireworks and the keys to a new car.

Which reminds me that girls can put me at ease and make

me feel pretty under fluorescent light, but there's also something powerful-feeling about rendering a boy semi-verbal and awestruck with nothing but yourself.

I reach out and put one hand on his chest, and one on his waist, touching his bare skin in a way I never have before. He shudders, and his eyes close halfway. We kiss, and it's good like it always is, but better because I can feel his skin against mine. I climb into his lap, straddling his legs.

"Is this okay?" I ask.

He takes a deep breath and nods, and I try to relax. I think about the things that feel good to me, the way I touch myself when I'm alone.

We love each other. We're meant to be together. We can fix this, I think.

The thought doesn't hold because almost immediately I'm thinking about Risa.

What is wrong with me? Why can't I feel how I'm supposed to feel?

Vincent wants to be with me, wants me to leave town with him—that's supposed to change things. I'm supposed take whatever feelings I had for Risa and cancel them out with Vincent's kisses. Because he's the one I'm here with now, in this minute, not her, which means I must have chosen him.

But that's not how I feel about it.

The last time Claire and I hooked up, she was buttoning her shirt after and I heard her mutter, "Ugh, why do I keep doing this?"

At the time it hurt my feelings, but now I think I understand what she meant.

Every time, I feel like I'm fumbling toward something I can't quite describe. I feel like there's a way to ask for what I want. But I can't figure out how to ask it, so instead I make the same mistakes over and over again. I'm so tired of making those mistakes. I'm so tired of myself.

Why did he just shut down, why did I just cheat? We were two people who could talk about art, love, and the universe, so why could we never talk about this?

I pull away from Vincent, slide off his lap, onto the hard ground, my hands splayed out behind me.

"I can't do this," I say. "This isn't right."

Vincent looks confused.

"I thought this was what you wanted."

"I thought so too."

Tell him everything, I think. *Tell him the truth.*

"This is happening too fast," I say. I'm talking about all the Washington, DC, things Vincent has promised me. They glitter and draw me, but I don't quite believe in them. They seem too close to the other future Vincent promised me, the one that turned out to be a figment of our imaginations.

Vincent still thinks I'm talking about sex, though, because he lets out an exasperated sigh.

"First I move too slow, then I move too fast. I don't know what you want, Lee."

"I don't want to go back to being us," I say. "I don't want things to be the way they used to be. I don't want sex to be something you get talked into because you're afraid of losing me."

Vincent sighs again and puts his T-shirt back on, which

makes me realize I'm sitting on the ground in a tent in my ex-boyfriend's backyard with my tits out.

"I'm sorry I didn't say it in exactly the way you wanted me to say it. I'm working some stuff out, Lee. I'm trying here."

"You're *leaving*," I say.

He gestures to the pictures on the wall, the Victorian house, the park with the fountain.

"I. Just. Said. I. Want. You. There."

I throw my shirt back on. I don't even bother with my bra, just crumple it up in my hand and stand up in the tent as far as I can. I'm hunched over, my neck craning down at an awkward angle.

"Then why'd you break up with me?" I ask, and before he can answer, I unzip the tent and step outside.

It wasn't *the* truth that I'd intended to tell him, but it wasn't not true either. When you put it off long enough, the truth gets too big and unwieldy to say all at once.

CHAPTER 26

Italian Luggage

Before I drive home, I check my phone again. Still no word from Risa.

It only takes me a minute to find her on social media, where I see she's posted a picture of the mic stand and guitar amp set up in the corner of Java Cabana for the open mic night, and the pile of shoes by her front door along with a post that says, *I'm taking a poll: Is this a shoe problem?*

I don't know if she's posted them for me or in spite of me, if she expected me to follow her, to comment on them. I almost log in to one of my dusty old accounts so I can, until I realize how embarrassing it would be if she saw me liking her two-day-old posts from an account with practically zero followers that hasn't been updated in a year. I can't let her see me like that.

Instead I put on my bravest face and send her a text that I hope sounds really low-key and upbeat and laid-back: **Heeeey, just thinking about you! Hope you're having a good night!**

I loathe myself the second I hit send. I might as well have texted, **Write to me so I don't panic!** The desperation is palpable.

When I pull into the driveway, I see Greg standing on the front porch with his suitcase. He has his phone out and is texting furiously but stops and puts his phone away once he sees me.

"Hey there," he says when I get out of the car.

"Where's everybody else?" I ask.

"They rented a truck and took some stuff over to your dad's new apartment."

"Even Max?"

"I think he said he was meeting someone named Risa. You can probably still catch them if you want to."

So she'll talk to him, I think. *She'll make plans with him.* I imagine the two of them sitting together at Java Cabana, talking about me. In my head, Risa asks, *"What's her deal, anyway?"* and imaginary Max shakes his head sadly and replies, *She's kind of a mess right now.*

It's too mortifying to consider further, so I turn my attention back to Greg.

"Are you going back to California?" I ask.

"Yeah, looks like it. I'm sorry I didn't get to see more of you this trip, Lee."

I cock my head to the side. "Are you?"

He's apparently not offended by this because he laughs and says, "I was about to call a Lyft, but maybe you could drive me to the airport instead. We can have a chance to catch up."

I hesitate because I don't feel like catching up, or driving to the Memphis airport, and because the last time we had a conversation, he walked out in the middle of it.

He can tell I'm about to turn him down because he quickly adds, "You can bring your recorder if you like. You can ask me anything you want to."

Greg gives me his practiced LA smile. I wonder who he uses it on in California. Probably movie producers and maître d's and the millionaires who buy his art. I think about Harold's untucked shirts and my dad's bushy hair and plaid pajama pants. Greg's clothes look like a grown-up's clothes. They look like they were purchased in a store, not haphazardly acquired at rock shows and rummage sales. When we used to go on family vacations to Destin or Gulf Shores—about as far away from Memphis as my dad could be dragged—he would pack everything in a black canvas duffel bag. Greg has a royal-blue hard-shell suitcase with the iridescent sheen of a bowling ball. If I ever traveled anywhere, I'd want one just like it.

"Where'd you get your suitcase?" I ask.

"Italy," he says. "It's easy to find on a luggage carousel."

His tan, Italian-luggage-owning face annoys the shit out of me, and yet, I can't help considering the possibility that he might be my biological dad and that I might never get another chance to talk to him again, on the record, or at all. One side of me says, *Well, then fine, maybe you don't get to know.*

But the artist side of me says, *Do it. Talk to him. Follow this story where it leads, because it's yours, and if you don't get to the bottom of it, who will?*

"I'll drive you," I say.

Greg flashes his whitened teeth at me again. "Great!"

I pop the trunk for him and he loads his expensive suitcase among the garbage bags full of stuff we meant to take to Goodwill but haven't yet, the bag of potting soil, my mom's bike helmet and running shoes.

"All right, let's do this," Greg says, slamming the trunk

closed. I can't tell whether he means the drive or the questions I'm going to ask him, but that seems like a good place to start.

I press record as we pull out of the driveway.

"Why did you come?" I ask. "You always say you will, and then you never do."

"I wanted to be there for your folks," he answers.

"You saw my mom when you were in New Orleans, didn't you?" I ask. "That's why you weren't on the flight to Memphis."

Greg nods sheepishly. I could tell him how I stood at the luggage carousel, waiting for thirty minutes, but somehow the apology I'd get from him doesn't seem worth the effort.

"So how was my mom when you saw her?" I ask.

"Sad," he says. "She misses you. She's worried about you. You should call her."

I want to tell Greg to mind his own business, that he's not my dad and he doesn't get to tell me what to do. Instead I try another approach.

"I saw a video of you and my parents at your literary salon. The one right before they got married. You gave a very bleak toast."

"Did I?" he asks like he doesn't already know what I'm talking about.

We pull up to a stoplight, and I turn to look at him.

"You did some other stuff too," I say.

I keep staring at him, even after the light turns green. I don't move until I see it in his eyes, him admitting that he remembers, and he knows what I'm talking about, and he knows what he did.

The little shops and houses of Midtown fall away on the road to the airport, and soon it barely seems like we're in a city at all. The streetlights begin to thin out. It's a long expanse of nothing—billboards, factories, warehouses, and graveyards. Nothing that would make a person want to stay.

"Why'd you ask her to come with you?" I ask. "Why then?"

Greg thinks for a minute, then says, "Maybe I was jealous."

Greg takes a black pen and Moleskine notebook from his shoulder bag and begins to draw while he talks to me. Having something else to focus on seems to make him less guarded. And he doesn't have to look at me.

"Jealous of my dad?"

"I couldn't love your mom enough to hold on to her. He could."

"Not forever, though."

"No, I guess not."

"Greg, did you ever figure out what love was?"

He takes his time answering me. He pulls out his phone and props it up in the crook of his elbow, turns on the flashlight to illuminate what he's working on.

"Not really," he says once he's gone back to sketching. "I think that's why I came this time. I was looking for some kind of sign."

"You mean if my mom was standing in a terminal at the New Orleans airport holding a picture of me that looked just like you and said, 'I'm still in love with you?'"

Out of the corner of my eye, I see Greg cringe in mortification. If I haven't landed directly on the truth of his feelings,

I'm pretty sure they're in the same zip code. I keep my eyes on the road, and he keeps his eyes on his sketch. More importantly, he keeps talking.

"At certain points in your life, Lee, you hit a wall. And you realize that everything that's gotten you through this far, all the tricks that used to work for you, don't work anymore."

"What do you do when that happens?"

"You fly to New Orleans and try to convince your ex to get back together with you," he says. "Or you find some other way to be happy."

We drive into the departures terminal at the Memphis International Airport, and as I pull over to the curb by the Delta sign, it occurs to me that I may never see him again.

"Let me open the trunk for you," I say. We go around to the back of the car and he gets his iridescent-bowling-ball luggage out, then hands me the picture he's been drawing on the way to the airport.

It's my mom and me. We're standing side by side on the bluffs by the Mississippi River, the Hernando de Soto Bridge behind us. He's drawn us with our hands on our hips, the wind blowing our hair, and it looks like something that might be stamped on the front of a coin, or used as a recruitment poster for some kind of artist army.

I give him an awkward hug goodbye and say, "Hey, Greg, what if you're really my dad?"

He takes a step back, jarred that I've said it so directly. But after a moment or two, he regains his composure and puts his hand on my shoulder.

"If you ever want to find out for real, I'll take the test. And if you ever need anything financially, I'd help you. But at this point, you're fully formed, you're already you, and I can't take any credit for it."

I give him another awkward hug, because what else would I say? Don't worry about it because I already have a great dad?

I guess I potentially also have this whole other parallel-universe life, one where my mom moves to LA with Greg, and I grow up there, and instead of the problems we have now, we all have an entirely different set of problems.

But I'm in this universe.

"Have a safe flight, Greg."

In this universe, that's all I have to say to him.

CHAPTER 27

Imp of the Perverse

Max is sitting on the front steps when I pull into the driveway, headphones in his ears and playing with a lighter. By his side, there's a paper sack from the Circle K with a beef jerky stick hanging out of it.

Traitor, I think, even though I know that's not fair, and I'm just jealous that he got to see Risa when she won't even text me back.

I lock the car, then sit down on the step next to him.

"Where have you been?" he asks, taking out the earbuds. "It's late."

"Taking Greg to the airport. What's up with the lighter?"

Max gives me a look that I've started to think of as his Imp of the Perverse face. It's the face that talks you into ordering an extra basket of fried pickles, or showing up at the coffee house you're banned from. He rolls his thumb over the wheel, and the flame shoots up from the hood.

"Did you and Greg talk some more?" he asks.

I play him the audio I recorded on the way to the airport. When it's done playing, he asks, "Are you going to get the DNA test?"

"I don't think so," I say.

"Why not know? Why not be entitled to that famous art-ist money?"

"I'd rather keep things the way they are. He can be Schrödinger's Dad."

"You should give that one to Harold. It can be the name of his next band."

I don't want to talk about Greg or Harold or who my dad is, though. Right now, there is a more pressing undiscussed matter.

"So, you and Risa ended up hanging out?" I ask, angling toward him so I can read every bit of his body language.

Max laughs in a way I wouldn't exactly call friendly, and says, "Remember how you left in the middle of a pretty heavy conversation we were having?"

"You were right, by the way," I say. "It was a mistake to go."

To his credit, Max doesn't gloat, even though I deserve it.

"I felt like talking some more," Max says, "so I texted Risa to see if she was free. We hung out over at her place."

"Oh, cool," I say, like I'm just casually interested in this and not bursting at the seams to ask, *Did you talk about me? What did she say? Tell me, tell me, tell me . . .*

"Do you still want to know what's up with the lighter?"

I mean, no, not right now, is what I'm thinking, but I smile politely at Max.

"Because before, you asked me what was up with the lighter. I thought you might still want to know."

"I suppose I moved on in the conversation," I say. "To the part where you tell me what you and Risa talked about."

"I just thought you'd be curious," Max says. "Maybe I'm planning to take up smoking. Maybe I'm planning an arson spree."

I giggle and roll my eyes at him.

"Would you like to tell me, Max, or would it be more fun for you to keep jerking me around?"

"You make it very easy when you're this transparently self-absorbed," he says, cracking up. He reaches into the Circle K sack and pulls out a pack of sparklers.

"It's not Fourth of July yet," I say.

"It's Fourth of July adjacent. Besides, I always liked doing these with you."

He opens the pack and takes out one for each of us and lights them. We hold them over our shoes and let the sparks fall onto the porch steps and the sidewalk. It's not very exciting, but it does keep the mosquitos away.

"She played me some of her songs," Max says at last, giving me the information I'm desperate to have. "She's a cool girl. I see why you're so into her."

I shake my head and look down at the concrete step. "I don't even know if she wants to see me again."

"Oh, I think you'll find that she does," Max says. "She was very disappointed I didn't bring you with me. She wanted to know where you were."

And now I panic. "What did you tell her?"

"That you went over to your ex-boyfriend's house."

"Max! What the fuck?"

With a shrug, he gives me the Imp of the Perverse grin again and lights each of us another sparkler. This time he stands up with his, and I follow him into the yard.

"I was feeling spiteful," he says. "You ditched me in the middle of a very intense conversation, and besides, it was true."

"Was she upset?"

"You'd have to ask her. But no, she didn't act upset. She was more, like, 'Oh, I see. Cool.'"

He writes out the word *COOL* with the tip of his sparkler. Each stroke leaves a trail of light behind before it disappears.

"That sounds upset."

"Maybe in a nineteenth-century English manor house."

"Fuck. Well, then, did she happen to say why she hasn't texted me?"

Max sticks out his tongue at me. "Actually, we didn't talk about you that much."

I'm being self-absorbed again, I think. The whole reason he went over there was because I bailed on him.

SORRY, I write with the tip of my sparkler, and then I say it too.

"What *did* you talk about?"

"Some more of my stuff. With my family and everything. My horrible, exciting new sexual fluidity. My fucking summer. I don't have a lot of people in Chicago I can talk to about it. When I broke up with Niko, most of our friends took his side. I should probably feel more upset about it, but the people I really miss are Xochitl and her friends. I hadn't known them as long, but they got me and saw me, and I felt good around them. It was the first time I'd gotten a sense of what it might be like to have people in my life who were queer and brown—"

"And not your mom," I say.

"Exactly," Max says, emphasizing the point with the tip of his barely flickering sparkler. "Anyhow, talking to Risa made me realize how much I need that kind of community in my life again. She's good to talk to."

He says this with a hint of accusation at the end, like he's suggesting I'm *not* good to talk to. Maybe he also notices, because he quickly says, "You've been great too, Lee. It's just sometimes, it can be hard talking to you about certain things. Your life is a fairy tale."

"No it's not."

He rolls his eyes. "Worst-case scenario, you get to have two dads, one who loves you, one who can give you money. Do you know anything about my dad, Lee Swan?"

Usually, I like it when Max calls me by my full name, but not right now.

"No."

"Yeah, me neither."

Up until he was eight, it was just Max and his mom, living in Chicago where the rest of Maggie's family lived. Maggie was never happy staying in one place. That was how my mom always talked about it. To Maggie, settling down was something to rebel against, so first it was Memphis, then Berlin.

When Max's mom died from a pulmonary embolism, nobody expected Maggie to do anything about it. Everyone assumed she'd stay in Europe, writing her doorstopper novels and living like a bohemian. Everyone assumed Maggie's parents would raise Max. But Maggie got on the first plane back to Chicago, talked to her parents, and got them to agree that she should have custody of Max.

You don't have to be old to die, and you can't promise a little kid that they'll never lose someone they love again. But Maggie looked at her aging parents and little eight-year-old Max and thought, *You will never be alone in this world. I can promise you that.*

That was how I'd always heard my parents talk about it, sitting at the kitchen table when I was supposed to be in bed.

"You do have family, though," I say.

"That's what Risa said."

"Who love you."

"That's what makes it worse," Max says. "Because I expected better from them. I know they still love me. It's just that I know they used to *like* me better when I was their sweet little *Love, Simon* adorable baby gay."

"Instead of an untidy queer."

"Exactly."

My second sparkler burns out, so I go back to the porch steps and light two more, hand one to Max. This time we run around the yard with them, spinning like we're trying to bind ourselves in a circle of sparks and flame.

"So, what do you do?" I ask, sitting down in the grass dizzily. Max plops down next to me, lays the spent wire on the sidewalk like we were taught when we were kids so we didn't accidentally set the lawn on fire.

"In a couple of months, I'll be moving two hours away. I won't see them every day, and eventually, it won't bother me so much."

I think about the way Maggie and Sage were the first few times they brought Max to visit us in Memphis. They were sort of awkward and showy about their parenting then. They made a lot of bad jokes and talked to Max like he was a small adult they were trying to impress. But they always listened to every word he said. They took him seriously. They paid attention to how he was feeling. And they got better at the other parenting stuff. Once, I left a bunch of my toys out on the living room floor when they were visiting, and when Maggie yelled, "Lee Carrington Swan, get in here and pick up your LEGOs before I step on another one," I thought it was my own mom.

"I get it," I say. "I just wish it could be some other way."

Max nods. "It's not what I want, but I don't know what else I can do."

"What *do* you want?"

"I want them to apologize for making me feel like who I am is somehow disappointing or gross to them. I want them to say they accept me, and I want it to be the truth."

"I think you should ask for what you want," I say.

"I didn't ask what you thought."

It stings when Max does this, lets me into his life most of the way, and then slams the door shut on me, like he wants to take it back, like he wishes he'd never let me in.

"And my life isn't a fairy tale," I say. I can slam doors too.

Only Max doesn't flinch at my words. He falls into the grass, throws back his head, and cackles.

"Are you kidding me? Mysterious artifacts. Long-buried secrets. Your true parentage revealed, and what ho! You are potentially of noble birth. You even have Prince Vincent and Princess Risa fighting to win your heart."

I should like the idea of being the heroine of a story like that, but I don't. I don't want to be that person. I don't want that kind of story.

"It's my heart," I blurt out. "It belongs to me. I don't want anyone fighting to win it."

"So, what do *you* want?" Max asks, using my own words against me.

I fall back on the ground next to him and look up at the patches of night sky visible through the trees.

"I want to find a way to ask for the things I want."

"See, it's not so easy, is it?"

I roll over onto my side in the grass, and Max does too. It's like we're kids having a sleepover, whispering secrets in our sleeping bags after everybody else in the neighborhood is asleep.

"I can't ask Vincent for what I want. I had two years to tell him the truth, but every time, I got scared. It wasn't just telling him I liked girls too, or that I'd cheated on him with Claire, or that I'd met Risa and had feelings for her, too. If I wanted to be all the way honest with him, I'd have to say . . ."

I roll over onto my back and look up at the sky while I say it.

". . . that I don't think being with one person works for me."

Max doesn't say anything. I wait as long as I can stand it, and then I let my head roll to the side, trying to catch a quick glimpse of Max's expression.

"You can look at me," he says.

I cover my face with my hands.

"It's easier like this," I say. "If I can just say it into the air like this and pretend nobody's listening, just long enough to get it all out."

"Okay," Max says. "Then get it all out."

I take a deep breath. "I'm queer, and I don't think I want to be with just one person. And I wish I could find some way to tell Vincent the truth before he leaves. I don't want him wondering whether he was enough, or if there was something else he could have done. He deserves to know this wasn't his fault."

"Why can't you just tell him?"

"Because it's entirely possible that this just makes everything worse."

"Telling the truth doesn't make things worse."

"It does make them more complicated."

Next to me, I hear Max get up, and I spread my fingers to see him standing over me, holding out his hand.

"Come on," he says. "Let's go up to the attic. We can probably finish putting the first episode together tonight."

I take his hand and let him help me to my feet. It sounds nice, thinking about my parents and their friends and their problems instead of my own.

We work until two in the morning. The episode isn't finished, but the things left to be done are too difficult to do well with middle-of-the-night brains. I realize the only reason I'm still working is because I want to be here in the attic with Max.

He must feel the same way, because at two thirty, he goes downstairs and comes back up in his pajamas with extra sheets and pillows and a toothbrush hanging out of his mouth.

"I don't feel like being alone," he says.

"You aren't," I say. A few minutes later, I come back up the steps in my pajamas too. We turn off the lights and snuggle up on the air mattress like sleepover buddies. The only thing we're missing are the old matching Star Wars sleeping bags we used to have.

"I love you, Max," I say.

"I love you, too, Lee."

I close my eyes and drift off to sleep, and for a moment, I'm happy, and there's nothing complicated about it.

CHAPTER 28

The Family Scab

I'm in that gauzy stupor that exists in the morning when my mind is awake but my body isn't. I'm aware of being on the air mattress, where I fell asleep with Max last night. I'm aware of light coming in through the window, but I'm not ready to get up yet.

In that peaceful, still place, my mind begins to unfold a thought. It begins with me, alone in the center of my brain, suspended in midair, and then a world begins to fill in behind me.

I see myself running the soundboard at a real Memphis club. I see myself at one of the famous local recording studios like Ardent, engineering Risa's record, and then that image fades and is replaced by something even better—a recording studio of my own. Not in an attic or a corner of my apartment, but a whole building with soundproofed booths and all the gear I've ever tinkered around with yet never known how to use: Moog synthesizers and Hammond organs and Leslie speaker cabinets. I see Risa in the booth with headphones on, recording a vocal track while I sit behind the mixing board.

Next, I see Risa and me walking in the front door of my apartment. It pops into my head fully formed. There's a couch in the living room that I've never seen before, and it's *my* couch. There's a television mounted on the wall, and it's *my* television. There's art on the walls that I picked. There's a whole room for my sound equipment. In the kitchen there's a dish rack and a coffee maker, and I say, "Hey, can I get you anything?" to Risa as she puts down her guitar case, and she asks, "What do you feel like doing tonight?"

Before I can answer her, suddenly, I see myself at an airport pulling an iridescent blue hard-shell suitcase, and then I'm getting into a cab. It lets me out in front of Vincent's Victorian house near the park, and then I see Vincent taking my bag, kissing me hello. I see us walking together through museums and galleries, talking about art. And as we do, I can tell things are different between us, that the versions of ourselves that we show each other are bigger and truer than the ones who told stories in my attic.

And then I realize that I haven't had to choose between these lives, that both of them are mine.

There's an ache in my throat when I open my eyes, the kind you get when you're trying not to cry. I'm trying not to cry because they're so good, these scenes in my head. And I'm trying not to cry because I know it's too much to want, and nobody is ever going to let me have a life where I get to have all of it. It's a dream. It's a fantasy.

Max was right. I'm living in a fairy tale.

When I sit up on the air mattress, all the way awake now, I'm alone. My skin is sticking to the sheets; my mouth is dry. There's no sign of Max.

This is what you get in the real world, I tell myself. *You wake up alone on an air mattress. Remember that next time you start wanting things.*

When I get downstairs, I can tell that I've slept late. The house is bright and already warm, and the kitchen smells like a pot of coffee that someone made hours ago and forgot to turn off. It's quiet, too, except for the sound of water running in the bathroom.

"Anyone?" I call out. No one answers, so I make a fresh pot of coffee. While I'm waiting for it to finish brewing, I peek out the kitchen window and walk around to all the rooms just to make sure no one else is here.

"Max?" I call into the bathroom. There's music playing along with the running water, so maybe he can't hear me.

Then I stick my head in my parents' office, and what I see there stops me cold.

Everything on my dad's side of the office is gone—the books, the papers, the desk and chair.

Panicked, I walk down the hall to my parents' bedroom. It's full of boxes. The lamp by the side of the bed that used to be my dad's side of the bed is gone. The closet is empty. This must be what Sage and my dad were doing last night, what they're doing now.

Signing the lease on a cursed fourplex feels abstract, but this is real. My dad is moving out of our house. My life, and everything in it, is about to change. I can't stop it; I can't put it back how it was.

I hear the front door open and then my dad's voice, belting out one of his favorite gospel songs. The refrain goes, *You've got to live the life you sing about in your song,* and it's about how you can't go to church and sing hymns on Sundays, then act like a jerk the rest of the week. He's been singing this song since I was little even though we've never really gone to church. I think a Memphis punk band covered it once, and that's probably why he likes it.

He's still singing when he finds me in the hall, tears streaming down my cheeks.

"Oh, honey, what's wrong?" he asks, giving me a hug.

"You're really leaving," I say, and he squeezes me tighter.

"I'm not going far."

"I wish you weren't going at all."

"I thought I'd get halfway moved in today, and tonight, we can have a housewarming party over there. See if we can't make it feel festive."

He looks upset, and I can tell he thought he was moving out in a way that would make things easier on me, less disruptive. I can also see how much he wants me to like the idea of having a housewarming party at his new apartment, and even though I don't, I manage a weak smile.

"That sounds like fun," I say.

"Does going to Target with me sound like fun as well?"

It does not, and we both know it, but I also know he's asking me because it will suck less if I'm there. And he hasn't asked me to help him pack or carry his boxes out of the house. This seems like the least I can do.

"What do you need?"

"A colander. A spatula. Garbage cans. Bathmat. Shower curtain. We might as well get two of everything. It'll save us a trip when you move out."

Suddenly, the fantasy I'd been having seems even more ridiculous. The thought of my mom, my dad, and me all living in different places seems so wasteful and lonely. We didn't hate each other's guts—why did we need to live in different places?

"I'm not moving," I say, more forcefully than necessary.

"Well, you don't have to get anything," my dad says. "It was just an idea."

Max emerges from the bathroom with a towel wrapped around his waist. Before he can say good morning, or rush down the hall to get dressed, my dad has detained him. My dad sees his houseguest, half-naked in the hallway, and decides this is an appropriate moment to ask, "Max, what do you appreciate most in a bathmat?"

Max gathers the towel around his waist more securely and considers this for a moment before replying.

"Something plush but not fluffy, with good grip. A neutral shade that won't look dingy. Maybe dark gray."

"See, I knew you were the person to ask."

I help my dad pick out a colander, a spatula, some garbage cans, and a bathmat. He's indecisive about everything, especially for a man who signed a lease on a cursed fourplex without a second thought. He ponders each item like a wrong choice might haunt him for years. Metal or plastic? Round or square? I start pointing to the ones I like best, to speed things up. He seems to appreciate this, nods as he puts the items I suggest into his cart. But then two aisles later, he doubles back and switches them out. The bathmat, however, I notice that he selects precisely according to Max's specifications.

I think about the kind of apartment he'll have. Will it be neglected like Harold's? Cluttered like ours? Will it have style, or will it look temporary and sad? Will he keep it clean, or will the toilet be disgusting and the fridge stuffed with moldy takeout? With my dad, it's hard to say. He's a surprising person, for all his routine.

"Have you called your mom yet?" he asks as we wheel our cart out of the bed and bath section.

"No."

"Lee, call her," he says. "If you're trying to make her feel terrible, congratulations, you've succeeded."

We walk past the luggage aisle, and I think about Greg's blue hard-shell suitcase. How would I even get to Washington, DC? I've never been on a plane. I've never gone anywhere by myself.

"I'm not trying to make her feel terrible," I say.

"Then why are you avoiding her?" he asks.

"Because I feel guilty," I say. "I started off feeling like I had a right to know what happened between you two, like it was my job to find it out. Now I'm starting to wonder if I'm just picking a scab. Someone else's scab, actually, so it's extra disgusting."

"It's the family scab," he says. "It's ours. You can pick it all you want."

"Please stop."

"It's a good metaphor. You should tell your mom about it. Maybe she'll call her next collection of poems *The Family Scab*."

"Absolutely not."

"Do you need a suitcase?" he asks me.

"No, why?"

"You keep looking at them."

"Where would I go, Dad?"

"Maybe you'd want to stay at my place sometimes. There's a room for you. At some point I'll put a bed in it."

"Air mattresses are fine."

"What I'm saying is, you might want to pack a bag for a weekend. Or a week, even."

"I have a duffel bag," I say.

"Suit yourself," he says. "But on the topic of the family scab, I will say this. If you're sitting around waiting for someone to give you permission to tell your own story, don't."

I try to figure out what my dad means by this. He doesn't want to talk to me about the past. He doesn't like being written about, so why's he telling me this? And that's when it hits me that he's called it *my* story. Not his. Not theirs. Mine.

It's not mine because I'm in it. It's mine because it's a love story, and nobody's ever told it before, and that's what I do.

I tell love stories all the time.

People talk about love like it's secondary, sex like it's business. They act like romance novels are fluffy and the way people feel about each other is nice, but less important than wars or court cases or old men battling marlins at sea.

Boil the whole of human existence down to its essence, and what you have is how we feel about each other and what we decide to do about it. Even if it ends. Even if we end up regretting it.

"What on earth are you thinking about?" my dad asks in

the checkout line at Target. "You look like you're about to climb on top of a mountain and sing."

"My story," I say.

It's a love story about confessional poets and thwarted playwrights, about sad rock stars and tattoo artists who are fighting with their kids, about messy bisexuals and untidy queers and evangelical Christians who make podcasts about art and girls who write beautiful songs in their bedrooms. About old lovers, new lovers, friends.

I think it's a story worth telling.

Because it's true.

CHAPTER 29

A Funny Way of Showing It

On the way home from Target, I check my phone and see that I have texts from Risa and Vincent. I open Risa's first. It's the first I've heard from her since we said good night at her house the night before last. She makes no mention of my five previous, increasingly desperate texts, and doesn't say why she didn't write back until now. Instead she's written, **I had no idea we would sound so great together—we're geniuses! Hang out soon?**

I'm so excited to finally hear from her and to hear that she wants to hang out with me again that I don't dwell on the fact that I don't totally understand the rest of what she says.

I text back, **I would love that.**

Then I go to the text from Vincent, which I'm more nervous to read. Part of me is stunned to hear from him after what happened in his backyard last night, but part of me isn't surprised at all. It's like we can't seem to let go, can't seem to get out of each other's systems.

I know it would be easier if I just ended things once and for all, but I don't want easy. I want to tell him everything. I want to tell him what happened with Risa. I want to tell him about my beautiful dream with the recording studio and the suitcase and the apartment. The funny thing is, of all the people I know, I feel like he's the one who would understand it the most. Vincent was always someone you could talk to about your dreams.

He might not share them, or like them, but he always got them.

When someone gets you, you keep that person around, I think as I open his text.

I don't expect it to be easy.

I know that I have to face him and tell him the truth. I'll lay everything out on the table, and trust that Max is right, that the truth will make everything better.

I still have a chance to fix this, I think.

But then I open Vincent's text, and it just says:

I could have forgiven you for anything except this.

Oh god, I think. Oh no. There's so much I've done, I'm not even sure which part he's talking about: my sexuality, the way I stormed out of the tent during our fight, what happened with Claire, or Ian, or Risa.

I text back, I wanted to tell you everything, but I didn't know how. I'm sorry I hurt you, Vincent.

He replies almost immediately.

You have a funny way of showing it.

Then he texts me a screenshot, an image of Man Ray's metronome and Lee Miller's eye, an image I do not have any legal right to use, and over it I see printed in a bold-stamped font the title *OBJECTS OF DESTRUCTION: A podcast by Lee Swan and Max Lozada, with original music by Risa Bryant.*

No, I think. *This is a mistake.*

It only takes me a minute to find the first episode of *Objects of Destruction*, uploaded two hours ago to the same platform where Vincent and I put every new episode of *Artists in Love*. I don't know how it got there, but I know that every one of Vincent's and my subscribers got a notification about it. The same subscribers who went to school with us, who loved Vincent, who only tolerated me because Vincent loved me.

It's already been downloaded a few dozen times, and there are already comments.

Not even a week since they broke up . . .

She was cheating on him the whole time, and now this. Poor Vincent.

The whole thing leaves a bad taste in my mouth.

It leaves a bad taste in my mouth too. It looks like I'm trying to cash in on what little popularity Vincent and I had, to spin it into something for myself in the tackiest, least respectful possible way.

It's too late to fix things now. I'd waited and made excuses, and I'd been a coward, and what was I even afraid of? Because anything, anything in the entire world, would have been better than him finding out like this.

Never mind the fact that it wasn't finished. I'm not even sure which version of it has been uploaded, but from the sounds of it, it was a version full of things that I'd only said out loud for myself, things I'd never intended anyone else to hear. The parts about Claire must be in there. I feel exposed, knowing that something I made was released into the world raw and unfinished like that.

When my dad pulls into the driveway, I jump out of the car the moment he puts the car in park.

"Lee, is something the matter?" he asks, but I slam the car door without answering, run up the front porch steps and into the house.

"Max!" I call out. There's no answer, so he must be in the attic. I pull down the steps and call his name again, louder this time, as I rush up the stairs. I find him there, lying on the air mattress with his headphones on.

"Max!" He sits up and takes out the earbuds.

"Hey," he says with a grin. "Did you get a bathmat?"

"Max, what did you do?"

It's the only explanation, and as soon as I see the look on his face, I know I'm right. He knows exactly what I'm talking about.

"You said you wished you could find some way to tell Vincent the truth. You said he deserved to know it wasn't his fault."

"He didn't deserve to find out like this!" I say. "Max, you had no right!"

Max looks genuinely surprised that I'm not grateful for what he's done. I sit down at the computer and log into the *Artists in Love* hosting site, pull up the social media accounts to see if it's gotten any worse since the last time I checked.

"I thought it was what you wanted," Max says.

"Do you think that I wanted this?" I ask, pointing to the page of disgusted comments.

He gets up from the air mattress and reads over my

shoulder, the ones I'd already seen, as well as the new posts that have shown up. Not every post tears me to shreds for being a terrible person. Some of them simply say that *Objects of Destruction* isn't as good as *Artists in Love*. And I know they're right.

I pull up the admin page and delete the episode of *Objects of Destruction* before anyone else can download it.

"Maybe it's not so bad," Max says.

"Vincent told me he could have forgiven me for anything except this, so don't tell me it's not so bad."

"Well, whose fault is that?" Max mutters.

"Excuse me?"

"You heard me."

"I don't care what you do with your own life, Max, but don't be a dilettante with mine."

I smack the wall with the palm of my hand and cry out. I can't believe Max would do something so thoughtless, so reckless, much less that he'd do it to me.

"Max, I trusted you."

I can't stand to look at him any longer. I go down the attic steps and into my bedroom, slamming the door behind me.

I try calling Vincent, but he doesn't pick up. I text him, explaining that I'd just made the recordings for myself, that they were never supposed to go up, but someone else uploaded it.

Please forgive me, I type. **I'll do whatever it takes to make this right.**

I wait for the dot-dot-dot that always follows immediately when I text Vincent, but it doesn't come. He's always been a prompt replier. Then again, I used to be the same way with him. I think about my three days of silence after we broke up, and wonder if it felt like this to him, like I was never going to speak to him again. What if he'd blocked my number? What if the last thing he ever said to me was, *You have a funny way of showing it*?

I don't know what to do. I don't know how to begin to fix this, and the only person who knows won't speak to me.

Then I remember there's someone else who will know what to do.

And I owe her a phone call.

CHAPTER 30

What You Do Next

By the time I call, she's already listened to it. My mom is an unconditionally supportive person, even when her love life is the subject of a podcast.

"You're going to get through this," she tells me when I call her. She doesn't lecture me for not calling her. She doesn't even mention it.

"But how can I *fix* it?"

Wherever she's calling from, I can hear jazz playing softly in the background, sounds of traffic on the streets outside her window.

"You can't," she says. "You can't take it back. You can't do it over. You just have to live with it."

The walls of my room feel close and claustrophobic. I hate the art posters on my wall, the clothes in my closet, the duvet on my bed. I want to crawl out of my own skin and abandon all of it.

"People make mistakes, Lee," my mom says. "We hurt people we love. All of us do it, and there's no getting around that. The only difference is what you do next."

"What does that mean?"

"Give him space, Lee. And time. Maybe that will be enough, maybe it won't be."

"Mom, when are you coming home?"

"Soon," she says. "After your dad's moved out."

"Why does it have to be like this? Why can't you and Dad just figure it out?"

"Because we just can't. We tried for a long time, Lee."

"Then you didn't try hard enough. You gave up."

"I wouldn't call twenty years of my life giving up. I'd call it a success. Sometimes things are over, and it's time to let them be over."

"Are you talking about Vincent and me?" I can't tell whether she's doing that poet thing of saying something that means two things at once.

"I'm saying this new project of yours isn't *Artists in Love.* I'm not surprised your listeners didn't like it."

"Thanks a lot, Mom."

"What I mean is, that's not your audience anymore. *Objects of Destruction* will find its own audience. In any case, it inspired me."

This gets my attention. My mom saying something inspired her is one of her highest compliments.

She continues, "I did some reading. Do you know what happened to the original *Object of Destruction* after Man Ray and Lee Miller broke up?"

"No."

"A group of anarchists came into the museum where it was on display, and they smashed it. Man Ray wouldn't let the police press charges. I mean, the piece was called *Object to Be Destroyed.* They were just taking him up on the suggestion.

"After that, he made six more of them, and when people

asked why, he said, 'The work has already been done.' And then he renamed it *Indestructible Object.*"

"What does that mean?"

"Even things that are over aren't over. The work has already been done," she says. "And, Lee, I know your podcast isn't finished, and I know you must want to walk away from it right now, but I want to tell you, I found it to be very meaningful."

"Are you just saying that because I made it?"

"I'm saying it because it's helpful to find out what your life looks like from the outside. You helped me, Lee. You gave me the courage to do what I need to do next."

"What's that?"

"Well, for starters, catch up on *The Bachelorette.* Apparently, Lindsey and Evan get busy in a lighthouse off the coast of Maine, but she's still exploring her feelings for Lucas."

"I love you, Mom."

"I love you, too, baby. I miss you, and I'm so glad you called."

She tells me she'll see me in a few days, and we hang up. A few minutes later, she texts me a picture from her hotel room in New Orleans. She's holding her notebook open to show me what she's written in Sharpie:

YOUR HEART IS AN INDESTRUCTIBLE OBJECT.

I think about Max and me, trading inscriptions for our tombstones. Maybe I'm not like Max, floating through the world and finding all of it endlessly fascinating. I don't know what to do about the fact that I'm a mess and a cheater and an artistic fraud. I don't know what the next year of my life is supposed to look like, and even if someone told me I could have the beautiful life from my dream, I don't begin to know how to get it. But as I look at the picture my mom sent, a sense of calm washes over me, and I know whatever happens, I can withstand it.

Because the work has already been done.

CHAPTER 31

Wiring Explosives

When I hang up with my mom, my situation is every bit as bad as it was before, but instead of asking *Why me?*, I find myself wondering, *What next?*

I do what an artist would do.

I sit down, and I make something.

A STATEMENT FROM LEE SWAN:

There are things about my life that I want to say out loud. And then, some things are personal. Some things are private. Some parts of love stories are just for the people involved in them.

I'm sorry that I've caused pain to someone I love. I'm sorry, Vincent.

And to anyone else reading this, I'm sorry for taking a story that meant something to you and putting an ugly ending on it. That's not how you tell the truth.

I hope someday I'll get it right.

Before I post it, I want to find Max. I want him to see what I have to say, and more importantly, I want to apologize for yelling at him. Not that he's apologized to me yet for what he did, but fuck it, I don't even care anymore.

Apologies aren't about who is right. They are about who is sorry.

Max had spent nearly a week humoring me, helping me, keeping my mind off my breakup, and following me down rabbit holes that involved confessional poetry and VHS cassettes. And yes, he fucked up, but when I think about how much I wish Vincent would call me up right now and say, "Lee, I understand. It's all right. I forgive you," I can't go on being angry with Max.

Whatever it is that I want, I don't have a lot of role models for it. I can't even look to Lee Miller and Man Ray for advice. She just dumped him, moved to another country, and didn't speak to him again for seven years.

My question is, what are you supposed to do when people who have loved you and been good to you and treated you well for a long time let you down? You can't just go around wiring explosives and blowing up the bridge every time someone disappoints you. If you did that, eventually you'd have no one left.

I want my life to look different than that.

When I go up to the attic, though, Max is gone. I check the porch, the office, the backyard, my room, but there's no sign of him.

He probably went for a walk to clear his head, I think.

When I sit down at the computer to post my statement to the *Artists in Love* social media accounts, I see that someone else has beaten me to it.

This is Max Lozada, and I want to make it clear that Lee Swan never gave me permission to upload her new project.

Lee likes doing things well. I thought what she'd made so far was good enough, but Lee is always trying to do better. Please don't hold this against her, and accept my most sincere apology.

Oh, Max.

I post my statement beneath his, and then I go back downstairs, calling his name. I text him, **Where are you?** But five minutes later, there's no response, only a text from my dad, asking if I'll check his office for the clip-on reading lamp that he'd attached to the closet door, angled over the spot where his writing desk used to be. I tell him I'll look and bring it over when I come.

Surprise. There is insufficient lighting in the cursed fourplex.

When I go into the office, something's missing. It's emptier than it was this morning. And that's when I realize that Max's suitcase is gone.

CHAPTER 32

Back to Chicago

I text my dad, **Is Max over there?**

No, he writes.

A minute later, my dad texts again.

Lee, we should talk about Objects of Destruction when you come over.

Shit, I think, he's heard it. I imagine the scene, him and Harold and Sage sitting around a half-unpacked cardboard box, furious with me for airing their personal business to the world.

It wasn't my fault, I want to text back to him.

But I know that's not true. I said those things. I asked those questions. I committed the answers to digital format. It was my idea. If I'd really wanted to keep it from getting out into the world, I would have left it in my head.

That was the reality of what Max had done.

It didn't matter whose fault it was. What mattered was, did I stand by what I'd said?

I didn't know.

It was entirely possible that I'd taken a situation where my parents were getting divorced and I'd been fired and dumped, and found a way to make everything about it worse.

Well, you certainly found a way to make it all about yourself, I can almost hear Max saying. I wish he were here right now to say it.

I don't text my dad back.

I don't know whether Risa will write me back or not, but I know she's gotten close with Max too. She'd want to know that he's gone missing. And of course, it's possible that he's over at her house at this very moment. She's good to talk to, he'd said so himself.

She texts me back almost immediately: **No, he's not with me. Everything okay?**

I don't know, I write back. **He took all his stuff.**

Where would he go? Risa asks.

The answer pops into my head immediately, though I have no evidence other than knowing him for ten years, knowing how much he didn't want to come to Memphis in the first place.

Back to Chicago, I text Risa.

Max has finally had it with me, with Sage, with being under the same roof as our bullshit. Not that he'd tried to make things right with either of us to our faces. He'd posted an apology to a bunch of strangers on the internet, then disappeared without even saying goodbye. I thought we were friends. I thought we meant more to each other than that.

He must feel awful, Risa writes.

I almost text back, **He has a funny way of showing it,** but then I remember Vincent using those words on me. I remember how misunderstood they made me feel.

I check the clock. There are still a couple of hours before the next train.

Do you have a car? I ask Risa.

Yeah, why?

Do you want to go on a mission to stop Max from getting on a train to Chicago?

I'll be there in ten minutes, she writes.

CHAPTER 33

The Life You Sing About

It's the last scrap of daylight when I get into Risa's car. Streetlights are beginning to come on, and the sky is a fierce golden pink. She tries to kiss me on the cheek, but it's an awkward angle and the kiss lands near my ear, and when I try to kiss her cheek back, I miss altogether and end up kissing the air.

Neither of us speaks as I buckle up. I'm wondering if I should have kissed her on the lips, or hugged her, or if, given the seriousness of the situation, we shouldn't have touched at all. I wonder whether she'd even be here if she knew what had happened between Vincent and me the night before.

"I'm so sorry," she says as she pulls out of the driveway. "If I'd known what would happen, I wouldn't have told Max posting it was a good idea."

"You knew?"

"He had a crisis of conscience right before he posted it and asked me what I thought he should do. I told him to go for it."

"Oh."

I don't have any energy left for feeling angry about this, or blaming other people. Instead I change the subject.

"Max told me you had a good conversation last night."

"You would have been invited if you hadn't been over at Vincent's," she says in this very cool, tossed-off way, adding, "How'd that go?"

"It was a disaster."

"Anyway, you were invited," she says.

I can't tell if she's being sincere or sarcastic, or whether she's angry with me but trying to be low-key about it, because it's not even clear whether we have the kind of relationship where you *get* to be mad at someone for hanging out with their ex.

I decide to do things like Risa would, the honest way.

"When I didn't hear back from you, I guess I thought maybe you had second thoughts, or maybe you weren't that into me."

She looks surprised. "I'm a utilitarian texter."

"What does that mean?"

"I'm not a recreational, conversational, chatty, 'you up?' kind of texter. I'd been meaning to talk to you about that."

I thought about the giant paragraphs of text that Vincent and I used to send each other on an average Wednesday and wonder what Risa must have thought of my correspondence.

"I'm sorry. I hope I didn't stress you out with my . . . long-windedness."

"You weren't long-winded. Just enthusiastic." I must look mortified because she quickly adds, "Enthusiastic is good. It *felt* good, knowing you wanted to spend that many words on me. It's just not my style."

"Understood," I say, and I know that whatever kind of relationship this is, it doesn't have any lies or secrets in it yet, and I want to keep it that way. "I have to tell you something too."

"Did something happen with Vincent last night?" she asks.

"He asked me to move to Washington, DC, with him. He said that he wanted to be with me, and . . ."

"You hooked up." She says it like she's not even surprised.

"Not exactly. We started to, but then, like I told you, disaster."

"Cool," she says, and I can already feel her putting me back in the box of bi girls to watch out for.

"Are you sure?" I ask, because I'm not.

"We never said we were exclusive. Anyhow, I kind of knew better than to expect that from you."

Just a couple of days ago, Risa was writing me songs and taking me to underground video stores. Everything she's saying now sounds so casual and indifferent, like I'm more trouble than I'm worth.

"I like you," I say, "and I like being with you. I want to be around to see what happens next."

"Like an experiment?" she asks warily.

"Like a dream," I say. And then before I think better of it and stop myself, I ask, "Have you ever watched *The Bachelorette*?"

Cool Risa, guitar-playing Risa, bedroom studio–having, very-gay Risa looks at me like I've just asked if she's ever watched a snuff film.

"It's my favorite show," I say. "I've never told anyone that except my mom."

"Okay . . . ," she says, trailing off. I can tell that she thinks

I'm just trying to change the subject. If I have a point, I need to make it fast or I'm going to lose her.

"Hear me out. At the beginning, you have this model or beauty queen or whatever, and she's dating all these different people at the same time. They go out, they get to know each other, they kiss. And the feelings she develops for all of them are real. She cares about all of them for different reasons. And every week, people watch her do this, and they're cheering her on."

"But then she picks one, and they get married," Risa says, rolling her eyes like she's annoyed this *Bachelorette* knowledge is taking up real estate in her brain.

"I hate that part," I say. "I like to pretend that each season of *The Bachelorette* ends once she's sent home all the shitty people and given roses to all the cool people. She picks everyone she likes, and then everyone cheers."

And even though I don't know what Risa will make of it, or whether it will freak her out, I tell her about my beautiful dream. I tell her about how I want to have adventures and travel, but also stay here. I want to learn how to run sound and make records, not just fooling around in my attic, but for real. I tell her how I want my life to be filled with love, with people I love.

And then I tell her the same words I said to Max on my front lawn, only when I say them to her, I'm not staring at the sky or covering my face with my hands.

"I don't think being with one person works for me." I look right at her.

When I finish, Risa doesn't say anything. She's looking

straight ahead, her hands clamped on the steering wheel. She doesn't say anything when she signals and turns into the parking lot of the Kwik Chek convenience store. She doesn't say anything when she gets out of the car. I watch her walk through the front door and disappear behind the racks of chips, and I honestly don't know if she's planning to come back, or if she's just going to hide out inside the store until I give up and go away.

This is what I'm about to do when Risa finally comes out of the Kwik Chek with two bags of chips and two fountain drinks, which she puts on the roof while she opens the car door.

"Do you like either of these kinds?" she asks, holding out the bags of chips.

I take the salt-and-vinegar ones from her hands and mutter a thank-you.

She hands me one of the fountain drinks. "They're both Coke."

"That's fine," I say. "That's great."

All I care about is that she's back in the car and speaking to me.

"I'm sorry I stopped," she says again as she starts the car and backs out of the parking lot. "I know we're in a hurry."

"Risa," I say.

"We have to get Max."

I say her name again. "Are you okay?"

Risa puffs out her cheeks and slowly blows out the air while she's driving down Madison Avenue.

"The thing I like about you, Lee, is also the thing that scares the shit out of me."

I'm clutching the chips in one hand and the soda in the other, relieved she's talking to me again, worried I'm going to say something that screws it up.

"What's the thing you like?" I ask.

"That you're not sitting around waiting for anyone to give you permission to put your ideas out into the world. You just put them out there, and maybe people like them, maybe they don't—you don't let that stop you from being you."

"Why does that scare the shit out of you?"

"Because you're not who I expected to want."

I flinch. Her words aren't cruel, but they're exactly the reason I couldn't look Max in the eye when I told him. When you tell someone who you are, and they leave you sitting by yourself in the Kwik Chek parking lot, it's hard not to feel like a disappointment.

When we stop at a red light, she finally turns and looks at me.

"My last girlfriend told me she wasn't looking for anything serious. She told me that for six months. And every time I said anything romantic to her, or talked about the future, she'd remind me that she wasn't looking for anything serious. Like she was keeping her options open. I don't even know if it's accurate to call her my ex-girlfriend.

"I didn't really care if she dated other people. It wasn't jealousy. It was being held at arm's length like that that got to me, having someone set all the terms and conditions for what I was allowed to feel."

I swallow. Except for her music, this is the most personal thing Risa's ever shared with me.

As we pull into the parking garage, I want to convince her that I'm not the things she's afraid I'll be. I want to tell her that I'm not afraid of romance or seriousness, that she can be anyone she wants to be with me, that she can feel however she wants to feel.

And then, when I'm working up the nerve to say something impassioned, I notice the corners of her mouth twitching. Right in the middle of the garage, she puts the car in park and takes my hand, and looks at me with a seriousness that threatens to dissolve into giggles.

"And just when I get out of that, the next interesting person who comes along tells me she wants to configure her romantic life to look like a season of polyamorous queer *Bachelorette.*"

I've never been tremendously good at viewing myself in a comical light. I mean, for fuck's sake, I have confessional-poet DNA running through my veins, and I made a podcast about art in my attic for two years. But I can't help myself, and suddenly, I'm laughing too, to hear it put so simply, so bluntly. And part of me is laughing with relief because there's no judgment in the way she says it.

"I don't need to be put up in a mansion," I argue. "Just my regular house is fine."

"What about your various suitors?" Risa asks, still laughing. "What do they do while you're off with some other person?"

"Whatever they want. With whomever they want."

Risa's smile fades and she goes quiet for a minute, then says, "Nobody's going to cheer you on, you know that, right?"

"Not even you?" I ask.

We've been joking around, but I can tell she's serious.

The problem is, so am I. I've been serious about all of it, even though I knew there was a very strong chance that Risa would recoil from everything I'd said. I mean, there was nothing wrong with wanting a girlfriend who only wanted you. Lots of people wanted that. Probably *most* people who wanted girlfriends wanted a girlfriend like that.

"I'll always cheer for you," she says.

"And I'll always cheer for you, too," I say. "I want to be in the front row."

"I spent the last two years playing songs in my bedroom that nobody else ever heard," she says. "Since I met you, something feels different."

My breath catches in my throat.

"When I see the way you make art, the way you live your life—there's this passion in everything you do, and I want to be close to it."

I can't believe my luck. I can't believe my life, I think. We're still idling in the middle of the parking garage, but I don't care. I lean across the seat to kiss her. She draws her hand up to my shoulder, and I'm just about to close my eyes when I realize this touch isn't to hold me closer.

I pull away, press my back tight to the car seat, press my palms together in my lap.

"I'm so sorry," I say. "I thought . . ."

"That's what I'm talking about when I say that wanting you scares the shit out of me."

She puts her hands over her face, then smooths back her hair, tucks the strands behind her ears, like she's pulling herself back into orbit, back to herself. She puts the car in gear and circles around the garage. She drives past three empty parking spots before she finally says,

"Lee, I'm a lesbian in the Bible Belt. I just want something in my life to be easy."

She finally pulls into a parking spot and takes the key out of the ignition, but she doesn't move, doesn't look at me when she says, "If what you just told me is what you want, I don't think I can do this."

I feel like crying, like telling her, *Forget I said any of it. Never mind. I can be someone else for you.*

But then I remember that I gave Vincent a version of myself like that.

It didn't matter how much we loved each other when the whole perfect story of us was just a story. I don't want that again. I don't want to do that to someone else again.

Memphis may not love you back.

Max's words ring differently in my ears this time.

I think about what Sage said at the dinner table the other night, about the stress they felt during every interaction, waiting to see if the person in front of them was going to be a dick or not. Sage already knew what it felt like when Memphis didn't love you back. Risa already knew it. Vincent and Max must know it too.

It's been so easy for me. I don't know how it feels to move through certain spaces, bracing yourself for the things you know can happen. I hate that so many people I care about know what that feels like. I'd always been able to move through the world like a straight person because I kept my queerness a secret. I did it because it was easier that way. Easier on the surface, at least.

The life I saw in my beautiful dream is full of art and love, but more than that, it's a life that's out in the world, not hiding from it.

I can't be out in the world ignoring the parts I don't like, nodding my head like I already understand. I can't be out in the world putting my own reality front and center every time.

I think about the lyrics to the gospel song my dad was singing in the hallway this morning: *You've got to live the life you sing about in your song.*

If I'm going to stay in Memphis, that's the kind of person I need to be. If I want to be out in the world, I need to step outside myself, outside my tiny corner of experience, and be *all* the way out in the world.

If I'm asking Risa to crank up the difficulty setting on her life, to trust that having me in her life won't just pile more stress on her shoulders, I need to be worth it.

"I understand," I say.

"This is hard for me, Lee. I really like you."

"Can we do that, then?" I ask. "Can we just like each other?"

Risa tilts her head to the side and considers me for a moment. Then she takes my hand again, laces her fingers through mine and gives them a squeeze.

It feels good, just to sit there with her and not try to figure out what any of it means.

We stay like that for a minute, and then she lets go of my hand and says,

"Let's go find Max."

CHAPTER 34

Rhymes with Stax

My first mistake is in thinking what we've planned will be easy. The Memphis train station is not big. There are only two tracks, one southbound to New Orleans, one northbound to Chicago. The train to Chicago leaves once a day, always at ten thirty at night. I know the schedule by heart because it's how Maggie and Sage and Max have always come to Memphis. Max loves buying snacks from the club car; he loves staring out the window in the observation car; he loves staying up late in one city and waking up early in another one. He loved it when he was eight, and he still loves it. I've been dropping them off there for years, so I know we have plenty of time to find Max moping on the platform, convince him not to leave, and bring him back to Midtown with us before the train boards. It probably won't even be crowded.

But when we arrive at the train station, there's no sign of him. We check the lobby, the platform, up the stairs, but it's deserted except for a few paranoid tourists, terrified of missing their train and being stranded overnight here.

A few buskers are setting up around the station. I see an Elvis impersonator and a blues guitarist, neither of them unusual sights around downtown Memphis. But on the north-bound platform, there is a band setting up unlike anything I've ever seen before. There are seven of them, unpacking things from a refrigerator box: a saxophone, a harmonium, a leaf blower, an instrument I've never seen before that looks like a mandolin with a jack-in-the-box crank on the end.

"Where else could he have gone?" Risa asks.

I consider the possibility I was wrong, that Max went somewhere else with all his luggage. But no, Max doesn't have money for a plane ticket. What he has is an open-ended round-trip ticket back to a city he misses. I know he's around here somewhere.

"Maybe he went to the Arcade," I say.

The Arcade is a diner, the oldest one in Memphis. Some-times we came to the Amtrak station early so we had time to eat there before we put Maggie, Sage, and Max on the train home. They make a sandwich called the South Main, with ham and pear and Brie cheese and Creole mustard that Max loves. I have a strong suspicion we'll find him parked at a stool at the counter, ordering one up so his trip here won't have been a complete waste.

"What are you going to say when you find him?" Risa asks as we race down the steps to the station lobby.

This is a very good question, one I haven't thought about at all. I suppose I thought it would be self-explanatory. We'd show up, and he'd see us and realize that everything was fine now, because if it wasn't, we wouldn't have shown up, right? But that was assuming he wanted to see us, that he was inclined to go back with us at all.

I remember the way he told me my life was a fairy tale, the way he muttered *Well, whose fault is that?* when I yelled at him for ruining my life. It was my fault, and we both knew it. Maybe the message he posted was just a way to make a clean break before he left town, pretended the last week had never happened, and wrote me off forever.

"This is a mistake," I say as we open the door to the Arcade and go under a sign that reads, THROUGH THESE DOORS PASS THE GREATEST PEOPLE ON EARTH: OUR CUSTOMERS.

"Why?"

"Maybe he doesn't want to see me," I say. "That's why he left."

Risa and I scan the restaurant, but there's no sign of Max at the counter or in the booths.

"He left because he was ashamed, Lee."

"Ashamed of what? I'm the one who should be ashamed."

"He fucked up something that was important to you."

"So what." I say it like a fact, not a question.

"So what?"

"Seriously, so what. I'll make another one. The work has already been done," I say, quoting Man Ray, though I don't stop to clarify that point, not after I've already subjected Risa to my treatise on *The Bachelorette*. "What I mean is, he means more."

"Tell him that," Risa says.

I take out my phone for the fifth time in ten minutes, but there's still no reply to the text I sent Max an hour ago: **Where did you go? I'm worried.**

"Can you try texting him?" I ask. "Maybe he'll write back to you."

Risa snorts. "I already did, half an hour ago. Nothing."

We look around the Arcade one last time, then go back to the train station, where the scene has changed dramatically. Fifteen minutes ago, the station was deserted, but now the train has arrived, and all kinds of specifically Memphis pilgrims have come off it. The Beale Street blues fans, the Elvis nuts, the people in Redbirds jerseys in town for tomorrow's baseball game against New Orleans. The retired couples with their knee socks and khaki shorts and reservations on a Mississippi River steamboat cruise.

The buskers strike up B.B. King–style blues and Elvis ballads as a bridal party streams across the platform, all the bridesmaids carrying their high heels by the ankle straps. The groomsmen have their ties undone and shirts untucked, and the bride and groom are sharing a beer concealed in a paper bag.

Risa and I fight our way through the crowd to the platform and see that the train has started boarding. For all we know, Max is already on the train.

I turn around and see an older white woman wearing a wig that's a waterfall of auburn curls and a red hat with a wide brim. She's leaning against one of the pillars, posing dramatically with a cigarette holder between her fingers, though there is no cigarette in it. She seems like a person who'd notice Max.

"Excuse me," I say, "we're looking for somebody."

"What does he look like, baby?" she asks in that Southern way, where people call you sweetie, baby, and darling all the time, and sometimes it's awful, and sometimes it's nice. When this lady says it, it's nice.

"Like a postapocalyptic rogue I picked up at the club," I say.

She adjusts her wig under the red hat, points down toward the end of the platform, and says, "I saw a young man in black patent leather boots board over there. Does that sound like him?"

Before I can hug her, she strikes a film-noir pose and pretends to take a drag off her cigarette holder with no cigarette in it, so instead I thank her, and Risa and I run over to the train car where Max allegedly boarded.

When we get to the front of the line, the attendant asks for our tickets.

"We don't have tickets," Risa explains. "We just need to get on for a second."

"I can't let you on without a ticket," she says.

"We're looking for our friend," I say.

The attendant looks at us like she's shocked we don't understand how the world works.

"And I can't let you on without a ticket."

We fall back from the line. I start to pace up and down the platform. I look up to the train's upper-level passenger cars, where I know Max likes to sit, cup my hand around my mouth, and call his name.

Risa joins me, and together we pace up and down the platform calling out his name. Over all the noise on the platform and the sound of the train, I'm not even sure he can hear us.

He probably has his earbuds in. Maybe he's seen our texts and ignored them. Maybe he has no interest in being rescued by two people who care about him.

Because this is what it's about, I realize. I'm chasing Max to the train station because I love him, because I want him around, because I don't care if he posted our podcast. Max Lozada is too lovable to be on the periphery of anyone's life, and I'm chasing him to a train station because he's worth chasing to a train station.

Suddenly, our voices are drowned out by a burst of feedback followed by the squawk of a saxophone. I turn around to see that the seven-piece band with the leaf blower is tuning up. They are curved in a semicircle around the refrigerator box, a woman on the saxophone and two more on drums and bass. There's a man blowing into the harmonium, and another fiddling with the knobs on his portable amplifier, strumming chords on the guitar until it sounds how he wants it to sound. I see someone else holding the instrument that looks like a steampunk mandolin with a crank on the end. He gives the crank a furious twist, and it makes a sound like a violin mixed with an accordion. I don't know what the seventh member of the band is going to do. Maybe he's supposed to play the leaf blower.

I don't know what it is, but it looks like art to me, and that gives me an idea.

The guitar player is barking instructions at the rest of the band, and because he seems to be in charge, I walk up to him. He doesn't seem terribly friendly, and I'm nervous to ask him what I'm about to ask him. There's a twenty-dollar bill in my pocket, left over from my next-to-last paycheck at Java Cabana, money I earned when Vincent and I were still together and my life was stable and happy. I decide that if I don't need to save that money for a deposit on an apartment, I might as well spend it on this.

"I'd like to request a song," I say to the guitar player.

"We don't really do that," he says, then bobs his chin in the direction of his guitar case, which doubles as a tip jar.

I throw in the twenty-dollar bill and say, "It's not really a song I want. It's more of an improvisation."

I can tell that my twenty dollars has bought me, if not a song, at least thirty seconds of the guitar player's patience in which to explain myself.

"Our friend is on that train," I say. "We think he's making a mistake. We want you to play a song that will convince him to get off that train."

The saxophone player has been listening in. She comes over and asks, "What's your friend's name?"

"Max," Risa says.

"Rhymes with *Stax*," the saxophone player says. She raises her fingers in a snap, just like the logo from Stax Records, the Memphis soul label that was around before my parents were born. We have a ton of Stax records in our house. Or we had a ton of Stax records, before my dad loaded them up in crates and moved them to a new apartment. "Why do you think he's making a mistake?"

"Because he's my friend, and I love him."

"What's so great about you?" she asks.

"My heart is an indestructible object."

While the saxophone player considers this, Risa opens her wallet and throws another ten dollars into the guitar case.

"Sold," the guitar player says.

He takes the mic and counts off, and the band roars to life, a fury of skronk and dirge. Gradually, a hook emerges and the drummer falls into a shuffle, and the song takes shape just in time for the singer to lean into the mic and begin to speak.

"This is a song for Max, which rhymes with *Stax* and *relax* and *panic attacks* and *train tracks.*" He doesn't sing it, or say it, so much as he preaches it, like he wants to save every Redbirds jersey and knee sock–wearing tourist in the Amtrak station from hellfire and brimstone.

He continues.

"This is a song for Max, who is on the train.

"Max, if you can hear me, and you are on the train, there are two fine women here on this platform who wish for you to disembark.

"These two fine women paid thirty dollars of their hard-earned money for me to make this announcement.

"I don't know what Chicago holds for you, Max.

"Maybe you've got a family there, or a job at the pet-food store, but Max,

"I'm asking you, as you consider the alleged charms of Chicago,

"that you look in your heart and report honestly what you find there,

"that you ask yourself,

"does the city of Chicago have in it two fine women who

will chase your narrow ass to an Amtrak station and buy a song to get you off a train?

"I'm going to answer that question for you, Max.

"It does not.

"Because shit like this only happens in Memphis."

And with that declaration, the band, which has been vamping behind the guitar player, erupts in a squalling fusion ecstasy. The member of the band whose role was unclear begins to dance wildly in front of the band, wielding the leaf blower. Then after a few bars, he puts it back in the cardboard box and pulls out his next trick, a baton that he twirls and tosses up in the air. He manages two full spins before he catches it.

"I want you to give it up for Leon Humphries on the hurdy-gurdy," the guitar player says, and I realize that's what the mandolin with the jack-in-the-box crank instrument is called.

During the saxophone solo, the man with the baton tosses it up so high that it almost hits the train station rafters, and somehow, it lands right in the cardboard box. He gives the audience a relieved smile, then reaches into the box with both hands and pulls out a bathroom sink basin with a mirror and an electric razor in the bowl. He sets it down on the train station platform and sits in front of it, then proceeds to shave off his lumberjack beard, all the hair falling neatly into the sink while the band plays.

I realize that what the guitar player said during his monologue was true. Shit like this only happens in Memphis.

Now the band is singing Max's name over and over with a refrain of "Don't go back to Chicago."

Through the whole song, I run my eyes up and down the platform, checking the doors of each train car, but there's no sign of Max. After ten minutes, I can tell the band is ready to wrap it up. I think about asking them for one more chorus, but I exchange a glance with Risa, and I can tell that she already knows it's pointless. If Max wanted to get off the train, he would have done it by now.

The guitar player gives me a shrug, and he and the band come rollicking to an instrumental finish. Disappointed, Risa and I give them a round of applause. I notice that a small crowd of curious train passengers have gathered around them, and while most of them seem mystified by what they've just seen, they throw dollar bills into the guitar case anyhow, and the band moves on to the next song.

Over the loudspeaker, the conductor announces final boarding to Chicago, and suddenly, I wonder if I'm ever going to see Max again. He's eighteen. When we were kids, we'd been thrown together once or twice a year because our parents were friends. Now that was all going to change. If we were going to be in each other's lives now, it would have to be because both of us wanted to make the effort. And what if Max didn't think I was worth the effort?

I remember one of the last things I'd said to him before he ran off: *I don't care what you do with your own life, Max, but don't be a dilettante with mine.*

When you go around saying asshole things like that to people you love, they get on trains to Chicago without saying goodbye to you, and you deserve it.

"Are you okay?" Risa asks, and I shake my head.

"Come on," she says. "I'll buy you another Coke at the Arcade."

"No, you won't," I say. "We gave all our money to the band."

"Fuck," she says. "Never mind. I'll take you home."

The train doors close, and the crowd that had gathered to watch the band floats away, waving goodbye to their friends and family in the passenger cars. The band wraps up their song and starts packing all their gear back in the cardboard box, probably getting ready to move to Beale Street, or outside the bus station. Or, this being Memphis, they're probably all in two other bands apiece, half of which are playing shows later on tonight.

The saxophone player empties the spit out of her horn before putting it in its case. There must be a cup of it in there, and I watch in horror as it splashes onto the concrete, onto the side of the cardboard box, onto a pair of knee-high black patent leather boots.

My eyes shoot up, and I see Max standing in front of us, looking like the spit on his boots is penance for all of this.

"You came," he says.

"Of course I came," I say.

His eyes well up with tears. "I'm sorry, Lee."

"I'm sorry too," I say.

He takes my hands in his hands and squeezes them, and then we fling ourselves into a hug that feels like a promise.

Max sees Risa standing to the side, watching the train as it pulls out of the station. He lets go of my shoulder and throws his arm wide, inviting her into our reunion hug.

"The *Objects of Destruction* team is back together," he says.

Risa gives me an odd smile before she steps forward and finds a semi-gracious way to mostly hug Max. She gives my shoulder a cursory touch so I know that I'm not being brushed off, but also that this shouldn't be considered a group hug in the truest sense because the three of us aren't picking up in the same place we left off—things have changed.

If Max was the kind of person who picked up on nineteenth-century English manor house detail, I wouldn't even have to tell him what had happened.

Or maybe I've rubbed off on him because he looks back and forth between the two of us, suddenly anxious, and asks, "What's going on? Did someone *die?*"

Risa and I both burst out laughing, a little harder than the situation warrants. It relieves the awkwardness, puts the level of shittiness and disappointment into perspective.

"Nobody died," Risa says. "We're just happy to see you."

It's only the three of us on the train platform now. Even the Elvis impersonator is gone.

Max looks down at his boots. There's still a splash of the saxophone player's spit on one of them. After a moment he looks up and meets my eyes.

"I know you're not happy with the podcast, and there's stuff you would have taken out. And I'm sorry I posted it without your permission. But that doesn't mean it's not good, Lee," he says. "Even before I heard the band playing that song for me, I was already thinking about getting off the train because I didn't want to stop working on it with you."

Risa gives him a shove. "You mean we spent thirty dollars, and you were about to get off the train *anyhow?*"

Max gives her his Imp of the Perverse smile. "I said I was *thinking* about getting off the train. The song really sealed it, though."

"So what do you think we should do?" I ask. Earlier today, the only version of this that I'd bothered to imagine ended with me deleting everything. But after talking to my mom, after finding out Max feels the same way, I know that I'm not finished with this story either.

"We figure out how to turn it into something better," Max says. "Just because it's not perfect doesn't mean it's not art."

"You sound like my mom."

I take out my phone and show them the picture my mom sent me, standing in front of her New Orleans hotel window, holding a sign that says, *YOUR HEART IS AN INDE-STRUCTIBLE OBJECT.*

I've looked at it a lot since she sent it, the calm, reassuring look on her face, the comfortingly familiar loops and flourishes of her handwriting. The words that I can't fully wrap my head around, but that I know mean something fierce and true about the person I want to be.

They're comforting now, too. They remind me that the pain of losing your family, of being left behind, of being rejected—even the faintly ridiculous pain of being dumped three times in one week—is endurable.

Hearts are made for this. They're made to be battered, filled up with big feelings, emptied out again. They're made to swell and ache and break and piece back together again.

They're made to be *used*, even if everything you're ever going to use them for ends.

"My mom is a very wise person," I say.

Max isn't paying attention to me, though.

"I thought you said she was in New Orleans."

"She is," I say as Max takes the phone out of my hands and zooms in on the picture, away from her face, away from the sign she's holding.

"No, she isn't."

That's when I see what's behind her, what's out the window in the top right-hand corner of the photograph: the Hernando de Soto Bridge; the bridge tattooed on my dad's shoulder; the M Bridge; *M* for Maya; *M* for Memphis.

"She's at Harold's apartment," Max says, and I know that he's right. I remember that view from the last time we were over, the corner of the bridge that's visible from the window near the recording-studio setup. "Why didn't she tell you she was back?"

For a moment, I'm too stunned to speak, but Max doesn't wait. His brain immediately starts spinning strategies and conspiracy theories.

"We could go there right now and ask her," Max says. "It's right around the corner from here."

Part of me wants to dive back into podcast-making, mystery-solving mode, go racing through downtown Memphis so we can bang on the door and demand answers, but then Risa touches my shoulder and asks, "How do you want to find out, Lee? How much do you want to know?"

I appreciate the way she slows everything down and gives me a chance to ask myself what I really want, to consider all the possible explanations, which ones I can live with and which ones I can't.

After a minute, I look at her, then at Max, and I say, "I want to know everything."

CHAPTER 35

Weird Relationship Ghosts

The three of us walk over to Harold's apartment building together, but when I punch in the security code, Risa holds back.

"I don't think I should go up," she says, stopping in the doorway.

"It's okay," I say. "You can come along if you want to."

"It's a family thing. I don't want to make it weird."

The door buzzes while we hold it open, the sort of buzz that's annoying enough to keep people from propping it open or navigating complicated interpersonal dynamics there.

"You've been part of this since the beginning," Max says. "Don't go developing healthy boundaries on us now."

Risa smiles, but says, "I think I'll just wait in the lobby."

"Are you sure?" Max asks. It's nearly eleven o'clock, and the apartment lobby is dim and deserted.

"The gloom is kind of nice," she says, sitting down in a worn armchair and putting her feet up on the ottoman. "You go ahead, I'll give you a ride back to Midtown when you're done."

As soon as the elevator doors close behind us, Max turns to me and asks, "What happened between you two?"

"She told me 'I don't think I can do this.'"

Repeating her words makes me start rehashing the whole thing in my mind. I cringe thinking about the moment she left me in the Kwik Chek parking lot, the moment I let myself hope that maybe she wanted to be with me even though it scared her, the moment I leaned over to kiss her and she held up her hand to stop me.

"And that's it? That's the end of it?"

"I think so."

I want to tell Max all of it, but I don't. The things Risa told me, the reasons she decided to break things off, they don't feel like mine to share.

Fortunately, I only have three floors to wallow before we're on Harold's floor. As the doors open, Max looks at me like we're about to rob a bank but he's having doubts about my reliability as a heist partner.

I walk down the hallway with purpose, my arms pumping at my side because I am about to face my mom, a person I'd actually called "wise" just a few minutes ago. Only, a wise person wouldn't lie to her kid, come sneaking back into town without telling anyone except her former, secret lover. A wise person wouldn't make such a goddamn mess of her life.

I bang on Harold's door so hard it sounds like both of us are knocking. Everything Harold's done the past week suddenly seems suspicious to me. I find myself scrutinizing all the times he wasn't with us, the way he looked up and down the hall before he let us into his apartment before. How long had my mom been here? How long would she have stayed, not telling her own kid she was just a few miles down the road, and not hundreds of miles away?

Suddenly, I feel bad for my dad and Sage, waiting for someone to show up to the housewarming party at the cursed fourplex.

How could she do something like this to him? I don't care how angry you are, how badly you want to get divorced. You don't tell your family you're in an entirely different city. You don't get your friends to lie for you.

"Mom!" I shout as I pound on the door. "Open up, Mom. I know you're in there!"

There's still no answer, and finally, Max takes my shoulder lightly until I stop knocking.

"She's not here, Lee. Come on. Let's go home."

"What home?" I ask, and tears fill my eyes. "There's no one there."

My lip starts to tremble like I'm a little kid who's skinned her knee on the blacktop.

"I want my dad," I say, and then I can't hold it in anymore, and the tears come leaking down my cheeks.

"Let's go," he says.

Risa drives us not to my house in the Cooper-Young neighborhood, but to my dad's apartment on McLean. Max takes the front seat, and I ride in the back, watching the gas stations and bars and barbecue restaurants out the window. There aren't as many houses in this part of town, but there are lots of apartment buildings, most of them identical to my dad's, all with big balconies and wide stairwells that make it easy for people to move in and out of them as often as they do.

Risa hugs Max goodbye when we pull up in front of my dad's building.

"In case I don't see you again," she says. "And if you don't call me the next time you visit, I'll be very cross with you."

"And Chicago's not far," Max reminds her. "You can crash on my couch anytime."

Risa looks over the back seat at me. It's too awkward an angle to hug, even if she wanted to, but she holds an arm out to me and I take it.

"I still want to go to Shangri-La Records with you sometime."

"I still want to hear your new songs," I say, giving her arm a squeeze before I let it go. "Thank you for everything today."

"Everything?" she asks.

"All of it."

Max and I go around to the back of the building, the same way the landlady took my dad when she showed him the apartment. The rickety back staircase leads to a screened-in porch with a washer and dryer on it, and the doors to two apartments. I can't remember which one is my dad's, but there's a dead plant on the shelf above the dryer, and my dad hasn't lived here long enough to kill a plant. Then again, maybe the last couple who lived here abandoned it when they broke up horribly and left their weird relationship ghosts all over the place.

While I'm trying to solve the dead-plant logic puzzle, Max has put his ear to the door.

"They're in here," he says. "I can hear your dad's records."

He tries the doorknob, which opens. I make a mental note to remind my dad to lock his door at night so people don't wander in off the street.

We enter through the kitchen, where the garbage can we bought at Target earlier that day is overflowing with paper plates and beer bottles. There are a couple of mostly empty boxes from Memphis Pizza Café on the counter as well. The clock on the stove says 11:34, so though we're late, at least we're before-midnight late. We cut through the kitchen, past the bedroom my dad had said could be mine. We go through the bookshelf secret passageway, which bypasses his bedroom. I expect to see my dad sitting on an upturned milk crate eating a slice of pizza and looking forlorn, while Sage sits by, exhausted from helping with the move, and only staying awake with my night-owl dad out of politeness.

But when we come out the other side of the secret passageway, there is a small party in progress. A tame, middle-aged party, but a party nonetheless with records and pizza and beer and milk crates, and it doesn't feel depressing at all; it feels nice and neighborly. I see my dad in the front room, adjusting the air conditioner. Sage is sitting on an orange velvet couch I don't recognize, talking to Trudy from Java Cabana and her girlfriend, Kyra. Maggie is there too, talking to someone I don't recognize, possibly one of my dad's new neighbors. It's an unusual guest list, and I wonder if he invited every person he ran into today. Then again, even if he did, they all showed up.

Max freezes as soon as he comes out of the secret passageway, and I realize it's the first time he's had to be in the same room with both his parents since they arrived in Memphis.

"Are you okay?" I whisper.

"It's fine," Max says.

Then my dad sees me, and from across the room, I see his face light up. He opens up his arms, and because my eyes are still red from crying like a little kid, I go running into his bear hug.

"I didn't think you'd come," he says.

"Dad . . ." I start to speak, but I don't know where to go from there. The last time I saw him, I hadn't been outed as a cheater and a liar. I hadn't been worried about betraying him by digging into his life, his pain, and turning it into a story. I hadn't known that my mom was secretly back in Memphis and apparently hiding out at his best friend's apartment.

I don't know whether it would be better to tell him the truth or not. I look over his shoulder and try to meet Maggie's eye for some clue, but she won't even look at me, like she feels guilty for helping my mom keep her secrets.

My dad doesn't wait for me to figure out where to begin. He pulls back, studies me, and asks, "Are you okay?"

"Not really," I say, and then I start to cry again. "I'm sorry."

"What do you have to be sorry about?" he asks. "Besides being grossly late to my housewarming party, but that's hardly anything to cry about."

"You never wanted to talk about the past, and instead, your past ended up spewed out into the world for anyone to hear, and I know you must hate that, and I'm sorry for all of it."

"I don't hate it," he says.

"You said we needed to talk about it. Nobody ever says 'we need to talk' when they're happy about something."

"I'm not happy with the way I've handled things," he says. "Maybe that's what I was trying to say. There was a joke I used to tell your mom, 'Why would I talk about my feelings with you when I could just bury them in the backyard?' Only she never thought that joke was very funny, and I don't even have a backyard anymore, so what I'm saying is, it's occurred to me that I may need to find a new place to put my feelings."

Max hovers nearby, trying to give us space for our conversation while also trying to look like he's part of it, avoiding making eye contact with Maggie and Sage. My dad notices him and falls into hosting mode.

"Come back to the kitchen with me," he tells us. "I'll get you something to eat."

I've barely eaten anything all day, and when I remember the boxes of Memphis Pizza Café in the kitchen, my mouth starts to water. We follow my dad back through the secret passageway, and in the kitchen, he gets us paper plates and pours glasses of sweet tea.

And he's just about to go back through the secret passageway when the bookshelf opens and Maggie comes through looking like she's on a mission, and Max, whose mouth is full of garlic-and-tomato pie, dodges around her and cuts back through by himself, like his mom is invisible, and why would you acknowledge someone who isn't there?

Maggie is tiny, with a bouncy ponytail and bright red lipstick and a dress that's printed with cats in rocket ships, and yet, when she's as angry as she is with Max right now, all the cuteness of her style turns huge and ominous. She turns on her kitten heel and storms after Max through the secret passageway. I follow behind them, in case Max needs backup or moral support.

Before Max gets to the other end of the secret passageway, the false bookshelf swings open from the other side and Sage appears. Max freezes, blocked in by both people he'd hoped to avoid, with no way to escape them.

"Where have you been all day?" Maggie asks, livid. "Why is your suitcase sitting in the front room?"

Max tilts his head back and sighs loudly.

"I'm here now, aren't I?" he says, ignoring both of her questions.

Maggie turns around and sees me hanging back like we're trying to melt into the walls.

"Lee," she says, "would you mind giving us a minute?"

"I want her here," Max says, so forcefully it seems to catch Maggie off guard.

"I don't know what's going on with you, Max, but I'm sick of it."

"Which part of this are you sick of?" Max asks. He turns to face her, holding his shoulders back, his chin lifted. And yes, he's wearing a tank top and vinyl pants and black patent leather boots, but when he straightens up and gives Maggie his star-pupil posture, I can see him projecting the Max she's talking about, the sweet, preppy gay boy who attended formal dances wearing bow ties.

I take a deep breath. He's practically daring her to come right out and say it.

"You're different," she says.

"And different is bad?"

On the other side of the secret passageway, Sage has been quiet, perhaps relieved to have someone else sharing Max's anger.

Before Maggie can answer, Sage clears their throat and speaks up. "Max, when you're a parent, you think you know who your kid is. And when it seems like something has changed, the first thing you do is worry."

Max folds his arms across his chest and slouches into a pose that's both indifferent and impenetrable. I can't see his expression, but the earnest optimism on Sage's face vanishes.

"If there was one person I thought I could count on to understand this, one person I thought might know what I was talking about when I said, 'The way I used to understand myself doesn't feel true anymore,' it was you, Sage. I thought you'd get it."

"I do get it," Sage says, but their words are drowned out by Maggie, who bursts in.

"But you didn't say that to us. You started dressing like . . . I don't even know, and you were awful to Niko, and started sneaking that girl into your room. And you didn't tell us what was going on with you; you just started treating us like we were the enemy."

I can see how angry Max is. He looks like he's about to say things that can't be taken back, and Maggie looks like she's going to go there right along with him. There's a reason my mom is tight with Maggie, and my dad is closer with Sage. They have similar fighting styles.

"Her name is Xochitl, and if I'd believed you were capable of treating her like a human being, I might have let her in through the front door."

"You want to be mad and say I'm being judgmental, but really, I'm just looking at my kind, considerate, happy kid and wondering why he's acting like such a jerk all of a sudden."

"That's really loving and supportive. Thanks for the feedback, Maggie."

Maggie's about to tear into him again, when Sage steps between Maggie and Max and meets Maggie's eyes.

"Honey, stop this," Sage says, then puts their hand on Maggie's shoulder. To my astonishment, Maggie backs down, and Sage turns to look at Max as well.

"Nobody has acted perfectly here. But also, nobody has acted unforgivably. And so, Max, the question I have for you is, if we, your parents, can admit to you that we have messed up, what do you propose we do about that? What do you want?"

Neither Max nor Maggie speaks. Maggie's eyeing Sage like they're a traitor, waiting to see what Max does, and I'm worried because I don't know whether he'll speak up or shut down. Max isn't stubborn like Maggie is. He isn't someone who goes out of his way to win fights by getting in the last word or proving he's right. In fact, a few hours earlier, he tried to flee Memphis rather than face a conflict.

After a long silence, Max finally speaks.

"I'm not always going to be the same person," he says. "I mean, I'll always be me, but whatever it was that made you like me so much better before—being that person was crushing me. And I had to do something because I knew I was either going to be crushed, or I was going to explode. I guess I exploded."

Sage puts a hand on Max's shoulder, and he doesn't brush it off.

"You didn't explode, Max," Sage says. "You bloomed."

Sage hugs Max, and I see his shoulders heaving as he sobs onto their shoulder.

Sage holds out an arm to Maggie, who steps into the family hug.

"I'm sorry, Max," Maggie says.

"I'm sorry, Mom."

"Will you let me into your life, though?"

"What do you mean?" Max asks warily.

"I mean that I will love you always, but will you let me know what's on your mind and how you feel about the world? Because if it seems like I liked you better before, maybe it's just that I knew you better then. I miss knowing you like that."

"I'll try," Max says. "You don't get to know everything, though."

"That's okay," Maggie says.

"That's how it should be," Sage adds.

"But we are here for whatever you want to tell us because we love you more than anything."

As Sage and Maggie wrap Max up in another hug, I realize that Max doesn't need me there now, and I'm just intruding on a personal moment. I back out the way we came, to join my dad where I'd left him, standing in the dining room, awkward and alone.

But when I push open the bookshelf, I see that he's not alone at all.

In that tiny room, a room you can hardly call a dining room because a single card table almost fills it up, my dad is standing face-to-face with my mom, and I can tell from the look on his face that she was not invited to the housewarming party.

CHAPTER 36

Finish This with Style

W hat are you doing here?" I ask.

The last time I saw her, she looked fresh and crisp and together. Now she looks like she's been sleeping in her clothes.

"I was looking for you," she says.

My dad glares at her. "That doesn't mean you can just show up here."

"I wasn't planning on making a habit of it, Arthur."

I can tell that they're winding up for one of their circular fights that take place about two kilometers west of the thing they need to discuss, so I step in.

"You found me," I say to my mom. "What do you want?"

"I was worried about you," she says. "I knew you were going through a lot right now, and I wanted to be here for you."

I want to believe that she missed me, that she wanted to take care of me after what happened with Vincent and the podcast, and that's what brought her back to Memphis so fast. Maybe that's part of it, but I've seen the VHS tape of her engagement party. And Harold knows I've seen it.

"So you came home from New Orleans and decided not to tell anyone about it?"

Her eyes widen in surprise, and I can see her trying to figure out how I know, who ratted her out, who to blame for getting caught.

"How long have you been back?" I ask. "How long before you were going to tell someone?"

She's flustered for a moment because I never talk to her like this. I've always been an appreciative audience for her free-spirit spontaneity, not the person who was yelling at her for it. Finally, though, she plays it cool, like I'm the child with the wild, rangy emotions and she's the adult with a rational explanation for all of this.

"I needed a little more time alone to collect myself," she says.

I'm not buying it.

"But you weren't by yourself," I say.

"Lee, I've only been back in town for a few hours. I got a flight this afternoon."

"And then you went right to Harold's apartment. Were you two getting your stories straight or something?"

My dad tenses up. "What were you doing with Harold?"

My mom pulls back like she's been slapped and her cool I-don't-have-to-explain-myself-to-you look fades, and for a second, she looks like she might cry.

"He's my friend too, you know."

My dad looks disoriented by this, though he does not dispute that it is true. Maggie has always been Mom's friend, and Sage has always been Dad's friend, but Harold has always belonged to both of them, insofar as you can assign the custody of a friendship.

"He's here, actually," my mom says. "On the back steps."

"Why on earth is he outside on the porch like a dog?" my dad asks. "Why doesn't he just come in?"

"Would you want to walk into the middle of this?" she asks.

He's just on the other side of the door, and I'm sure he can hear them, sniping at each other, talking about him like he's not even there. I slip out from between them and out the back door. I'd rather be sitting on the porch with Harold and the dead plant than trapped in a galley kitchen with my parents.

Harold's sitting on the back stoop where my mom left him, his knees tucked up to his chin, looking out over the parking lot.

"I'm sorry, Lee," he says. "Your mom was pretty upset when I told her you'd seen the tape."

"So she came back to Memphis to hide out in your apartment?"

"She needed a few hours to think. She wanted to explain herself to you, but then you weren't at the house, and we couldn't find Max. We came here because it was the only other place we could think of where you might be at this hour."

"It's been eighteen years," I tell him. "Why did she have to track me down tonight?"

He picks at the rust on the staircase railing, and it rains down on the steps in chunks so big, I'm amazed it doesn't dissolve in his hands.

"You're her kid," he says. "She cares what you think; she cares how you feel about things."

He looks down at his shoes again, then says, "Come on. We should go inside. I'm sure they're done fighting by now."

I know he's right. We've both seen enough of my parents' fights to know their rhythms. My parents stop mid-sentence when we come in the door. I don't even want to know what they were in the middle of saying to each other.

"Nice of you to join the party," my dad says. "What were you two talking about out there?"

"Lee has the videotape from your engagement party," Harold says. He can't quite look my dad in the eye, like he's blaming himself even though the tape was in our house.

My mom clears her throat and stands face-to-face with my dad, her back against the refrigerator, him leaning against the sink.

"The thing is, Arthur, she's already seen it."

"Oh, that explains why you two are so damn twitchy," my dad says.

"So I'm *twitchy* now?" my mom spits back at him.

My dad ignores her and turns to me. "I take it that's going in your podcast too?"

"It doesn't have to, Dad," I say. I think about my parents, rubbing my shoulders when I was little and saying *I am calm, I am calm.* Right now, all I want is for them to do that to themselves.

Harold nods to my bag where my recorder and microphone are.

"How'd the sound quality come out, ripping VHS to digital?" Harold asks.

My parents both turn and stare at him in astonishment.

"How'd the *sound quality* come out?" my mom asks. "*That's* what you want to know?"

My dad can't keep himself from laughing, and when he turns to look at my mom, something in his face softens. I can tell she sees it, and they size each other up, until finally my dad says, "So, how about it, Maya?"

"How about what?" she asks tentatively.

"Shall we listen to it for old times' sake? Go back to the spot where it all went wrong?"

She squints like she's trying to get a read on him, trying to figure out whether he's messing with her, or being cruel, or whether he's serious about this.

She sees the smile in his eyes and decides to call his bluff.

"Yeah," she says, slow and drawling like a cowboy in an old western movie standoff. "We should."

"It's my party," he says, "and I say it's time for a show."

She folds her arms across her chest, sticks out one of her hips, and smirks, while my dad smirks back at her, and I see something friendly and conspiratorial between them. They could always do this. When their old friends were around, they could rally and turn into this wacky, happy couple. Maybe their marriage could have worked out if all these people were constantly around, eating hamburgers in our backyard and frying bacon in the kitchen, and they had an audience to show off for—the carefree and bohemian domestic hipsters. The Spitfire and the Derelict. The Poet and the Playwright.

Maybe they want to play those roles one last time.

"Then let's do this," my dad says, and my mom lets out a whoop, and he leads everyone through the secret passageway. And then my dad, the man who never wants to talk about the past, is circling up his friends, explaining what we're about to do, what they're about to listen to, as I plug my recorder into the speakers.

"You're about to hear one of the worst engagement parties in recorded history," he says, gesturing to me to begin. "Let's finish this in style."

CHAPTER 37

Right Where I Already Was

It's almost one when everyone gathers round in my dad's living room to listen: Trudy and Kyra; my dad's new neighbors, who are medical students and used to late hours; and my parents' inner circle—Maggie, Sage, and Harold—and Max and me.

Maggie and Sage sit on the orange velvet couch, Maggie's legs thrown over Sage's lap, just like she does in the video of my parents' engagement party. I wonder if they remember.

Harold sits on one of the milk crates, and my mom sits with her back against the wall, legs stretched out in front of her.

Trudy, Kyra, and my dad's neighbors stand near the front door, leaning against the walls like they're not sure whether they should be here, but are also worried it would be rude to leave now.

The audio I'm playing isn't finished yet, but I've been able to pull the sound from the digitized VHS and edit in my commentary. The levels are all over the place, in a way that makes my inner perfectionist cringe. Still, I can hear the thing it *will* be, and even now, it's beginning to sound like a real story.

And people seem to like it. Everyone in the inner circle giggles and exchanges knowing glances when I describe

Greg's goatee and indoor sunglasses. Maggie rolls her eyes at his bleak toast, and when he tells my mom she'll regret staying in Memphis with my dad, Sage gasps. "I knew he said something dumb, but I didn't remember *how* dumb," they say.

Even the people who weren't there when it happened seem to be connecting with it, feeling the things I hoped they'd feel when I edited it.

"Mosquito-infested shithole?" Trudy says, scoffing. "Ahem, Memphis is a *cockroach*-infested shithole. Everybody knows that."

"Yeah," Kyra adds. "Get it right, *Greg.*"

It's interesting to watch Sage, Maggie, Harold, and my parents while they listen. Even though it's part of their shared lore, I can tell they all remember it a little bit differently. Had they forgotten how my mom flipped the coffee table, or how it was Harold, not my dad, who caught my mom in his arms and stopped her from lunging at Greg? Did they remember that my dad didn't do anything, didn't say anything, didn't even get up off the floor when it happened?

We listen to the part where Greg storms out of the house, and everyone goes outside to smoke, and my mom is sitting alone in the living room with her head in her hands.

I look over my shoulder and see that she's in a similar pose now, in the present tense. She's drawn her knees up to her chest and is looking down at them, rocking slightly.

"Is this okay, Mom?" I ask.

"Yes," she says, sitting up straight, eyes on the recorder almost like it's projecting an image above.

And then we listen to the rest.

OBJECTS OF DESTRUCTION, EPISODE #3:
"A Book, a Passport, a Tape"

LEE SWAN: (studio)

When we reach the end, my dad gets up and walks out of the room. Kyra whispers something to Trudy, but otherwise, nobody speaks. Harold looks like he's torn between following my dad or putting his arm around my mom, but isn't sure either of them want that, so he does nothing. He avoids looking at Maggie and Sage.

The person my mom can't seem to look at is me. Under her breath I hear her whisper, "I thought I was doing what was best."

Stories are supposed to have villains. Stories are supposed to have people who do the right thing and people who fuck up. Stories are supposed to have wronged parties and people who get what's coming to them, people you cheer for and people for whom you only wish bad things. Stories are supposed to have a romance where two people find each other and live happily ever after.

So what I ask myself, as I sit in my dad's cursed fourplex, as I watch my mom looking like she wants to vanish, what I ask myself is: *Do I want a story, or do I want the truth?*

Do I want a villain, or do I want my family?

I sit down next to my mom. I haven't even hugged her since she's been back, so I do, because I missed her, because my heart hurts for her, and I still have my arms around her when my dad comes back into the room holding a photo album.

He crouches down beside my mom and hands the album to me. On the cover, there's a picture of my parents and me standing on the front porch of what I realize now is the big house on Belvedere that wasn't really that big.

"Turn on your recorder," my dad says. "Let's talk about the past."

ARTHUR SWAN:
Lee, by the time I was your age, all the family I'd ever had was gone. My dad left when I was exactly old enough to remember how scary he was, but young enough to be completely gutted by losing him. And then my mom got a new boyfriend who didn't want to raise another man's kid, so she left me with my grandparents.

They did their best, but they were very old, and I could never really shake the feeling that I wasn't supposed to be there, and maybe that was somehow my fault.

And then I got a scholarship to college, and I met your mom and Harold and Sage and everybody, and it was like, *whoosh*. Magnetic. Instant family. And just when I started to relax a little and trust that I wasn't going to lose it, we graduated. I panicked. I was losing everybody.

That's why I applied for the passport.

LEE:
Where were you going to go?

ARTHUR:
I was going to follow them. I didn't have any plans of my own, so I daydreamed about following Harold's band on tour and selling merch at their shows. And I thought about following Sage and Maggie to Berlin and getting a job as a tour guide or a nanny. I even thought about getting an apartment with Greg in Santa Monica and waiting tables until someone decided to put me on a reality show.

LEE:
But then you found out about me.

ARTHUR:
I was working as a nanny, and your mom worked day shifts at the TGI Fridays, so we were in the house together a lot while everyone else was out at night working or hustling or partying.

LEE: (studio)
I already know this part, but there's something comforting about hearing him tell it the same way my mom did, knowing that if nothing else, they agreed about this.

MAYA:

We got really close that summer. We'd always been friends, but then suddenly, he was the person I was always looking for at the end of the day. I wasn't over Greg, but I didn't care.

ARTHUR:

And when she told me she was pregnant, I wasn't sad. I was scared out of my mind, but I didn't have any doubts about what I wanted to do.

MAYA:

I didn't want to be pregnant, but at the same time, I didn't want *not* to be pregnant. I wanted to be your mom. I wanted your dad to be your dad, so that's how it happened.

LEE: (studio)

I page through the plastic sleeves of the photo album, and see pictures of my parents feeding me applesauce, pushing me on a swing, holding me by the hands, helping me take my first steps on the half-rotted hardwood floors.

Partway through the book, I recognize the kitchen in the house I remember growing up in, the back porch on Cook-out Night, my mom reading me stories in my own bedroom, in my own bed.

ARTHUR:

Lee, do these people look like they're consumed by regret?

LEE:

No.

MAYA:

Just because we're not happy now doesn't mean we never were.

LEE:

But why take that chance? You didn't know each other that well. It was so complicated. You both had a lot of reasons to walk away.

ARTHUR:

I wanted a family. I would have chased it to Berlin or Los Angeles or followed it around the world. But your mom wasn't telling me, "Sure, tag along if you want." She was inviting me to be a family with her, right where I already was.

MAYA:

If I could go back and do it all over again, I'd do this part the same way. I knew it might not work out, but your dad and I chose each other. We knew what we were doing.

ARTHUR:

Uh, our daughter's diaper is on backward in this picture. We did not know what we were doing.

MAYA:
Arthur.

ARTHUR:
What?

LEE: (studio)
I hear the sharp edge she gets in her voice when she's being serious and he makes a joke. The one she gets when he forgets to pay the gas bill and she says his name like he's the most disappointing person who's ever lived.

And I hear the exasperation in his "What?" The tone he gets when he knows why she's annoyed but acts like he doesn't. The one he gets when she wants to talk about something and he doesn't.

When I hear that, I remember that they fell in love for a reason, and they fell out of it for a reason too, and putting them on a podcast to reminisce isn't going to get them back together.

When you get right down to it, this is the story: my mom wanted someone who chose her, and my dad wanted a family, and even though it doesn't have a happy ending, it's my favorite story of artists in love.

Because it ends here, with me in this place, with these dreams, and it all could have been otherwise. I could have been an entirely different person. Maybe a tidier person, or a more practical person, or a less romantic person. I might want a little less, or dream a little less.

But whoever I turned out to be in those alternate realities, I'm glad that in this one, it all happened like this.

CHAPTER 38

Pentagram in My Heart

The sun is coming up when we finish the recordings.

A little after one, Trudy, Kyra, and the medical school students bail on the party. Maggie and Sage crash in the spare bedroom around two, and even Harold goes home. I don't know if there's anything between him and my mom now. If seeing Greg in person settled that question for her, once and for all, Harold might pose a more complicated question. After all, she's seen him almost every day for the past twenty years. If she hasn't made up her mind about him yet, maybe she never will.

Max is by my side until the very end, though. He listens, makes coffee, goes across the street to the Circle K for beef jerky and Coke. Mostly, though, he listens.

At dawn, my dad tumbles toward his bed, but before he does, he pulls me aside.

"Trudy said to give her a call next week so you can talk about when you might be ready to come back to work." He slips a phone number into my hand. "And she asked me to give you this. It's Wire Mother's road manager—she said you'd know what that meant. Anyhow, they want you to run sound for a show he's doing at the P&H Café in the fall."

I tuck the paper into my bag. It's an unexpected bit of sweetness and relief at the end of a sleepless night.

"Thanks, Dad," I say.

"And she told me to yell at you until you made a website or got business cards or something to let people know you do this."

I know this is the extent of the yelling at me he will do.

For a moment, my mom looks like she isn't sure where she's supposed to be, but then she gets her bearings and calls us a Lyft back to Cooper-Young, back to my house that feels a little bit less like my house than it used to. My mom sits in the front seat, and I'm amazed at her ability to make small talk with the driver like nothing is out of the ordinary. Max and I sit together in the back, holding hands, our heads slumping onto each other's shoulders, then jerking awake. We climb into my bed without getting undressed and fall asleep the moment our heads hit the pillows.

I don't know what time it is when I wake up, but the heat of the day has seeped into my bedroom and I'm hungrier than I've ever felt in my life.

Max is still asleep, so I open the door quietly and go out to the kitchen. There's a note on the counter from my mom saying that she's gone out to eat with Maggie and Sage before their train back to Chicago. At first I'm offended that we weren't invited, but then I look at the clock and see that it's two in the afternoon.

I check the fridge for breakfast fixings, but it's empty except for two beers and half a package of hot dogs. I can almost imagine my mom's thoughts when she saw that this morning. It's while I'm closing the refrigerator door that it hits me: I just pulled Max off an Amtrak train yesterday so he could get on another one today and leave me all over again. We've fallen into such an inseparable rhythm this week, I can't imagine it ending.

When I turn around, he's there, leaning against the kitchen doorway like he'd collapse if it wasn't there to hold him upright.

"Is there bacon?" he asks. I shake my head sadly. "Is there at least coffee?"

I open the cupboard and realize that my dad has packed it with his few belongings and taken it to his new apartment.

But it's okay, I tell myself, because I am a woman of means, a woman who has gotten her sound-guy job back. I can dip into my savings for a special occasion like Max's last day in Memphis.

"Let me buy you breakfast," I tell him. "I know a place you'll like."

We walk down my street, into the center of Cooper-Young, and even though I've made this walk hundreds of times, my heart suddenly swells with love. I know how lucky I've been to grow up in these few blocks, this neighborhood that isn't perfect, but has nearly always loved me back. I want to carry that feeling with me to all the places I go next.

I take Max to a restaurant that used to be a beauty shop in the 1970s, but because this is Memphis, they turned the stylists' stalls and old-fashioned bonnet hair dryers into part of the booths. And because this is Memphis, you can get biscuits with sausage gravy and cheese grits, which Max does. Anyone who orders cheese grits in Chicago is just setting themselves up for disappointment.

We're about to dig into our feast when I see Claire walk into the part of the restaurant where we're sitting. She weaves between the chairs, setting up at a small table in the corner. She has her notebook with her, but she hasn't opened it, and when she sees Max and me, she raises her fingers from the tabletop in a small wave.

"Do you mind if I go over there?" I ask.

Max gives me a pained look, which I realize is only because he thinks I might ask him to go with me and leave behind his Southern feast, all of which will congeal into glue if it's not consumed within the next five minutes. That's what you get for ordering the sausage gravy *and* the cheese grits: desperation.

"You eat," I say. "I won't be long."

I walk over to Claire's table and finally do the thing I never did when we went to school together.

"Hi."

"Hi," she says, cocking her head to the side and folding her hands under her chin. "I'd offer you a seat, but I don't have another one."

"That's okay," I say, nodding toward her notebook on the edge of the table. It's a plain college-ruled notebook with a black cover, the kind you can buy at Walgreens for three dollars, but I can tell it's as much of an artist's notebook as the fancy Moleskine Greg kept in his shoulder bag. "I don't want to keep you from your writing."

"I heard you're coming back to work next week," she says, then adds, "Brent's been an absolute dick since you've been gone. He thinks you getting fired—semi-fired—is some kind of vindication for him."

"When I come back, let's finally ban him from the open mic."

Claire nods enthusiastic approval of this plan. "Did you know he once put one of his baby teeth in the tip jar? Unironically. He thought I would appreciate it more than money."

"Why did he have one of his own baby teeth?" I ask. "Wait. I don't want to know."

"He's so vile even the tooth fairy wouldn't come to his house."

We laugh, and it feels good, like we've reeled back around to where we started, where we were when we realized that we liked each other as people but before we fucked it all up.

"Before I come back to work, I just want to say . . ."

At that moment, the server comes over and sets down Claire's coffee. Claire picks up the cup, holds it to her lips, like, *Oh, you just want to say . . .*

"I'm sorry for putting you in the position that I did."

Claire chortles into her coffee cup. "Interesting phrasing choice there."

I'm mortified but decide to try for a better apology.

"I'm sorry for being a person you probably regret hooking up with."

"I wouldn't say I regret it. I just wish you'd treated me a little more like a person than a logistical problem."

"Yeah, that was shitty," I say. "I'm working on some self-awareness in that regard."

I say it, and about halfway through the sentence, I realize that I don't know what makes me say ludicrous, pretentious shit like *I'm working on some self-awareness in that regard.* But maybe, with Claire, it's because I know it amuses her so much.

She purses her lips and nods, like she's a high school wrestling coach who is proud of me, but also emotionally repressed, and this amuses us both.

"Yeah, well, good start," she says, "but don't get lazy on me."

"I should let you get back to your writing," I say.

"It'll be good to have you at work again," Claire says. She even sounds like she means it.

When I return to our table, Max is laboring to finish every scrap on his plate, his face flushed with the effort.

"You got the meat sweats?" I ask, spreading my napkin across my lap and digging into my pancakes.

"Wouldn't be a trip to Memphis without them," he says.

"Do you really have to go?" I ask. It still hasn't quite hit me that his visit, which began so abruptly, is ending in the same way. "Can you stay a few more days, now that things are calmer? We could work on the podcast. Or not. We could do nothing. We could watch *The Bachelorette.* Really, I just don't want you to go."

"Maggie and Sage already have the tickets, and we *just* patched things up. I feel like they probably want me to go back with them so we can talk."

"What about what you want?" I ask.

Before he even opens his mouth, I can tell that going back to Chicago isn't just Maggie and Sage's idea, it's what he wants too.

"How about you?" he asks. "You're not going to go back to kissing girls and lying about it the second my back is turned, are you?"

"I won't if you won't," I say, giving him a playful slap on the shoulder. I want this trip to end on a happy note between us. I'm afraid that if it doesn't, he'll think of my house as a place he was forced to come when he was a kid, where weird and upsetting things happened and everyone was a mess.

And then, the older he gets, the further away it will be, and then it will just be a story he tells sometimes, on the rare occasions when Memphis comes up in conversation. *Oh, Memphis*, he'll say. *I spent a lot of time there when I was a kid. What a backward-ass place.*

"Hey, what's wrong?" Max asks. "I was just kidding."

"What if this is the last time we're ever in this city together?" I ask.

Max looks down at his plate, mops up the last of the sausage gravy with his biscuit, and takes a deep breath, like he's summoning his inner resources to finish it.

"Then we will have to visit each other in other cities."

"I'm afraid of losing you," I say.

"I'm afraid of losing you, too," Max says. "Your life always seems very crowded. I'm afraid you won't have room for me in it."

"There is always room in my life for you, Max. Whatever shape you want that room to be."

"Can it be a hexagon?" he asks, stuffing the last bite of Southern breakfast into his mouth and grinning.

Some people deploy jokes like they're trying to trick you

out of being sad, but when Max does it, he's like a generous magician who shows you the silks up his sleeves, then dazzles you into feeling better anyway.

"For you, I'd build a hexagon," I say. "I'd build a pentagon. A pentagram. Max Lozada, there is a pentagram in my heart with your name on it."

"Lee Swan, that's the sweetest thing anyone has ever said to me," he says with his mouth full.

CHAPTER 39

Another You

We say goodbye the way we always do. Harold picks us up in his gear-toting SUV so we can all take Sage, Maggie, and Max to the train station together. It's early evening when we make the drive, and Max has sufficiently recovered from the meat sweats in time to have his beloved ham, pear, and Brie sandwich at the Arcade, and then that's it. Walking them to the train platform seems too formal and final, so we've always said goodbye outside the Arcade, like our lives aren't really so far apart, and we're just going back to them for a little while, until we do this again.

Both my parents are there, and I realize this is our last goodbye like this, which makes me sad until Max hugs me and whispers "Hail Satan" in my ear, and I draw a pentagram over my heart with the tip of my finger.

Then Harold drives us home, just like always, except this time he'll drop off my dad at his apartment and my mom at our house. As we make our way toward Midtown, they start to bicker over who gets the car which days next week, and I'm grateful to be distracted by a notification on my phone.

Can we talk?

That's the text that Vincent sends me.

I don't even think about what to write back—it comes flowing out of my fingertips as easily as breathing.

Always.

As soon as my mom pulls into the driveway, I ask for the keys, tell her where I need to go. She doesn't tell me what to do or how to feel or why it's a bad idea. She hands me the keys and tells me to drive carefully.

"What a surprise, Lee," Mr. Karega says when he answers the door. I don't get the feeling he thinks it's a very nice surprise, but I don't let that stop me.

"Hi, Mr. Karega, is Vincent home?" I ask.

Then Vincent's standing in the doorway too. He looks at his dad and says, "Can we have a minute, please?"

Mr. Karega frowns and stands glued to the spot, like anything I have to say to Vincent, I can say in front of him. And who knows. I needed to say it all so badly, I probably would have apologized to Vincent and come out as a bisexual, polyamorous reformed cheater right there on the doorstep.

But then, the most remarkable thing happens.

"Dad, excuse us, please."

Then Vincent takes my hand and leads me inside the house, up the stairs, and into his bedroom, where he shuts the door behind us.

I've never been here before, and I pause in front of the

door, taking in the twin bed with the reading lamp clipped to the headboard; the tidy desktop recording setup—laptop, mixer, and microphone all positioned just so. There's not so much as a dirty sock on the floor. I can't tell whether everything's packed or whether it's always like this, and I'm shocked that after all this time, I don't know the difference.

When I look at the walls, though, I feel better. On the walls, that's where I see Vincent. There's art—a framed poster of the Kehinde Wiley presidential painting of Barack Obama, an Ernest Withers photograph. There's a Memphis Grizzlies poster on the wall too, and I don't know where it fits in, whether it's one of the things he hasn't packed because he's leaving it behind, or because he can't bear to spend a night in his room without it.

Vincent motions for me to come in, to sit down at the desk. He pulls the laundry hamper up beside me and sits down. He hands me a pair of headphones, puts on another pair himself, and sets the microphone between us. And then he says, "Okay, let's talk."

ARTISTS IN LOVE, EPISODE #86, POSTSCRIPT:
"I Hope I Gave You a Good Love Story"
Hosted by Vincent Karega and Lee Swan

LEE SWAN:
I can't believe you even want to talk to me right now.

VINCENT KAREGA:
I want to talk to you all the time. Sometimes you're the only

person I want to talk to. Even when I'm angry with you.

LEE:
You have a lot of reasons to be angry with me.

VINCENT:
And you don't have to be here right now, but here we are. After everything that's happened, what do we have left to say to each other?

LEE:
I'm sorry. That's one thing I have left to say to you. I'm sorry for everything, Vincent. Sorry that I lied, and that I didn't tell you I was bi, and that I cheated, and for the way that it all came out.

That's part of it.

VINCENT:
What's the other part?

LEE:
I know that Howard, and NPR, and everything that's waiting for you in Washington, DC, is a great opportunity, Vincent. It's going to change your whole life. And I've spent the past two years thinking that I knew you so well, but I didn't even know you wanted to change your whole life. That seems like a pretty big thing not to know about someone you love.

VINCENT:

I could say the same thing about you.

LEE:

Why didn't you tell me you wanted to get out of here so much?

VINCENT:

When it was just you and me recording stories in your attic, everything about that felt so right. And when I was there, I could make all these plans with you, tell you about the things I wanted to do with you, and in the moment, I meant them.

LEE:

What about when we weren't in my attic?

VINCENT:

Everything got so much more complicated.

Maybe my parents shouldn't have come back to Memphis at all. They're so afraid of everything, and I can't even get mad about it because most of what they're afraid of has to do with me.

My whole life I've felt like I can't slip up once. My parents act like being a brown boy in Memphis makes me a time bomb, and they're just holding their breath, waiting for me to make one mistake that ruins my life.

And the scary thing is, Lee, they're not right to think that way. But they're not wrong, either.

It's like they have this book of rules—not just the Bible, but another one too—and they believe that as long as I follow them, maybe everything will be okay. Homeschool, go to church, no parties, no going out, no dating, no sex.

But the rules don't change anything. They just make everything smaller until it feels like my whole world is a book of rules that don't help and wouldn't protect me even if I followed every single one of them.

I needed to get out of here, away from that anxiety and control. Even if Howard University and NPR had never happened, I still needed to find a way out.

I've known it for a long time, Lee, and I should have told you.

LEE:
I'm sorry, Vincent. I wish I'd done a better job understanding. I wish I'd asked more.

VINCENT:
I wish I had too. I mean, if I'd known from the beginning that you wanted to have other people in your life, I probably would have told you that you should explore it.

LEE:
Really?

VINCENT:
It's not like I was exploring any of those things with you. It would have been a relief.

Sex always seemed like one more thing that was lurking out in the world, waiting for me to make a mistake so it could ruin my life. It's hard to want something when you feel that way about it.

And I never talked to you about it because it was easier to pretend it was your problem. I'm sorry for that, Lee.

LEE:
So, if we'd been honest with each other about what we wanted from the beginning, we both would have gotten exactly what we wanted?

VINCENT:
It's kind of funny when you put it like that.

LEE:
I'm not sure if I'm ready to laugh about it yet.

VINCENT:
Then why are you laughing? I wish there had been another

you before there was you. Another you to make all these mistakes with so that by the time we met, we could be perfect for each other.

LEE:
I wish we could be like Man Ray's *Indestructible Object*. I don't want to try to recreate what we had. I want to build something new.

VINCENT
What does new look like to you?

LEE:
My life is in Memphis. And yours isn't.

VINCENT:
But I still want you in it.

LEE:
Not the way we were, but I still want you in it too. I want to know who you really are when you're out in the world, not just in my attic.

VINCENT:
I want to know you, too. The real you.

LEE:
I can't wait to see what that looks like.

VINCENT:

I think it will be beautiful.

LEE:

I think the thing I said is the better last line, though.

VINCENT:

But I wanted to say the last line.

LEE:

Ha. Finally.

VINCENT:

Finally what?

LEE:

Eighty-six episodes I've been trying to get the last line, and you always act like it's a coincidence that you get it every time.

VINCENT:

Do you really think I'm that petty?

LEE:

About last lines? Oh yes. Absolutely.

VINCENT:

Well, then, fine. You can have it.

LEE:

But I don't have anything else left to say.

VINCENT:

Then I can't help you. "It will be beautiful." Last line. I stand by it. Will see it in the final mix.

LEE:

I can't wait to see what that looks like.

CHAPTER 40

What Art Is For

I take my time driving back from Vincent's house. The streets are dark and quiet; everyone's turned off their porch lights and settled in for the night. I'm in no hurry to get back to my house because I know that Max won't be there. Sage won't be there. My dad won't be there.

If I'd known that Risa was there, though, I wouldn't have made her wait.

She's there when I pull into the driveway, sitting on the porch swing. She's rocking with the kind of purpose that makes it seem like this is what she came over to do, and that any other motives are secondary at this point. She's rocking the way that I used to when I was a kid, the way that would make my parents tell me I was going to pull the whole swing out of the ceiling.

When she sees me get out of the car, she puts her boot down hard and comes wobbling to a semi-dignified stop.

"Your mom said I could wait for you," she says before I can even say hello.

"Can I get you something to drink?" I ask Risa. "I think we have iced tea."

"You do," she says. "You mom is making me a glass right now."

"Oh," I say, wondering what Risa and my mom chatted about long enough for her to take a drink order.

"Is it okay that I'm here?" she asks. "I can't tell if you're glad to see me or not."

"I'm glad you're here," I say to Risa. "Just surprised. You did dump me in a train station parking lot yesterday."

Risa flinches, and for a second, I think she's going to get up and leave, but then my mom calls out through the front door, "How do you take your iced tea, Risa? Sweet or unsweet?"

And then I hear the creak of the screen door, and she sticks her head out and sees me, and says, "Oh, Lee, you're back from Vincent's. How did it go?"

Now it's my turn to flinch.

But Risa stays where she is. She doesn't look upset. She doesn't look annoyed. She looks like she wants to know what I have to say next.

"Sweet, please," she says.

"It was good," I say. "We had a really good talk."

They both look at me expectantly, and I can tell they want me to say more. I'm not trying to be coy or difficult. It's just that Risa's on my front porch right now. She's right here, and I don't want to talk about Vincent anymore. I want to be here with her.

My mom goes back inside, and Risa says, "Are you going to go with him, then?"

"No," I say. "I'm staying right here."

Risa pushes off with her foot and gets the swing going again. Over our heads, the chains creak against the rusty ceiling fixtures.

"That's what I'm doing too," she says.

My mom brings Risa a glass of sweet tea, and she brings me one too, even though I didn't ask her to. Then she goes back inside and leaves us sitting side by side on the porch swing, scraping the sugar slurry at the bottom of the glass, lifting the cold spoons to our tongues.

"When we were in my car yesterday, I told you that you weren't who I expected to want," Risa says.

"It's okay," I say. "I understand how I might not be."

She sets her glass down on the steel luggage trunk my dad had once fished out of a trash bin, and which had been our front porch coffee table ever since.

"I'm not sure that matters, though," she says. "I think it was an excuse."

"An excuse for what?"

"An excuse to talk myself out of something I want because I'm too scared to want it."

I stop the swing and turn to Risa and take her hand. I think about all the things I'd once expected from my relationship with Vincent. Just because they hadn't happened didn't mean they should have, didn't mean that I even wanted those same things anymore.

"I don't know what I'm doing either," I say. "I never feel the way I'm supposed to feel. I never want the things I'm supposed to want."

Risa looks down at our hands. With one of her fingertips, she starts to trace up and down the back of my wrist.

"I think that's what art is for," she says. "For when we don't want the things we're supposed to want, and the answers that were supposed to be right don't work."

I'm stunned by her, because she is stunning and because she says things like this, things that make me see the world as I most want it to be. I want to tell her something profound in return, give her a bouquet of beautiful words right there on the front porch.

What I say is, "I wish people on *The Bachelorette* talked like you. It would be such a better show," and even though she laughs at me, I think she knows what I mean.

When she's stopped laughing, Risa takes a deep breath and says, "I was thinking about your beautiful dream. And mine. I think we both want a lot. And we could decide to be afraid and want less. Or we could decide to be brave and want more."

"So, what are we going to do?" I ask.

She squeezes my hand, and I know that the feelings spilling out of her don't have to be everything because they are big enough to include me.

"We'll be brave," she says, and she kisses me.

OBJECTS OF DESTRUCTION, EPISODE #3, EPILOGUE

LEE SWAN: (studio)

When Lee Miller and Man Ray were old, they met at an art museum. There was a tube installation in the gallery, and she crawled in one end, and he crawled in the other, and they met in the middle, laughing.

There's no such thing as perfect love. You can't say that love failed when love ends, because everything ends.

But when you've loved someone, some version of it lasts. It keeps being important. It lives somewhere within you, and in that way, you carry the people you've loved along with you, not just in your memories, but in the person you are.

It's worth the weirdness. It's always there. It cannot be destroyed.

ACKNOWLEDGMENTS

I wrote this book with a heart full of love and gratitude for so many people, and now I'm going to do my best to thank some of them properly.

Patricia Nelson, thank you for helping me find a story only I could tell, and for being this book's champion, even before I was.

Kendra Levin, you edit with the wisest brain, the biggest heart, and the deepest care and understanding for others. Thank you for seeing what this book could be, and for editorial letters that employ the dreaded sandwich structure, but with very thick bread.

Thank you to the editors and designers who brought everything together and made it beautiful. I'm so grateful to Amanda Ramirez, Jen Strada, Beatriz Ramo, and Krista Vossen for their work and art.

Many thanks to Shenwei Chang, Eileen King, Jessie Maimone, Alexandra McCarty, and Iva-Marie Palmer, whose artful insights gave clarity, language, and empathy.

Richard Lemarchand, I couldn't have written this book without you. Thank you for celebrating my wins, talking me through the tough spots, and asking after Lee, Vincent, Max, and Risa like they were old friends.

To Rebecca Anderson, John Argroves, Melody and Stephen Deusner, Barrett Hathcock, Jason Knobloch, Beth Land, Henry Murphy, Brady Potts, Matthew Shipe, James Spears, Karen Wilmoth, Amanda Winters: thank you, friends, for exploring Memphis with me and teaching me how to live the life I sing about.

Memphis music was playing in my head while I wrote this book. Thank you to Julien Baker, Shelby Bryant, Greg Cartwright, and Dave Shouse for writing it. And while they are not from Memphis, I'm quite grateful to the Montreal band Jo Passed, whose THERE IS NO MUSIC UNDER LATE CAPITALISM t-shirt both Lee and myself have been known to wear.

Thank you to my parents, John and Karla McCoy, who raised me with love, humor, encouragement, and the ability to make ordinary days feel like they were full of magic.

And at last, Brady (you are getting thanked twice, just go with it) and Shelby, I am constantly overcome with joy that my one wild and precious life has you in it.